ROMANCING THE ALPHA

ALSO BY ALICIA MONTGOMERY

Daughter of the Dragon

Shadow Wolf

A Touch of Magic

Heart of the Wolf

THE BLACKSTONE MOUNTAIN SERIES

The Blackstone Dragon Heir

The Blackstone Bad Dragon

The Blackstone Bear

The Blackstone Wolf

The Blackstone Lion

The Blackstone She-Wolf

The Blackstone She-Bear

The Blackstone She-Dragon

ROMANCING THE ALPHA

BOOK 3 OF THE TRUE MATES SERIES

ALICIA MONTGOMERY

ABOUT THE AUTHOR

Alicia Montgomery has always dreamed of becoming a romance novel writer. She started writing down her stories in now long-forgotten diaries and notebooks, never thinking that her dream would come true. After taking the well-worn path to a stable career, she is now plunging into the world of self-publishing.

facebook.com/aliciamontgomeryauthor

twitter.com/amontromance

bookbub.com/authors/alicia-montgomery

To D and M, my parents, who are celebrating their 50th wedding anniversary this year.
I tell them every day that I love them and am inspired by their love and dedication to each other.

PROLOGUE

The tall man in the dark robes stood silent, looking out the massive windows that overlooked the mountains. The moon was full, shining light down over the trees and rocks, making them look craggy and intimidating.

"Lord Stefan," a voice from behind him boomed. "You called for me, Master?"

"Sit, Daric." He motioned to the large table behind him with his long, claw-like fingers.

The other man, a tall, intimidating figure with long blond hair nodded and took a seat by the head of the table. Opposite him sat a beautiful redhead dressed in a blood-red coat. She gave him a feral smile.

"Hello, Daric," Victoria Chatraine purred. "How was your trip to New York? We've missed you here."

"Tell me what you have found out." Lord Stefan turned to them, his voice cold.

After the Lycans had run their forces out of New York, Daric, Victoria, and what was left of their mage contingent retreated to one of their secret hideouts on the East Coast. The raid on their upstate mansion had dealt a devastating blow to their cause, but not all was lost. Stefan had numerous secret hiding places all over the world, most of them protected by magic. After a few months, they were able to regroup and gather their strength.

"The birth of the True Mates' child is drawing nearer," Daric said in a flat voice.

"And?" Stefan continued.

"As you feared, a second will soon be brought into the world. Cady and Nick Vrost's child will also be a True Mate offspring."

Victoria flinched, remembering her failure at bringing her daughter Cady in before she could start breeding witches. She and Daric were going to be the sires of a new generation of witches, who Stefan would then turn into mages by making them use forbidden blood magic. But Lycans were able to stop them, and now Cady was pregnant with a Lycan child.

Stefan roared in anger, and, with a wave of his hand, several chairs flew against the wall.

"Master," Victoria soothed, "once they leave the womb, the True Mate children aren't immortal or indestructible."

"But they have already begun the cycle!" Stefan shouted. "Soon, this world will be overrun with those filthy dogs!"

"We must act quickly," Daric began. "We must recruit more witches and warlocks, bring them to our cause."

"No, we must stop the Lycans first!" Victoria countered. "Those vile creatures have corrupted and poisoned my daughter, making her carry one of their dirty pups!" Her lips curled into a cruel smile. "Nothing would please me more than to get revenge for you, Master."

"We will do both those things and more." Stefan's eyes narrowed. "But first, we will hit the New York clan where it will really hurt them. Knock out their base of power and then corrupt them from within."

"How do we do that, Master?" Victoria asked.

"I've already begun forming an alliance with powerful allies. The Lycans will not know what hit them."

"And knocking out their base of power?" Daric raised a blond brow.

"Why, my dear protégé, we will kill their Alpha, of course."

CHAPTER ONE

Grant Anderson scanned the room, his deep green eyes keen and sharp. He was like a predator looking for its next meal, but, tonight, he was looking for a different type of prey. Cool, modern, and hip, decorated in black and gold, Luxe looked like any typical high-end bar in Manhattan. But, it was unlike other establishments in the city.

It was a members-only bar, though getting in wasn't as simple as paying a fee and filling out an application form. No, all members were fully vetted with background checks, signed an iron-clad NDA, and, of course, had to be of a certain net worth to get in, both for men and women. The membership manager assured him that everyone who walked into Luxe's doors was discreet and didn't go blabbing to the media about what went on inside and who frequented the establishment. He didn't have to worry about running into women who expected payment for their companionship either. Luxe also didn't allow actors, athletes, entertainers, or other celebrities on their membership list, as these types of people attracted a lot of unwanted attention.

There was a reason Grant preferred to come to this club,

and it wasn't just for the atmosphere and the beautiful women. He valued his privacy above all, not just because he was rich and powerful but also because he guarded a more precious secret, one that could change the world. He was Alpha to the New York Lycan clan, a secret community of werewolf shifters. Lycans weren't just hiding in plain sight in the Big Apple but all over the world. Grant had a lot of responsibilities as leader of one of the biggest and most influential Lycan clans, and keeping his people safe was top priority.

That was why, when he did find himself in need of female company, he kept to exclusive clubs like Luxe. It was one of a handful in the world, though Luxe was the best and most secure one in Manhattan. The women were always sexy and gorgeous, but, more importantly, they never asked questions, never wanted more than what he could offer, and always knew when it was time to leave.

He used to go to regular bars, where he found many willing and beautiful companions who provided pleasant company in and out of bed. Most of them were happy to leave once their time together was done. Of course, he had his fair share of gold diggers, as power and money attracted those types in droves. Most were happy enough to be sent on their way with a shopping spree or some trinket, but some were eager to sink their claws into him, thinking they had hit the jackpot. He had learned to spot and avoid those kind of women, but it was much easier to just go to places like Luxe.

Grant sensed a presence approach him from behind and settle to his right.

"Well, now, I thought I'd never see you again," a deep baritone voice said.

The voice was familiar, even if he didn't know the name. He turned to his right and a man stood next to him, leaning on the sleek, onyx-colored bar. The other man was tall, probably three or four inches taller than he was, with broad shoulders encased in an expensive navy suit. His dark blond hair was styled up into a short faux-hawk, and he sported neatly trimmed facial hair. He was good-looking, Grant supposed, and, from previous meetings with the man, he knew his left forearm was covered in tattoos. Probably former military, based on some of the ink he spied. Plus, the man was built like a brick wall.

"Yeah, well, been busy." Grant took a sip of his whiskey. "Crisis at work."

"Oh, sorry to hear that." The man signaled the bartender, who nodded back and began fixing a drink. "I thought you'd gotten into some trouble or an accident. Or something worse."

"Worse?" Grant asked. "Like what?"

"You know. Got your head lost over some girl. Or married." He nodded his thanks as the bartender set a glass with a measure of bourbon in front of him.

Grant laughed. "Right. Well, work's much too busy for that."

"Glad you're back. You're the only other guy around here who doesn't act like a jerk." He raised his glass to Grant, who raised his own in reply.

Grant liked Tattoo Guy (as he'd called him in his mind) and chatted with him when they both happened to be at Luxe at the same time. But neither man was inclined to introduce himself. He did know that a lot of the women were drawn to the mysterious man, perhaps sensing that bad-boy vibe he radiated.

"Find something you like yet?" Tattoo Guy asked.

He scoured the room again. All gorgeous, sexy women, of course. One particular woman seemed to stand out, a blonde in a slinky red dress. She took a sip of her white wine, her eyes flickering from the glass to the two men.

"Ah," the other man saw his gaze, "she's new. Never seen her before."

"Did you spot her first?" Grant took another sip from his glass.

"Yes, but I think she's definitely got her eye on you," Tattoo Guy observed.

"You don't mind?"

"No, please, go right ahead." He nodded to a gorgeous brunette on the other side of the bar. "That one's been eye-fucking me since she sat down. Good luck, buddy, not that you need it." He clapped Grant on the shoulder. "And next time, don't stay away so long."

"Thanks. I won't." Grant finished his drink and placed his glass on the table. Getting up, he walked over to the blonde.

"Excuse me, Miss," he said with a practiced smoothness. "Can I get you a refill?"

She turned toward him, her movement graceful and cat-like. "Of course," she replied, her red-painted lips curling into a smile.

"Excuse me," he called to one of the bartenders who hurried over to their side. "One more whiskey, please. Neat. And she'll have another glass of wine, please." The bartender nodded and went to get their drinks.

"Now," he turned to the woman, "tell me all about yourself ..."

"Andrea," she supplied, leaning into him.

"Andrea, I'm Grant," he said. There was no need to give fake names at Luxe, though he knew most people did. Grant sat down next to her and proceeded to flirt and chat, asking her what she did (lawyer, recently made partner at one of the big firms downtown) and where she was from (California, but she moved to New York a few years ago). Andrea mostly talked about herself, not asking Grant any questions, which he preferred.

After about 20 minutes, Andrea swirled the remaining wine

in her glass. "So, how about we finish this up ... in my room?" She gave him a wicked smile. Luxe also happened to be located in one of the nicer hotels in downtown Manhattan, which made it easy for trysts and one-night stands.

"Lead the way." Grant put his glass down and signaled the bartender to close his tab.

Andrea took his arm and pulled him toward the exit. As he walked past Tattoo Guy (who was already getting cozy with the brunette on one of the couches), the other man gave Grant a thumbs-up and a wink.

They walked toward the elevators, and, as soon as the doors closed, the blonde pushed him against the wall, her breasts pressed up against him, the soft mounds threatening to spill out of her low-cut dress. She trailed kisses up his chest to his neck and jawline, but just when she was about to press her lips to his, he put a hand on her shoulders and pushed her away.

"Sorry." He shook his head and took a deep breath.

The blonde looked confused. "I thought you wanted to come up with me?" she asked with a slight pout.

"Oh, I do, baby." He grabbed her hips and pulled her to him. "I'm ... let's wait until we get to your room. You never know who's watching."

Andrea nodded and, after the elevator doors opened to her floor, she led him down the hallway. "It's just over here, sweetie," she cooed.

Grant followed the blonde, admiring her assets from behind. Andrea was charming, beautiful, sexy as hell, and willing. He bet she was probably a wildcat in bed, too. "Wait," he called as she stopped in front of a door, ready to open it with her keycard.

"Yes?" She looked up and gave him another bright smile. "C'mon, tiger, let's not waste any time."

"Um, yeah, about that ..." He let out a breath. "I'm sorry. Sorry, Andrea, I just ... I can't."

Her face crumpled in disappointment. "What? What do you mean?"

"I just remembered, I have an early meeting tomorrow, sorry."

"But ... I thought you ... you were flirting with me and ..."

"Look, you're gorgeous." He ran his fingers through his hair. "I'm just ... I can't right now, okay?" He kissed her on the cheek. "Maybe I'll see you around." He turned to the elevators and left her standing in the hallway.

The elevator was, thankfully, still there, and he was able to catch it without having to wait. When the doors closed, he banged his head on the wall.

What the heck is the matter with me? For the first time in months, he had some spare time, finally free (if only for one night) of the responsibilities of being Alpha and the CEO of a major corporation, and yet he couldn't seal the deal. Grant never struck out, much less backed out when it came to beautiful women. By this time, he should have had Andrea on her back, already moaning and screaming her way to her first orgasm. But, somehow, it felt wrong.

He bumped his head on the door again. It had been too long —way too long—since he'd taken a woman to bed. His body practically screamed at him, craving soft curves and sweet feminine scents, but, each time he got close, it was like being doused with a bucket of cold water. This was his third attempt in the last month, and, although he had gotten closer than tonight the previous two times, they ended the same. Something inside him was telling him all those women were wrong. If it wasn't for work and Lycan business to keep him busy, he would have gone insane by now. He drove himself to near exhaustion with work, meetings, exercise, and even sparring and training with his Lycan security team.

Grant considered going back to Andrea, telling her he

changed his mind, or even finding another companion at Luxe, but, as the elevator doors opened to the lobby, he decided against it. *Air,* he thought, *I need some fresh air.* Instead of going to the garage where his car and bodyguard were waiting, he walked out the front doors. It was strangely empty outside, but, then again, the building was tucked away on a side street, which meant less traffic, especially at night. He stood on the sidewalk, staring up, trying to find the stars in the polluted Manhattan skies. It was cold outside in the early spring weather. Good thing his Lycan physiology made him almost immune to the cold, his body heating up to make sure he didn't freeze.

Suddenly, the hairs on the back of his neck stood up, warning him. *Danger.* He turned around, and Andrea was standing behind him.

"Grant," she called. "I was hoping you were still here."

"Yeah, well, I needed some air," he explained. "Is there something you needed?"

"Why yes, in fact there is," her lips curled into a smile, one that didn't quite reach her eyes. "I need you ... to go to sleep."

"What?"

A cloud of blue smoke blew up in his face. Andrea's cruel smirk was the last thing he remembered before the world went black.

CHAPTER TWO

Francesca "Frankie" Muccino let out a long, tired sigh and rubbed her eyes as she sat back in her chair. It was another Sunday night, and she could hear the kitchen crew finishing up outside, cleaning and scrubbing away, making sure everything was spotless. Meanwhile, she had just finished with the books.

Another depressing month, she thought glumly, trying not to look at the spreadsheet on her screen.

As manager and part owner of Muccino's Italian Restaurant, it was her job to make sure all the books were balanced. While they weren't going under, profits were down for the fifth straight month and they barely broke even again for this one.

At least everyone gets paid, she mused. She herself had taken a pay cut to make sure all the employees could at least get their full salary this month, but the servers were definitely balking at the lack of tips. Hopefully, the spring break slump would be over soon and the students from the nearby colleges and universities would be packing Muccino's on weekend nights again.

"Yo, Frankie!" Dante, the oldest of her younger brothers and co-head chef, popped his head into her office. "I'm headin' home. And so's Matt," he said, referring to their half-brother.

"And Enzo?" she asked, crossing her arms over her chest as she mentioned the name of Matt's twin.

"Where do you think he's headin'?"

Frankie rolled her eyes. "Right. He's going out clubbing with his friends until morning. Tell him I said to drink plenty of fluids before he goes to bed!"

"Yes, yes!" a voice from behind Dante called sarcastically. "See ya Tuesday, Frankie!" Enzo shouted right before the back door slammed shut.

Frankie shook her head. "That boy!"

Dante chuckled. "C'mon Frankie, give him a break. He's young, and he's got no responsibilities yet. What else is he gonna do?"

"I know, I know," Frankie sighed, "I just hope he keeps out of trouble."

"You know him," Dante sat down in front of his sister's desk, "the last time we had to bail him out, he got into a fight protecting some girl. He loves girls, can't stand to see 'em in trouble."

"And the women sure do love him back," she said with a smirk. Her middle brother was a true charmer, which was why he was the perfect host for Muccino's. Enzo could effectively talk little old ladies into ordering the evening's specials as easily as he could charm the younger ones out of their pants. No woman between the ages of 18 and 90 years could resist his handsome face; tall, toned body; sandy blond hair; and those chocolate brown puppy-dog eyes. "I just wish he'd grow up. Like Matt." Despite their identical looks, Enzo's twin brother Matt was his complete opposite. He preferred to stay at home and tinker on his computer in his free time, though he did help out in the kitchen on busy nights.

"We all know Matt's your favorite!" Dante joked.

"He's not!" Frankie tossed a wadded up post-it at him. "I hate all of you equally!" she joked.

While growing up with four younger brothers wasn't easy, Frankie took her role as oldest sister seriously. Matteo had always been a painfully shy and awkward child, overshadowed by his more boisterous and outgoing twin. That why she paid him a lot of attention, to make up for it. She even encouraged him to go to college and take up computer engineering. He was the first one in their family to graduate from college, just last year and on a full scholarship. Frankie was so extremely proud of him. He was currently working for a startup in Jersey City, but he still helped out at the restaurant out of loyalty.

Dante glanced over at the screen, and then looked at his sister. His mismatched eyes—one blue, one green, a hereditary quirk in their family that he shared with Frankie—looked worried. "Not another good month, huh?"

She shook her head. "Afraid not."

"How bad is it?"

"Bad enough to worry," she confessed.

"I told you, Frankie, we gotta start using the internet to bring in more people! Set up a website, go on social media and stuff! Matt could help!"

"Matt is busy, and he should have his own life," Frankie stated. "Besides, the college kids will be coming back soon; we don't need to advertise or go online. People already know us, and we'll do it like Ma did and Nonna did, by making great food!"

Dante threw up his hands. "Frankie, we can't stay stuck in the past! Yes, Ma and Nonna were able to start and build up

Muccino's all those years ago, but we need to take it into the future! We'll get some reviews and—"

"*Basta*! I don't wanna talk about this now!" She slammed her palm on the table.

Her brother sighed and shrugged, then glanced at the spreadsheet on the screen.

"I'm sorry, Dante ... I'm just worried." She slumped back in her chair in defeat. "Fine. Talk to Matt, but only if he has time! We can get one of those Facethingys."

"Facebook," Dante corrected. "Jeez, are you really 28 or 68? Are you gonna start talking about that time when soda pop was 10 cents?"

"Yes, Facebook." She stuck out her tongue. "Whatever. You guys work on it."

"Thanks, Frankie!" He leaned over and kissed her on the cheek. "Oh and, by the way, cousin Eddie called again."

"What is it now?" she asked in an irritated voice.

"He keeps saying Gary Fontana is encroaching on his land again, poaching his chickens."

"And why is this my problem?"

"Well, he says he caught Gary in Lycan form on camera this time."

"Argghhhhhh!" Frankie let out a frustrated groan. Aside from being head of the family, she was also Alpha for the entire New Jersey Lycan clan.

There weren't many of them, and most were related to her, so there wasn't much to do except settle small disputes like this. Of course, she also had to send "incident reports" to the Lycan High Council whenever there were any problems. They had to keep the lid on their secret, after all. She wondered how many of the reports the council actually read, and if they were as tired of her redneck cousins as she was. "Fine, fine, I'll deal with it tomorrow. Now go." She shooed him away. "You've been on your feet since three; go home and rest."

"Yes, Primul," he joked, and then ducked another flying object before heading out the door.

Frankie let out another sigh, leaned back in her beat-up leather chair, and looked at the two portraits hanging on the wall to her right. The first was a beautiful older woman with white hair, and the second was a middle-aged version of the other. Both had the same features—thick, wavy hair; dusky olive skin; an oval-faced shape; thick, arched brows; and, of course, the startling mismatched blue and green eyes. Frankie herself was a third doppelgänger for the two women, though she always thought her features weren't as striking. Plus, her hair was more curly and unruly. Her mother, especially, was a great beauty, and she remembered all the men who would flirt with her and try to date her when she was single. "Oh, Ma, Nonna, I miss you both," she said sadly.

———

After locking up the restaurant, Frankie got into her ancient Honda and drove back to her house. She lived close to the restaurant, just a ten-minute drive away. Barnsville, New Jersey was a typical small college town, usually bustling with activity during the school year. Since it was spring break, though, the town was much less busy.

Frankie knew the route home from the restaurant by heart, having basically grown up at Muccino's, either playing in the office by her mother or grandmother's feet or hanging around the kitchen and pantry since she could walk, then working there since she was fifteen. Drive down Main Street for about two miles, go past the old mill, and then turn into the driveway of her childhood home.

She still lived in their old, five-bedroom Victorian-style house, which had belonged to her grandmother, then her mother, and, now, to her and her brothers. Dante, Enzo, and Matt had moved out a while back, preferring to have their own bachelor pads, but their youngest brother, Raphael or Rafe, was still living with her at home while he finished his political science degree at the nearby NJU. Tonight, though, he was staying at a friend's house, studying for a test. He would be the second Muccino ever to graduate college, and, while Matt was naturally brilliant, Rafe was hardworking and whip smart, determined to go to Harvard Law School as soon as he finished his degree.

Frankie slowed the car down as she approached the driveway. As she turned in and her house came into view, she suddenly slammed on the brakes. "*Cazzo! Madre de dio!*" she cursed aloud as a figure suddenly appeared out of nowhere, bounced off the hood of her car, and rolled down to the ground.

She bounded out of her car and rushed to the front. There was a large man—a very naked man, she realized—slumped down on the ground.

No, wait ... She sniffed the air. "Lycan!" she gasped aloud.

She grabbed her purse, took her phone out, and dialed Dante's number. It rang a few times before it sent her to voicemail. "Dante! Where are you? Please come to the house now! I think ... I ran over a Lycan, and I think I killed him!" she shouted, her voice panicked.

A low groan made her gasp. "Wait, I think he's alive! I'll call you back!" Tossing her phone back into her purse, she ran to the man.

Stranger, a voice from deep inside her said. Her inner wolf, normally silent, growled softly at the unfamiliar presence.

As Alpha of her clan, she was much more in touch with her Lycan side, at least that's what her mother and grandmother said. It was a part of her, after all. Over the years, aside from learning to control the she-wolf, she also learned to listen to it like a second gut instinct.

Kneeling down, she inspected the figure on the ground. Taking another whiff, she sought to identify the scent. *Ocean spray, sea salt, sugar and fried dough, like going to the boardwalk.* She froze, stunned as the image the scent brought her felt almost real, with the ocean roaring in her ear. *Strange*, she thought.

Yum.

"Yum?" Her wolf never had that reaction before.

She placed a hand on him, hoping to shake him awake. He was hot, normal after transforming back from Lycan form, which explained his naked state. Touching his naked skin sent tingles of heat through her own body, and she nearly jumped back in surprise. However, she kept her hand on his shoulder, squeezing it and shaking him.

"Hey ... you! Mister!" she called. "Wake up! What are you doing here? You're not one of us! This is Jersey territory!" She flipped him over onto his back. Knowing he was Lycan, his body would heal much faster, even without medical attention.

When his face came into view, she bit her tongue, trying not to gasp. From what she could see, the Lycan was handsome, with dark hair, strong cheekbones, a straight nose and sensual lips. His muscled, well-defined chest was covered in a soft matt of dark hair, a line trailing down a tight six-pack, teasing to what lay below. Frankie blushed and turned her head away but not before she glanced at his impressive package. He let out another groan, his lids opening for a moment, revealing emerald green eyes.

"Hey! Are you awake?" she asked.

The man opened his eyes, but they were unfocused.

Frankie paused, gathering her thoughts. There was no way she could call 911, as the police and the ambulance would ask her tons of questions she wasn't prepared to answer, like what a naked man was doing in her driveway and why he healing so fast after being run over. Of course, she couldn't just leave him there where her neighbors would see him. Squaring her shoulders, she decided she'd have to take him in for now and figure things out later.

"Okay, if you can get up, let's get you into the house, okay? What happened?"

He seemed to nod, but his eyes remained glassed over. "Hurt ... can't see ..." he managed to moan. "Drugged ..."

"You were drugged?" she asked. "Okay, well you can shake it off at my house." She helped him get up by placing her shoulder underneath his left arm. "Jesus, you're huge!" The man was probably around six feet tall and towered over her own petite, five foot one frame. His upper body was broad and solid, his shoulders bunched with well-defined muscles. It was difficult, but she managed to brace him as they walked towards the house.

It was a feat to get him up on the porch and to prop him up against the door while she opened the lock with her key, but she somehow managed. She guided him to the guest bedroom on the ground level. She hoisted him off her and onto the bed, then turned on one of the lamps on the bedside table.

Looking at him in the soft lamplight, she realized just how handsome he was. His eyes were closed again, but she could clearly see all his features, his tanned skin, the slight stubble growing on his strong jaw. Something in her was mesmerized by the sight of him, and her hand caressed his cheek gently, brushing away a streak of dirt.

A strong hand caught hers, and she instinctively pulled back, but he was much stronger. He pulled her down and then rolled her under him, pinning her on the mattress with his body.

Frankie gasped as his nose nuzzled the spot under her ear,

and he breathed deeply. "You ... almond cookies ...," he said incoherently. She opened her mouth to speak and struggled to get out from under him but was silenced as his lips captured hers.

At first, she remained frozen, unable to move due to shock. But, soon, desire and heat shot through her body and she wasn't resisting at all. Instead, she was returning his ardent kisses. His lips moved over hers, devouring them, his tongue sought entrance. As soon as she parted her lips, he delved his tongue into her mouth, warm and delicious, seeking hers out.

His hands slipped under her shirt, yanking down the cups of her bra. Large, warm palms cupped the generous globes of her breasts, squeezing gently, fingers playing with her nipples until they turned into hard little buds. Something hard pressed against her hips, and he shifted his body so he was cradled between her legs. He was definitely fully erect, his naked and engorged penis pressing into the seam of her jeans.

A deep, appreciative growl came from deep within her, and Frankie pushed her hips up at him instinctively. Moving his hands away from her breasts, he trailed lower, over her belly, and his fingers clumsily clawed at the buttons on her jeans. She pushed at his hands impatiently and unbuttoned them herself. He yanked her hands away and pushed his own under the thick fabric and her panties, his warm fingers seeking out the wet folds of her sex. Slowly, he probed a finger inside her wetness and let out a low, feral growl as he continued his fervent assault on her lips.

Suddenly, the sound of the front door unlocking and opening brought Frankie to her senses. "Fuck!" she cursed and tried to push the man away. It wasn't an easy feat, but she braced her hands on his chest and then mustered all her strength to push. She must have caught him by surprise because he rolled over and fell back on the floor with a loud thud.

"Frankie! Frankie, where are you?" Matt's voice came from the main hallway. She heard footsteps run up the stairs.

"Frankie, what happened?" Dante called.

Fuck! Frankie buttoned up her jeans, straightened out her bra and shirt, then tried to brush her long, black hair back into some semblance of order. "I'm coming!" she said, scrambling quickly out of the guest bedroom

Matt was running down the stairs, and she nearly collided with him. "Frankie!" He grabbed her by the shoulders to steady her. "Dante said you called in a panic and that you killed someone! What happened?" Matt's brown eyes were filed with concern.

"Frankie, there you are!" Dante called as he entered the main hallway from the kitchen.

"What are you guys doing here?" she asked, her voice high and tense.

"You leave that message on my phone and then don't call back? What were we supposed to do?"

"Er ... sorry, I got distracted."

Dante's eyes scanned her from head to toe, his nose wrinkling, and when she blushed at his gaze, his eyes widened. But before he could say anything, Matt spoke up.

"Tell us what happened! Where's the guy you ran over? Is he dead?"

She shook her head. "No, no ... he's okay ... just drugged." She sighed and then relayed to them what had happened, at least up until the part where she got him into the house.

"A Lycan? Here in Jersey? Aren't they supposed to ask you for permission before entering your territory?" Matt asked. Although he was one of her fully human half brothers, he knew how Lycan society worked.

"Usually, but it looks like he was drugged and maybe dumped here. He was ... uh, naked, which makes me think he shifted to escape the people who drugged him, and then wandered off," Frankie thought aloud.

"Where is he?" Dante asked.

"I put him in the guest bedroom," she explained.

"Is he dangerous?" Matt asked, a worried look on his face. "Did he try to hurt you?"

"He's too weak to do anything, I think," Frankie assured him. Dante shot her a knowing expression and she looked at him with silent, pleading eyes. "Matty, can you please uh ... go and get him some clothes, please? I think he's about Dante's height, but a little broader in the chest."

"Check my old room," Dante instructed. Matt nodded and bounded up the stairs.

Dante turned to his sister. "Too weak, huh?" he sniffed the air around her. "You know you can't hide anything from me. Not when you smell like sex and—"

"Shush!" she held up her hand. "Can we please not ... I'm okay; he didn't hurt me ... we just ..." she stammered and Dante raised a brow at her. "Let's not do this now, okay? I'll explain later." *If I can find a logical explanation*, she thought to herself. *Other than I've gone insane from lack of sex all these years.*

"Fine. Let's go take a look at this guy."

The two of them went to the bedroom, and Dante flipped on the main light switch so he could get a closer look. The large man, still naked, had somehow hoisted himself up onto the bed and he lay on his back, his eyes closed.

"Huh," Dante moved closer, peering over the man. "He looks ... oh, holy shit!" Dante turned his head slowly to his sister. "Jesus, Frankie, don't you know who this is?"

She shot him back a look and shrugged. "Am I supposed to?"

"Frankie ... jeez, you're supposed to be our Alpha!"

"Just tell me who he is!"

"This is Grant Anderson. *The* Grant Anderson, billionaire industrialist, CEO of Fenrir Corp, and New York's Alpha."

Frankie looked at her brother, her mouth hanging open. Her eyes shifted from him to the man on the bed. "No way!"

Dante gave her an exasperated look. "I'm telling you ... that's Grant Anderson. He was on the cover of Fortune Magazine last month." He took his smartphone out of his pocket, tapped the screen a couple of times, and handed it to her. "See?"

Frankie's eyes widened as she saw the picture of the magazine cover. The handsome figure wearing a suit and a serious expression on his face was definitely the same person who was lying in bed, though the man on the cover was clean-shaven, his dark hair slicked back. "Oh my God!"

"Frankie, were you and him ...."

Her cheeks grew pink. "It just ... I can't explain it ... argh!" She groaned in frustration. "Never mind that! We need to contact his people! Maybe call the High Council."

"Wait, weren't you just in New York a few weeks ago?" Dante reminded her. "Didn't you meet him? Or his Beta or Liaison? It would be much faster than going through the Council, and they're our neighbors."

"Actually ..." Frankie thought back to the ball. "Even better! I met his sister! Her name's Alynna!"

She ran outside to the foyer, to the table next to the door where she kept the mail. After digging through the piles of bills and junk mail, she found the invitation. A few months ago, news of some long-lost Lycan had popped up. She was somehow special, but Frankie couldn't remember why. She was an orphan that the New York clan had discovered, half sister to their Alpha. Since she wasn't a pup, she couldn't have the more traditional welcoming ceremony so the New York clan invited everyone to a welcoming ball instead. Although Frankie did not

RSVP, Dante made her go at the last minute. It was at the ball, in the ladies' room, where she met the guest of honor herself, though she didn't know initially. The two had bonded, but Frankie had to leave unexpectedly and was unable to say goodbye.

She read the invitation. "Invited ... blah blah ... True Mate ... yada yada ... ah, here you go. Chase. Her last name's Chase."

Her brother took out his phone and typed the name into his browser. "Hmmm ... Alynna Chase, Private Investigator. Her number's still on this website. Could that be her?"

Frankie bit her lip. "Go ahead and give her a call. I'll talk to her and find out."

Dante tapped the number on his screen and handed his sister the phone. Placing it next to her ear, Frankie waited as the line began to ring.

"Hello?" a female voice answered.

"Hi ... is this Alynna? Chase?"

"Yes, this is she," the voice replied. "Are you calling about my PI services? I'm sorry, I'm currently not taking on cases, but I can refer you to some other investigators."

"No, I'm not ...um ... this is Francesca Muccino. I mean, Frankie. You know, from the ball. In the bathroom. With those women?"

"Huh?" The woman on the other side paused. "Frankie ... oh my God! Yes, I remember you! How did you find my number? I mean, I'm sorry, I've been meaning to look you up, but I couldn't find your name on the RSVP list and I didn't know which clan you're from and you were obviously alone so—"

Frankie laughed. "Yeah, sorry about leaving without saying goodbye. I kind of had to bail my brother out of jail," she explained. The night of the ball was also the same night Enzo was picked up for fighting at a local dive bar, trying to protect a girl who was being roughed up by an ex-boyfriend. Frankie mentally shook her head. It had cost her a lot of free meals at the restaurant to help soothe things over with the local PD.

"Ah, well, there are more important things than hanging around a ball, I suppose," Alynna quipped. "Hey, Frankie, listen, I really, really do want to catch up and chat, but, um, we're kind of having a ... a family emergency," Alynna explained. "But I have your number and I'll give you a call soon, okay?"

"Wait! Don't hang up!" Frankie pleaded.

"What's wrong?"

"Your emergency ... it wouldn't happen to be a missing ... Alpha?" Frankie lowered her voice.

There was a long pause. "What do you know about that?" Alynna's voice turned serious.

"I think we found him. He showed up in my driveway. Your Alpha, he was drugged and disoriented. He's safe, but he must have shifted to get away from whoever did this to him."

There was another long pause. "Give me your address," Alynna said. "I'm coming over now."

CHAPTER THREE

"So, Cady," Alynna Chase-Westbrooke said as the driver of her town car pulled out of The Enclave, the New York clan's home base on the Upper West Side of Manhattan. "Tell me what we know about Francesca Muccino." She closed the window between her and the driver so she could have the conversation in private.

"Hold on," Cady Vrost, Grant's Executive Assistant and the clan's Human Liaison, paused. "I'm pulling up what we have." Even though it was almost one a.m., Cady was alert and wide awake. Her husband Nick, the clan's Beta or second-in-command, didn't want her to go with Alynna because she was currently five months pregnant. Nick himself had to stay behind to hold down the fort in case there was any other emergency.

Alynna was over eight months pregnant herself, but there was no one else who could go to New Jersey. She was the only one who knew the New Jersey Alpha and invited into their territory. Alynna also requested permission for her husband, Alex Westbrooke, and their resident Lycan doctor, Dr. Tom Faulkner, which Frankie granted. So, Alynna decided that

Cady and Nick could brief her via phone during the forty-five minute drive to Frankie's house.

"Alright, here we go. Francesca Muccino, daughter of the previous Lupa, Adrianna Muccino. Twenty-eight years old, ascended to Alpha status two years ago when her mother died. Current residence, Barnsville, New Jersey," Cady rattled off.

"Hmmm ... Lupa? New Jersey is one of the few Lycan clans with female Alphas, right?" Alynna recalled from one of her earlier conversations with Cady.

"Yes, one of the few in the US," Cady explained. "I'm afraid that's all the information we have, really. We're not privy to all the records the High Council keeps, except for the name of the current and past Alphas, mates, and heirs apparent and presumptive, if any. As far as we know, Jersey has no Beta, no current Liaison or known Alliance families. She hasn't named an heir yet, which isn't unusual since she's young and currently not married."

"Why couldn't I find her name on the list at the ball? I searched through all the RSVPs."

"She actually didn't RSVP to your ball, but I guess she showed up anyway," Cadye said, referring to Alynna's coming out ball a few months ago.

"And that's where I met her," Alynna recalled. She had been in the bathroom, hiding in one of the stalls when a group of bitchy Lycan women started trash talking Alynna and her mom. Despite not knowing who she was, Frankie had defended her and the two women became fast friends that night. Unfortunately, Frankie was called away before they could exchange numbers, and Alynna was unable to track her. Plus, the events of the last few months had distracted her from trying to find her friend.

"You're sure it's her?" Nick Vrost asked.

"Yup, she remembered me and mentioned details only she

would know. Said she looked me up on the internet and found me on an old listing for my PI business," Alynna explained. "Apparently, Grant showed up in her driveway, drugged, but also appeared to have shifted into his wolf form at some point. I wonder if someone drugged him, tried to kidnap him, and then he turned into his Lycan form to get away?"

"That's most likely what happened, which is why he didn't call Miller to pick him up," Nick's voice was tense. "Sometime after ten p.m., he called me, saying that Grant had gone to one of his favorite bars, Luxe, but hadn't checked in for over four hours. He went to the bar and couldn't find the Alpha anywhere; Grant also wasn't answering his phone."

"And then what happened?"

"Well, I went down to Luxe and talked to the staff. Grant had apparently left with a woman for a few minutes, then went down to the lobby alone. The concierge recalled seeing Grant leave the hotel, and that was the last they saw of him. They wouldn't let me view the security tapes for privacy reasons, but I'm working on finding a way."

"Alex is also going to New Jersey, but took a separate car; he stopped to get Dr. Faulkner, just in case," Alynna relayed. "Unfortunately, Dr. Faulkner's all the way in Yonkers, attending to an emergency with a Lycan patient. They won't reach New Jersey for at least another two hours."

"What else did the Lupa say?" Nick asked. "Was it a human drug or something else?"

"Nothing really. All she said was that he appeared disoriented and couldn't see. He was also passing out intermittently." Alynna tapped her fingers on the leather seat.

"But what else could it be? It would take a hell of a lot of human drugs to knock Grant out. And he wouldn't just shift if he knew his captors were human," Nick said. Humans, except for a small number allied with the Lycans, were unaware of the Lycan werewolf shifters living underneath their very noses.

"This is going to get ugly," Alynna predicted. "The mages are getting bolder."

Ever since Alynna had joined them, the Lycans became a target of a series of attacks by an unknown force. Five months ago, it was revealed that a group of mages, former witches and warlocks who used dark blood magic, were responsible.

Their leader, Stefan, hated Lycans and wanted to kill all of them. He also wanted to get rid of Alynna, the first True Mate child for generations. His plan to kill her was thwarted, as Alynna herself became pregnant with her own True Mate child, which made her immune to poison and all other types of harm.

"I was worried that would happen." Nick let out a frustrated breath. "The mages probably have their next plan already in motion."

"Well, we'll deal with it," Alynna said. "For now, let's concentrate on getting Grant back."

———

After forty-five minutes of driving, they reached Barnsville, New Jersey, a small town near Morristown. Following the GPS, the car pulled up to a Victorian-style house outside the center of town. The driver opened the door for her, and she stepped out. She ascended the stairs slowly, trying to manage her large belly. After what seemed like an eternity, she rang the doorbell. A few seconds later, she heard soft footsteps approaching the door and it flew open.

"Alynna! *Madre de dio!*" Frankie's mismatched eyes grew wide as she stared at Alynna's obviously pregnant belly. "My God, you're huge! I mean, sorry! I didn't realize you were pregnant! When are you due?"

"Yesterday," Alynna replied sarcastically, then smirked at the other woman.

Frankie opened the door wider. "Come in, come in! Have a seat! Do you want water? Some milk or something? How about food?" The other Lycan seemed rattled. "Sorry, it's the Italian in me. We always want to feed people when they come to our house. Especially pregnant women!"

Alynna laughed. "I don't think you have enough food for us. Baby and I have been known to clean out a few buffets." She rubbed her belly instinctively. "But wait ... Grant. I need to see him first."

The other woman nodded. "Of course, come this way." Frankie led her to a bedroom, and flipped on the light.

"Grant!" Alynna exclaimed as she maneuvered to her brother's side. Grant was lying in bed, a sheet thrown over his hips. He lay still, but the even rise and fall of his chest told her he was alive.

"I'll leave you for now." Frankie stepped back. "I'll be in the kitchen, but just give a shout out if you need anything."

"Thank you," Alynna replied, not taking her eyes off her brother. She touched his forehead. He was warm, but not burning up. He looked like he was sleeping very deeply, probably fighting off whatever magical drug the mages had given him. She brushed away a lock of hair that had fallen over his forehead and wiped the sweat off with a towel Frankie must have left by his bedside. Giving her brother a kiss on the forehead, she eased off the bed and walked out.

The house wasn't that big, so she found the kitchen easily. Frankie was sitting on the large kitchen table, while another man—no, Lycan, Alynna could tell—stood in front of the stove, stirring a wooden spoon in a pot.

"Oh my God, that smells amazing!" Alynna's stomach grumbled loudly and the baby kicked.

Frankie shot up and walked to her side. "Come in, please sit down. My brother will have the pasta ready in a bit."

The male Lycan turned to Alynna, his handsome face breaking into a smile. He wiped his hand on his apron and held it out. "Hey, there, I'm Dante. Nice to meet you."

Alynna shook his hand. "Alynna, and same to you," she greeted as she gripped his hand. She could see the similarities in their features, but the most obvious were the eyes. Dante had one blue eye and one green, just like Frankie, though they were mirrored, she realized. Frankie's right eye was green and the left one was blue, while Dante's were the opposite.

"Sit, sit," Frankie ordered, pulling out a chair for her. A cup of tea and a glass of water were already waiting for her. "I didn't know what you want or what you could have. I can make coffee, too, but I'm not sure you can have that."

"This is fine." Alynna laughed as she sat down. "Really, please don't fuss. Not when I owe you guys. Thank you for taking care of Grant and sorry about him wandering into your territory."

"No worries," Frankie replied. "I figured he didn't mean to … is he alright? I mean, he couldn't talk or do anything else—"

Dante stifled a laugh and then coughed to cover it up. Frankie shot him a warning look. "I mean," Frankie continued, "he was able to mumble out that he was drugged or something. I kind of uh … ran over him. I mean, he just appeared out of nowhere and he bounced off my hood. But he should be okay; I don't think he broke anything."

"Our doctor should be on the way, so he'll get checked out," Alynna said.

"So, I didn't get an announcement or notice from the High Council, but … did you end up marrying Liam Henney?" Frankie asked.

Alynna giggled. "God, no! I mean, Liam's cute and nice and

all ... You've actually never seen my husband, but you do know of him ... from the ball."

Frankie's eyes widened. "You mean ... on the balcony?" She looked at Alynna's belly. "Well, congratulations! And good for him!"

"Yeah, well, there's a lot more to that story. Plus, you'll meet Alex when he arrives with our doctor."

"Excuse me," Dante said as he put a plate in front of Alynna. The plate was piled with pasta covered in a delicious-smelling red sauce.

"You didn't have to make me food." Alynna's eyes devoured the plate. Dante finished it off with freshly grated Parmesan cheese. "Did you make this? This is amazing!"

"Family recipe," Dante explained. "Same as what we serve in the restaurant so we keep lots of it around. Please, eat up."

"Thanks!" Alynna dug into the pasta, taking a forkful into her mouth. She closed her eyes, chewing and savoring the taste. "Oh. My. God." She took another bite. "Amazing. I'm gonna finish this entire thing!"

"Please, go right ahead, plenty where that came from," Frankie laughed.

"I'm a bottomless pit, thanks to this one." She pointed at her belly, then took another bite. "What's in this?"

Dante shook his head and wagged his finger. "Uh-uh, family secret." He winked at the pregnant Lycan. "You'll have to come eat at the restaurant to get more."

"Is that your game?" Alynna teased. "Tempt them with free stuff and then have them coming back for more? If so, sign me up!"

Frankie laughed. "We'll give you a jar before you leave. And you are most definitely welcome to come to New Jersey to eat at Muccino's."

"Thank God because I might ask to be transferred to your

clan if I wasn't," Alynna joked. The Muccinos were certainly an interesting bunch, and she was glad if Grant had ended up anywhere after being drugged, it was with them. Worry gripped her. Hopefully Grant would be able to recover from whatever was in his system.

CHAPTER FOUR

Grant swam in and out of consciousness, his thoughts and vision cloudy. *Where am I?* His hands gripped cool, soft sheets, and the scent of almond cookies, just like the ones he loved as a child, lingered on the pillows. He remembered full curves pressed against him, soft lips, and that heady scent. Placing his fingers against his nose, the sweet womanly scent teased him, causing his cock to spring to attention. His eyes flew open and, slowly, they adjusted to the low light. He spied a lamp next to the bed and flipped it on. Blinded temporarily by the light, he closed his eyes and collapsed back on the bed.

There was a weakness in his body, something he'd never felt before. It was like recovering from an illness, and he could already feel his enhanced Lycan immune system fighting whatever it was affecting his body. Searching his memories, he tried to remember what happened. Luxe. The blonde. She threw something in his face, a potion that knocked him out. But, after that, the next thing he could remember was the soft body against his, inhaling that amazing scent, and wanting to bury himself deep inside her. *No, not the blonde.* But who? The scent, it was definitely familiar, not just because it reminded him of his childhood. He had smelled it before, but when? He would have remembered meeting a female Lycan with such an irresistible scent.

He opened his eyes, took a deep breath, and slowly got to his feet. There was a pair of well-worn gray sweatpants hanging by the foot of the bed, which he assumed was for him since he was stark naked. *Did I shift?* That added to his confusion. Putting them on, he cautiously padded out of the room, into the main hallway. His vision was still blurry around the edges, but he heard voices from one of the inner rooms. Focusing on the voices, he followed the sound, which led him to a room at the end of the hallway, the only one in the dark house that was lit up.

"... tempt them with the free stuff and then have them coming back for more? If so, sign me up!"

Grant perked up when he heard the familiar voice. *What was Alynna doing here?* He walked toward the room and gripped the doorframe to steady himself. His mind and vision were now clear, though he still felt a little weak. "A—Alynna?" he rasped, his voice sounding rough and grating. "Where are we?"

Alynna shot to her feet. "Grant!"

Grant felt a spasm and clutched his side. He braced himself against the frame, and another man quickly ran to his side, helping him up. "Alpha, are you okay?" the young Lycan asked. He smelled like vanilla and something else familiar.

"Yes, sorry, I'm just—" He stopped short when he turned to the third occupant in the room. Once he set his eyes on her, his mouth went dry and he couldn't turn away. Sitting next to his sister was another woman, who was staring up at him, a look of surprise on her gorgeous face. Her pouty lips were parted; her dusky olive skin was smooth; her cheekbones were high; and her eyebrows were thick, dark, and delicately arched. Sweeping long, dark lashes framed gorgeous mismatched blue and green eyes that seemed to glow even in the harsh light of the kitchen. He could smell the subtle almond scent coming from her, or maybe it was all over the house.

Probably her house, he guessed. Something inside him lurched, and a low guttural sound rumbled softly in his chest. *What the heck was that?*

"Hello?" Alynna waved her hand in front of Grant's face. "Are you feeling okay?"

Grant blinked twice, not realizing his sister had gotten up and walked over to his side.

"Why don't I bring the Alpha back to the guest room?" the younger man offered.

"No, I'm fine ..." he looked down at the Lycan, "Thank you, uh ..."

"I'm Dante, Alpha," he introduced himself. Grant realized the younger man also had the same features and eyes as the mysterious woman, so they were probably related. "And this is my—"

The doorbell interrupted him.

"That's probably Alex and Dr. Faulkner," Alynna guessed.

The other woman quickly got up from her seat. "I'll get the door then." She swept past him, careful to avoid any contact with him. His gaze followed her as she left.

"Grant, if you're feeling weak, go back to the guest room." Alynna crossed her arms. He opened his mouth to protest, but she put her hand up. "Uh-uh. You mother hen me all the time, and now you're gonna listen to me, okay?"

"I'm fine," he grumbled and straightened up. "I don't need any help." He turned around and walked back out into the hallway with Dante and Alynna right behind him. When they neared the front part of the house, he saw Alex and Dr. Faulkner entering as the mystery woman held the door open.

"Grant!" Tom Faulkner called when he saw the Alpha. "Thank goodness you're alright!"

"Well, that's one way of putting it," he replied, rubbing his temples.

"We have some clothes for you, Primul." Alex handed him a sweatshirt. "Glad to see you're okay." He clapped him on the shoulder. Grant took the sweatshirt and nodded at him gratefully before putting it on.

As she stood next to Alex and Dr. Faulkner, Grant realized how petite the mystery woman was, probably two or three inches shorter than his sister. He also couldn't help but notice how her jeans and t-shirt molded to her curvy body. It was all coming back to him slowly. He remembered the soft hand on his cheek, pulling her to bed, how her lips tasted, and how her body felt beneath him. Again, that feeling came back, a strange sensation vibrating throughout his body.

"Grant, are you alright?" the older Lycan asked. "Your pupils are still dilated."

"I'm ... uh, still recovering, I think," he said with a cough.

Dr. Faulkner shook his head and turned to the woman. "Lupa, thank you for your help. Would it be an imposition if we stayed a bit longer, just so I can examine him?"

Grant's head snapped up in surprised. *Lupa*, he thought silently. *Oh, fuck me*. He felt like a sex-starved idiot, lusting and practically assaulting another man's wife. *Another Alpha's Lupa*, he added. Of course, he remembered her responding to his kiss and his touch, even unbuttoning her jeans when his hands wouldn't cooperate. Not that it mattered now. He did not sleep with married women, especially not mates of other Alphas.

"Of course," she nodded. "Please, take your time and don't

worry, it's not an imposition. I'm just glad ... your Alpha isn't hurt too badly. Let's go into the living room."

"Thank you, Lupa." Dr. Faulkner then turned to Grant. "Let's have a look at you."

They all filed into the living room and Grant sat on the plush, comfy couch. Dr. Faulkner kneeled in front of him and opened his medical bag, taking out his flashlight and stethoscope. He gave Grant a quick examination and also took a vial of blood from his arm. "Well, whatever you were drugged with, looks like your system is fighting it off. How are you feeling?"

"Still a little weak but much better," he replied. "Like I'm recovering from an illness."

"Good," Dr. Faulkner put away the small vial. "I'm hoping we can get some traces of whatever was in your system. I'll send these over to Dr. Cross in the morning."

"Good," Grant stood and turned to Dante and the woman. "Um, thank you, by the way. To both of you and your clan. Where is your Alpha, by the way? I'd like to thank him personally, if he's around."

Dante looked at the woman and let out a laugh. The woman, on the other hand, crossed her arms and gave him an annoyed look. "The Alpha is right here," she seethed.

Grant looked around, a baffled expression on his face.

"Hey, blockhead, maybe those drugs are still in your system," Alynna said in an admonishing voice. "She *is* the Alpha. We're in New Jersey."

Grant's face went from confusion to surprise. The woman's face turned sour as her eyes narrowed. "My apologies then, Alpha," he corrected himself. "I'm ... I just assumed ..."

"That I'm some Alpha's wife? Because of my title? Like I would just let a stranger—" She stopped short and her face flushed.

Despite her obvious anger, Grant couldn't help but notice how even more beautiful she was, especially with her blue-green eyes flashing. "Blame it on my drug-addled state. I meant no insult, Alpha. Not when I'm in your territory. I'm Grant. Grant Anderson. Alpha to the New York Clan." He held out his hand.

She raised a brow and looked at his hand, unsure what to do. "I ..." She hesitated and took his hand. Her grip was strong, her skin soft but slightly callused. The touch sent tingles up his arm, and desire bubbled deep inside him. "Francesca Muccino, Alpha to New Jersey clan," she replied.

"Nice to meet you, Alpha," Grant put on his most charming smile, not letting go of her hand. "Thank you for your rescue and generosity."

"It was nothing," she said dismissively, pulling her hand away from him.

"Hey, what's going on?" Another man entered the living room, dressed in a t-shirt and sweats. His hair stuck up in places as if he'd just gotten out of bed, and his chocolate brown eyes were sleepy. He was definitely a human, and all the other Lycans in the room, save for the Alpha and Dante, tensed.

"Matty," the Alpha greeted, her voice turning tender. "Sorry, did we wake you?"

"It's alright, Frankie," he said with a yawn. "Oh hey, everyone, I'm Matteo." He smiled at everyone, then turned to Grant. "Hey, man, are you okay? Glad you're up and about! Looks like Dante's sweats fit you okay. I wasn't sure, but I was hoping they would when I got them."

"Thank you, Matteo," Grant said with a nod. "And for your help. All of your help, I mean."

"Cool, well ..." He looked around. "Seems like you guys are discussing important Lycan stuff." He yawned again. "I'll leave you to it. Goodnight, I'll see you in the morning, Frankie, Dante.

I gotta go home and shower before I head to work." He turned and left.

"Who was that?" Alynna asked. "He's human, right?"

"Sorry." Frankie gave everyone a reassuring smile. "That's my brother, Matt. Half-brother, I mean."

"Brother?" Dr. Faulkner's brows knitted. He turned to Dante. "And you're her brother too, right?"

He nodded.

"You have two brothers, Lupa?" Alex asked in a curious voice.

"No," Frankie shook her head, "I have four brothers: Dante; Matteo; his twin Enzo; and our youngest, Rafe. Except for me and Dante, they're all human, since their dad was human."

"Four ... five of you?" Dr. Faulkner sounded incredulous. "That's ... fascinating!"

"Why?" Dante asked.

"Well, you must know ... most Lycans don't have more than one child, if at all, even those mated to humans. Yet, your mother had five," Dr. Faulkner explained.

Frankie shrugged. "That's the way it's always been with us. Ma had five, and her mother had four, though our mother was her only Lycan offspring. Grandfather died shortly after they moved here from Italy."

"Must be our Italian genes!" Dante joked.

"Still ..." Dr. Faulkner paused. "Sorry to pry, Lupa. Of course, as a man of medicine and science, I do understand that there are always outliers in such matters, an exception rather than the rule. I just wonder why we never hear about you or why the Lycan High Council didn't think such an occurrence, in at least three generations, was significant."

"Don't worry about it." Frankie shrugged. "Our clan isn't very big, certainly not as big as New York. It's mostly composed of my relatives and two or three families who have transferred over from other states, usually to get into better school districts for their children. We do what's necessary to keep the Lycan High Council up to date with our numbers and any problems, but that's about it."

"How did you know to call Alynna though?" Alex asked.

"Oh! I can answer that!" Alynna's eyes lit up. "Frankie threatened to tear another girl's throat out when she insulted my mother in the bathroom at my welcoming ball," she said proudly.

Frankie laughed. "Those bitches deserved it."

"You've met before?" Grant asked, his eyes darting to his sister.

"Yes. At the ball," Alynna explained. "I was hiding in the stall. You saw her there, right, Grant? She was the woman in green!"

"I didn't see your face," Grant confessed to Frankie. "And I'm afraid my Liaison takes care of invites and such."

"I wasn't going to go, but Dante said I had to," the Lupa explained. "To make nice with the neighbors."

"Well, I'm glad you went!" Alynna declared. "And that Grant found his way to you. Who knows what would have happened if he had shifted and went to your neighbor's house or something?"

Frankie's brows knitted. "What happened, by the way? Did you get kidnapped or something?"

He shook his head. "I'm not sure ... but it may be an internal matter."

"We will inform the High Council when we know more, Lupa," Dr. Faulkner assured her.

"Of course," she said nonchalantly.

"We should get going." Alynna yawned and stood. The rest of the New York Lycans agreed with her, citing the late hour.

"Hey Frankie, I got your number, don't be a stranger, okay?" Alynna said as they filed out into the front porch.

Frankie smiled. "Of course. And you need to come to the restaurant. Maybe when you have your little one? You look like you're ready to pop!"

"Oh, I hope so!" Alynna joked, rubbing her belly. "I'm ready to send this one an eviction notice! I just feel so fat and awkward ..."

"You look beautiful, baby doll." Alex put an arm around his wife and a hand on her stomach.

"Well, I wish you a safe delivery and look forward to welcoming a new life into your clan," Frankie said.

"Thank you, Lupa." Alex bowed reverently. "We accept your blessing and wish your clan happiness and health."

———

Grant watched as his sister and Frankie joked and chatted, so much at ease with each other. He was relieved Frankie wasn't married or mated to another Alpha, though he was surprised she was head of her clan. Not that he didn't believe women could be Alphas. He was also surprised to learn that he had been so close to her many months ago at the ball, though circumstances had prevented them from meeting.

"Grant?" Dr. Faulkner called his attention again. "We should head back. It's almost two a.m."

"Right," he turned to Dante and Frankie, "Alpha, Dante, thank you for your generosity. Our clan owes you, so don't hesitate to ask if you are in need."

Frankie nodded. "You're most welcome, Alpha," she said formally, avoiding his eyes.

"We're glad to help and that you're safe," Dante added.

Frankie gave Alynna a hug. "I'll talk to you soon. Come to the restaurant anytime."

"For sure! I can't wait to try out all your food!"

They said their goodbyes and the New York Lycans headed back to their cars. Alex drove Dr. Faulkner back in his car, while Grant joined Alynna in the town car. The driver opened the door, and Grant helped his sister ease herself into the back seat and then sat beside her. When the car door closed, Alynna crawled next to him.

"I was so worried about you," she said quietly, squeezing herself against his side.

"I'm sorry." He put an arm around her. "I was careless, and I can't afford to be these days."

"Was it the mages?" she asked.

He nodded. "Yes, but let's talk about it another time." His gaze drifted to the house, where Frankie and Dante remained standing on the porch, waiting for their guests to leave. His eyes remained fixed on the Alpha. Desire shot deeply through him, something he hadn't felt in months toward any woman, but, somehow, it felt much more than sexual attraction. Francesca Muccino was beautiful, and any man would be blind not to see that. He normally went for tall, willowy model types, but something about those lush curves and pouty mouth made him want to toss her over his shoulder and take her to bed. He wondered what would have happened if her brother hadn't interrupted them.

"Uh oh," Alynna said, interrupting his thoughts. She looked up at him meaningfully, her green eyes so similar to his own, sparkled with mischief.

"Uh oh?" Grant looked down at his sister. "What do you mean uh oh?"

Alynna gave him a smug smile. "Oh nothing." She turned to the driver. "Let's head home."

_____

CHAPTER FIVE

"You bumbling fool! You idiot!" Victoria railed at Daric. They stood in front of Stefan, who stood motionless and stoic as ever. "You *had* him! The Alpha of the most powerful clan in the world, and he got away!"

"I'm sorry, Master," Daric got on one knee and bowed his head. "Our mage team let the Alpha get away. He was able to shift and overpower our people. I take full responsibility." He closed his eyes, as if waiting for punishment to rain down on him like hellfire.

"Get up, Daric," Stefan's claw-like fingers dug into his shoulders. "No need to apologize."

"But Master, I failed you." Daric looked genuinely confused.

Stefan let out a cruel laugh. "Not at all."

"I don't understand, Master."

"Master!" Victoria screeched. "He let Grant Anderson escape when he could have killed him!" She looked at Daric. "Why did you kidnap him and let him escape. You should have put a knife to his heart the moment you got your hands on him!"

"The Master instructed us to bring him back here," Daric said.

Victoria, wild-eyed and confused, looked at Stefan. "Master?"

Stefan gave them a cruel smile. "Do you think I would just let the Alpha escape with a quick and painless death? No. This was part of the plan."

The redheaded witch's face twisted into a vicious mask. "Plan? What plan? Why can't we just kill the Alpha?"

"My dear," Stefan said haughtily. "Killing the Alpha now will only make the Lycans bloodthirsty for revenge. When that happens, the Beta will take over, and, with a strong mate, one that's connected with the witches and a True Mate offspring, it will only make them stronger and more determined to destroy us."

"So, what's the real plan?" Victoria asked in an irritated voice.

"I have set plans in motion with our new allies," Stefan relayed. "We will use them to hook in the Alpha by having him pledge his loyalty to them, and, then, once they have secured his legacy, we can kill him."

"Is that wise?" Daric asked. "How can we trust these new allies of yours?"

"We can't," Stefan declared. "We will keep them close, and, once we have what we want, we will kill them too. I have no use for creatures who would betray their own kind and for what? A patch of territory? No. We will get rid of these 'allies' and take over."

———————

CHAPTER SIX

"Now that is some story, Grant," Cady remarked. She was sitting on the couch in the Alpha's office at the Fenrir Corp headquarters in Midtown Manhattan. Her husband sat next to her as they listened to Grant relay the events from two nights ago. "And the New Jersey Alpha! I updated our database just before Alynna's ball, and she definitely got an invite. I didn't get an RSVP, though; otherwise she would have been introduced to you and Alynna directly."

"Well, apparently, she decided to go last minute," Grant said. "She just showed up and met Alynna in the bathroom."

Nick Vrost frowned. "We need to tighten up security, especially if anyone can just slip into our events." As head of security and Grant's Beta, Nick was in charge of making sure everyone at Fenrir and the clan were safe.

"Well, she wasn't just anyone." Cady put a hand on her husband's arm reassuringly. "She is a Lycan and an Alpha. Your guys probably just assumed she'd already been inside the ballroom."

"Sorry we're late," Alex said as he entered Grant's office with Alynna just behind him. "Primul, Al Doilea," he greeted

Grant and Nick by their honorific titles. Even though he was married to Grant's sister (and soon-to-be father to Grant's heir presumptive), he still showed respect to the two men, especially at the office or around other Lycans. "Cady," he greeted the other woman. Alex was a transferee Lycan, originally from Chicago, but he asked to move to New York to be part of Grant's security team. Human Liaison Cady Vrost (née Gray, before she married Nick) was his first friend when he arrived in the city.

"Alynna, you should have stayed home." Grant frowned as he watched his very pregnant sister struggle to sit down. "You could have called in."

"Uh, please, I'm fine, just didn't get enough sleep." She eased down on the plush seat, her hand on her belly. "Alex, we should definitely sign him up for football lessons. We're gonna have a kicker on our hands."

Alex sat next to her, placing an arm around her. "And if it's a girl?"

"Girls can play football, too, you know," she said with a sigh. "I wish True Mate babies weren't sonogram-proof, then we would know."

At the beginning of Alynna's pregnancy, Dr. Faulkner had discovered that the sonogram simply wouldn't work on her baby. One of the signs of having a True Mate child (aside from instant conception, barring any physical contraception) was that both the child and the mother were virtually indestructible. Alynna herself had survived a poisoning, and Cady recovered from what would have been a fatal stab wound. Unfortunately, True Mate fetuses probably had some type of protective shield, which also kept out sonogram waves. Alex and Alynna were worried, but they had to trust that their baby was healthy. They were a little disappointed that they would have to wait until after the birth to find out if it was a boy or girl, though.

"Anyway, now that we're all here," Cady began. "What do we do? It's obvious the mages were behind your kidnapping, Grant. What did they want and how did they get to you?"

"Well, there was a woman ..." he began.

Alynna grinned. "Oh, there's always a woman, I suppose."

"Contrary to popular belief, I'm not a monk," Grant said dryly. "The short version is I was at Luxe and when I went out to get some fresh air, this woman I had met followed me and hit me with some kind of potion. I can't be sure what she looks like, since she could have been using a glamour spell. Anyway, I blacked out. I remember shifting into wolf form and escaping from the back of a van, but the potion must have muddled my memories because, the next thing I knew, a car hit me and I was lying on the ground."

"Did you have blood on you?" Nick asked.

He shook his head. "No, and I didn't smell any traces of it either."

"You must have scared the shit out of the mages when you transformed in the back of the van," Alynna guessed. "And you were probably within the Jersey territory, since you couldn't have gone too far if you were still drugged."

"We should check for speed cameras, and maybe reports of crashes between New York and the Alpha's house, in case they lost control of the vehicle." Alex suggested. "Then we need to report back to the High Council and the Witch Assembly."

"How are talks going with the Assembly, by the way?" Alynna asked.

Grant sighed and shook his head. "Not good, I'm afraid. The witches and Lycans are still wary of each other, even after all these months of talks. And the mages have laid low, so neither side thinks there's anything to worry about."

"I'll talk to Vivianne," Cady said, referring to her aunt, who was also the head of her own coven, based in New York. "We need to get some progress on these talks. Hopefully the kidnapping of an Alpha should be good enough reason to start moving on a real alliance."

"Right," Grant said. "Now, let's move on to other business." He turned to Nick. "Nick, you said you were working on a plan to increase our security forces?"

"Yes, I wanted to start doing more recruitment drives. I know there are many Lycans in other clans that might be willing to transfer ...."

They all listened to Nick's ideas, threw in some of their own, and decided to continue the discussion another time.

"Can we get lunch, please?" Alynna begged.

Alex kissed her on the forehead. "Of course. Cady, Nick, Grant, come and join us? I asked Jared to have some Chinese food delivered to our office. There's enough for everyone, including two pregnant Lycans."

"Sounds great," Cady said, easing up slowly from the couch. Her own baby bump was showing and she had started wearing more maternity clothes. "You need to go home after we eat, Alynna."

"I'm not due for another two weeks," the younger woman pouted.

"Still, remember what Dr. Faulkner said—you need to be near The Enclave Medical wing this close to your due date," Grant reminded her. "And, knowing the mages are getting bolder, I'm not taking any chances."

"Neither am I," Alex said seriously. "I'll take her straight home after lunch." He nodded to Grant.

"Good, now," Grant moved to his desk, "I'll join you in a bit. I just need to send off one more email." He sat down as the others left his office, then turned to his computer screen.

"Grant?" Nick had remained where he stood after he urged his wife to go ahead without him.

"What is it?" Grant asked. "Something you need to discuss with me in private?"

"I'm just ... concerned about you, not just as your Beta but also as your friend," Nick began. He walked over to the desk and sat in one of the chairs.

Grant leaned back. "Alright, what is it?"

"Well, I don't meddle in your personal affairs, and I always let you come to me when you need advice." Nick hesitated. "But these past months have been difficult for all of us. For you most of all. You've got the weight of the world on your shoulders, being our leader."

The Alpha crossed his arms. "What are you saying, Nick?"

"You've been distracted and stretched thin. Sometimes, I see you just staring into space, thinking about God knows what. And then taking chances like going to Luxe and hooking up with random women ..."

"I don't know what you expect of me, Nick. You know how it has to be for me—I don't have time for relationships," Grant explained. "Especially not now. Sometimes I need female company, a distraction. You understand. You weren't celibate, even during all that time you weren't with Cady."

"That's different. First of all, I'm not the Alpha. And as your Beta, you need to let me help you."

"So, are you offering to find women for me?" Grant said in a light tone. "I think that's going a little bit above and beyond, even for a Beta."

Nick chuckled. "No, no, I'm just saying, if there's something I can do to help you ... get whatever it is out of your system, let me know, okay? I'll be your wingman, just like old times. At least if I'm there, I can protect you."

"Will do, but don't worry, I won't be making more trips to Luxe anytime soon. By the way, how are renovations going?" Grant asked, quickly changing the subject. Nick and Cady were having his entire penthouse redone, just for the baby (and possible future additions), so they had moved into her place a few floors below.

"Good, good, we're still on schedule to move in about two months from now," Nick said.

"And everything else is good?"

"All is well and good. The baby, from what we can tell, is healthy and strong. He or she kicked for the first time last night." Nick smiled, a rarity in all the time Grant had known him, but it has happened more frequently in the last few months. It was obvious his friend was happy, content, and completely in love with his wife. Grant felt a stab of envy, but he was glad Nick and Cady finally decided to be together after ten years. It was the one good thing that came out of all this mage business.

"Excellent news." Grant stood up. "Well, let's go and join everyone before Alynna and your wife finish off all the egg rolls."

———

At the end of the workday, Grant left his office, bid his admin Jared good night, and headed down to Fenrir Corp's private garage. Heath Pearson, his driver and bodyguard for the day, was already waiting for him.

"Good evening, Primul," he greeted as he opened the door.

"Thank you, Pearson." He nodded and slipped into the back seat of the town car. The driver closed the door and went to the front seat.

"Just back to The Enclave, Primul?"

"Yes," he replied. Pearson started the engine and drove the car out of the garage.

Grant stared outside as they went uptown. The day had been pretty busy, and he was able to get a lot of work done, but, now that his mind was winding down, he couldn't help but think of his conversation with Nick. His thoughts were also filled with a certain luscious Alpha who seemed to have gotten under his skin. Frankie was on his mind a lot the past two days. The memories of her scent and her lush body lingered in the corners of his mind, overtaking his thoughts when he had a free moment. He couldn't forget the way her sweet lips tasted and how they molded perfectly against his. Of course, he also imagined much more than just the taste he had. He wondered how her naked breasts would feel against his chest, what she would taste like when he licked her until she screamed his name, and how her beautiful face would look when she fell apart in his arms.

"Pearson?" He called the driver's attention.

"What is it Primul?"

"Do you have your GPS on? Can you do a quick search for me, please? I think I'd like to go to dinner first."

"Of course, Primul." Pearson slowed the car and pulled to the side of the road. "Where would you like to go?"

"Search for Italian restaurants. In New Jersey. Actually, just one restaurant, something with Muccino's in the name."

The other Lycan said nothing as he followed his Alpha's instructions. He entered the name into the GPS unit and waited a few seconds. "Okay, Primul. Muccino's Italian Restaurant in Barnsville, New Jersey. We can be there in an hour and a half. Traffic is a bitch, uh, I mean, it's heavy going into Jersey this time of day. Is that okay, sir?"

"No worries. Go ahead."

"Yes, Primul." Pearson put the car into gear and began driving toward their destination. There was heavy traffic in the Lincoln Tunnel, but, after they exited and got past the traffic, the scenery turned from the industrial area of Jersey to more pleasant scenery of rolling hills and rich greenery.

Finally, they pulled into a small parking lot on Main Street in Barnsville, New Jersey. The restaurant itself was housed in a low brick building with red awnings over the windows. The lighted sign in front read "Muccino's Italian Restaurant." He exited the car and walked right through the front door.

The dining room was decorated in a typical casual Italian restaurant style, done in warm tones with dark wood moldings and matching furniture, and all the tables were covered in red and white checkered tablecloths. Everything looked neat and in order, if a little old-fashioned. As he approached the host's station, he was greeted by a familiar face.

"Hey, Matteo," he said to the younger man. "How are you? Sorry, I didn't bring the sweatpants back. I can have someone send them back tomorrow."

The other man gave him a curious look. "Sorry, sir, I'm not Matteo; I'm his twin, Enzo. Enzo Morretti." He held out his hand. "He doesn't work here weekdays, but I can give him a call if you need to get in touch."

"Oh, sorry about that." Grant shook his hand, giving it a firm shake. "I'm Grant. Grant Anderson." He looked at the other man and upon closer inspection, he realized that, despite their identical features, this was definitely a different man. He had a more modern, hip hairstyle and was dressed in a tight-fitting gray shirt, skinny red tie, slim black pants, and wingtips.

"Oh," Enzo said, then lowered his voice. "You're that Grant Anderson. The Alpha, right?"

He nodded. "Yes, that's me."

"The one Frankie ran over?"

Grant smiled. "The same one."

"Well, I'm glad you're alive. I had my doubts, especially

with the way she drives," he added with a chuckle. "Was there anything you needed, Alpha?"

"Yes. A table, please," Grant said.

"A table?" The young man seemed confused, then shrugged his shoulders. "Okay, well, as you can see, we're not very busy tonight." He motioned to the almost empty dining room. Only two other tables were filled.

"Anywhere's fine," Grant said.

"Right, follow me." Enzo led Grant to one of the tables in the middle of the room. "So, aren't you like, supposed to get permission to come here or something?"

"Your sister invited us to come anytime. Also, I was hungry and in the mood for Italian."

"Of course." Enzo stopped as they reached the table. "Your server will be with you in a moment." He handed Grant the menus as he sat down. "Have a good dinner."

CHAPTER SEVEN

Frankie tapped furiously on the keyboard. "C'mon, you piece of shit!" she growled at the computer. It froze for the nth time, and if it didn't save her progress, she would have to start all over again.

A whole hour's worth of work gone. She looked at all the bills piled up on her table. *Ugh.*

"Frankie!" Enzo popped his head through the doorway.

"What is it?" she asked impatiently.

"You need to come out to the dining room," Enzo said.

"Arggh ... is Mrs. Clementi complaining about her gazpacho being too cold again? Just heat it up on the stove, I doubt she can tell the difference." Frankie turned back to the computer and let out a string of curses in Italian that would have made a sailor blush. She got on her hands and knees and then crawled under her desk to unplug her computer.

"Frankie, no, really. There's a Lycan out there. The Alpha you ran over."

A loud thud followed by another string of curses came from beneath the table. "What?" Frankie asked as she crept out from under the desk, rubbing her head. "Who?"

"Whatshisname ... Grant Anderson."

"He's here?"

"That's what I said the first time, didn't I?" her brother asked in an exasperated voice.

"What does he want?"

"A table. Said he was hungry."

"And he came all the way here to eat at the restaurant?"

"Jeez, Frankie, I don't got time to play twenty questions, okay?" Enzo grumbled. "Come out or not, I don't care. I just thought you'd want to know." With that, Enzo left.

What the heck was Grant Anderson doing in New Jersey? Frankie stood up and dusted off her jeans and blouse.

Tuesday was usually their slowest day, which meant she dressed more casually than normal. Looking in the mirror mounted behind the door, she frowned. Her hair was piled haphazardly on top of her head with pins, and, though her blouse was clean, there was definitely a small hole at the bottom. She didn't keep a spare outfit in her office, not even a blazer. Not that she had any reason to. At least she had thought to put on some makeup before she left the house.

Frankie yanked open the door and stalked to the dining room. She peeked through the doorway that led to the main room, and, just as Enzo had said, Grant Anderson was sitting at their best table, conversing with one of their servers. She quickly backtracked, pressing up against the wall, her heart pounding. *God, what was he doing?* She shook her head and walked the opposite way, toward the back door that led to the kitchen. Enzo and Dante were there, their heads close together in a hushed conversation.

"*Ciao,* Nonna Gianna," she greeted the older, heavyset woman standing over the stove before giving her a kiss on each cheek. She was wearing a white apron over her floral dress, and her white hair was pulled back in a neat bun and covered by a hairnet.

"Francesca, *mimma, ciao*," she greeted back. Nonna Gianna was her grandmother's human cousin and currently the one other person who knew all the secret family recipes they served at the restaurant. She trained Dante from the time he expressed interest in learning how to cook, when he turned sixteen. After nine years of training, she declared that Dante had perfected all of the recipes and was happy to share the title of head chef with him.

Not that she needed the extra help. At 77 years old, Nonna Gianna was still spry and independent, living by herself in her own apartment not far from the restaurant. She was also a tough old bird who didn't take crap from anyone.

"What's this I hear about some man you ran over the other night and now he's dining here? Did you promise him free food, so he wouldn't sue you? We can't afford to be giving away food each time one of you breaks the law."

Frankie slapped her hand over her forehead. "Ugh, no Nonna, I didn't."

"So, he's here because ...?"

She shrugged. "Maybe he's a glutton for punishment?"

"He's a Lycan," Enzo said.

"Another Alpha," Dante added. "The New York Clan's Alpha."

"Another Alpha? Here?" Gianna put her hands on her hips. "Francesca, why aren't you tossing him out if he's not been invited?"

"Because ..." She peeked through the small window where they sent the food out. She could see Grant having a glass of wine. "Did he order the 2009 Masseto Merlot?" she said, spying the label. It was the priciest wine on their list and one of only two bottles they kept.

"Oh yeah," Enzo said. "I had to go to the cellar myself to get it. He ordered two starters, a pasta, and the Osso Bucco, too."

"That's the most expensive thing on our menu," Frankie said.

Nonna Gianna's eyebrow shot up and, she looked at Frankie. "Sounds like he's trying to impress someone."

She let out a huff. "Maybe he was hungry."

"Go find out what he wants then," Gianna prodded.

"No way!" She shook her head and backed up against the door. Dante opened his mouth to speak, but she shot him a cutting look.

Unfortunately, at that moment, one of the servers decided to open the door to the kitchen, sending Frankie staggering out into the dining room. She fell back and was able to catch one of the potted plants to regain her balance, but it was too late. The one person she didn't want to see had spotted her. Her eyes locked with Grant Anderson, the expression on his face amused.

Taking a deep breath, she straightened her shirt and turned around, walking toward the table.

"Alpha," she greeted. "I hope this isn't a declaration of war, with you just strolling into *my* territory unannounced." She emphasized the *my*, hoping it made her sound confident.

Grant looked up at her, the smile on his handsome face revealing a set of perfect white teeth. "Alpha," he nodded, "I believe I was invited."

"By whom?"

"You, of course."

"I did not! When did I—"

Grant cleared his throat. "I believe you said, 'come to the restaurant anytime.'" He gave her another megawatt smile.

Frankie's face grew red as a tomato. "That invitation was for your sister."

"Oh, so you would invite my family into your territory and the mother of my heir presumptive, but not me?"

She considered rescinding her invitation, but it's not as if he would be back again. She would at least make sure of that.

"Fine." She turned to walk away, but a large, warm hand grabbed her arm. Her skin tingled where their bare skin met, and she shivered. "Please, let go of me," she said quietly.

"Alpha, I'm sorry, I don't mean to offend." He tugged at her arm until she looked at him. His green eyes sought hers out. "Please, will you take a seat for a moment, I have business I need to discuss. Life and death."

Frankie hesitated as she pulled her arm away from him. She sighed in defeat and then sat down in the other chair.

"Wine?" Grant offered with a grin. "I can't finish the whole bottle by myself."

"You can take it with you; we'll give you a bag," she said curtly. "Now, what's this business you need to discuss? And why life and death?"

"I'm afraid it's Lycan business," Grant said as he took a sip of the wine. "Excellent choice, by the way. As is the rest of your wine list."

"Thank you. Now what is it you wanted to talk about?" she asked impatiently.

"It's Lycan business, so we'll have to discuss in private."

"Fine." She stood up. "Enjoy your dinner and, when you're done, Enzo will bring you to my office."

"Thank you, Alpha." He raised his glass to her, and she gave him a curt nod before she walked away.

Enzo came up to her, but before he could say anything, she raised her hand. "Uh uh, no, not another word." She wagged a finger at him. "Now, when he's done eating, show him the way to my office." And without another word, she walked away.

——

After slamming the door behind her, Frankie sat on her chair, crossing her arms over her chest. Grant Anderson twisted her words, manipulated his way into her territory and restaurant, and now he even got her to agree to meet in private. She'd gone crazy.

Yummy scent Lycan.

She banged her head on her table, crossed her arms over her head, and let out a pained groan. *Oh shut up, she-wolf.*

Dammit, why did Grant Anderson have to be so sexy and hot? In the last two days, she found herself staring out into space, thinking about that night. His large, warm hands all over her, his lips on hers and on her neck. She shivered involuntarily when she remembered his fingers touching her, his cock pressing up against her. If Dante and Matt hadn't arrived at that moment, would she have let him continue? Her thoughts wandered that way, wondering how the sex would be. Hot, heavy, and intense, she guessed. Grant Anderson seemed like the type of man who knew how to make a woman scream and moan and beg for more. But, despite her traitorous body, something inside her screamed danger. He was exactly the type of man she should be running away from.

Lifting her head, she looked around the office and sighed. It was small and cramped, with papers, books, and knick-knacks all over the place.

Well, not like I can do anything about it now. She stood up, doing her best to make the office presentable at least. There was a dead plant in the corner she had forgotten to water a few weeks ago. With a sigh, she picked it up and threw it in the trashcan.

Frankie sat back down in the leather office chair and booted up her computer. It would be a while before Grant finished his dinner, so she should get some work done. When the screen came to life and she logged into the accounting software, she saw that at least half of her work had saved. "*Grazie a dio!*" she exclaimed and began to enter the bills and numbers again.

Work was a good distraction, and, after thirty minutes, she clicked on the "save" button on the screen.

A knock interrupted her thoughts, and she tensed, sensing who it was.

Was he done already? She used her fingers to brush her hair back, tucking some loose tendrils behind her ear. Quickly grabbing a tube of lip gloss from her drawer, she swiped it on. "Come in," she called.

The door opened slowly, and Grant Anderson stepped inside. His large frame made the already cramped room seem smaller. He gave the room a cursory glance and, in three steps, was in front of her desk.

"Take a seat, Alpha." She nodded to the chair.

"Thank you."

He sat, and Frankie groaned inwardly when the rickety chair creaked under his weight. *Really need to get that fixed,* she reminded herself.

"It was an excellent dinner, by the way." He flashed her a smile.

"Thank you, we're very proud of our food."

He looked at the two photos on the wall beside her desk. "Is that your grandmother and mother? The former Alphas?"

She nodded.

"I can see the resemblance," he commented.

"Right, well. What did you want to talk about, Alpha?" she asked.

"Grant," he said.

"Grant?" she echoed.

"My name is Grant. You don't have to be so formal with me, not when it's just the two of us, Frankie."

The use of her first name rankled her, but what annoyed her most was her reaction to it. His voice was dripping with promise and sex when he said her name, and her knees felt weak. "Fine. What did you want to talk about, Grant?"

He leaned forward, his voice taking a serious tone. "Have you been contacted by the High Council about the events of the last few months? With the witches? And the mages?"

Frankie's brows knitted. "I don't think so. I mean, no, definitely not. What are mages?"

Grant crossed his arms over his chest. "That's what I thought," he said. "Ever since Alynna showed up, she's been targeted in a series of attacks. First someone broke into her home while she was sleeping, then she was poisoned with belladonna, and then finally they attempted to kidnap her."

Frankie gasped.

"Then they turned to the clan," Grant continued. "They hit our night club, Blood Moon, and set off a firebomb in my office building, killing two employees. One of them was Lycan."

"I'm sorry." She shook her head, her anger and annoyance at Grant dissipating.

"We found out it was a rogue group of ex-witches. They're called mages, and their leader, Stefan, is hell-bent on killing our kind."

"What?" she exclaimed. Now he had her full attention. "Why weren't we informed? No one has told us anything about this!"

Grant shook his head. "That's what I was afraid of. Of course, we've reported everything to the Lycan High Council. But they've been slow on taking any action and, even though we've been in talks with the Witch Assembly, nothing's happened."

"That's crazy!" Frankie slammed her fist on the table. "What if ..." Her eyes grew wide. "They were the ones who kidnapped you, weren't they?"

The other Alpha nodded. "We can't prove it, but I can tell you magic was involved."

"And they were in my territory!" Her eyes flashed in anger. She thought of her clan, her relatives, her brothers. It was her duty to keep them safe, after all. "What can we do?"

Grant let out a frustrated breath. "The High Council is dragging its feet on sending out information to all the clans. They don't want to cause a panic, they said. But, they can't stop me from telling other clans about it, though I've been treading carefully, so as not to step on any toes. San Francisco has been informed, and so have Chicago and Connecticut."

Frankie paused. "New Jersey isn't exactly in the same league as those clans."

"But, so far, your territory and mine are the only ones we know of that the mages have been in."

She sighed. "Of course, I mean, we'll do what we can, but I don't have any security, bodyguards, or any spare resources. I don't even have a Beta or a Liaison."

"We don't have a solid plan yet, as I don't want to upset the High Council," Grant explained. "But I wanted to make sure you knew about this threat, especially since you're our closest neighbor."

"I appreciate the warning." Frankie clasped her hands together and sat back in her chair, her face pensive.

"You have a right to know," Grant stated.

"I'll have to call for a meeting with my clan, and tell everyone to keep their guard up. That's all I can do for now. Thank you for letting me know." She stood up. "It's getting late, and I'm sure the drive to Manhattan won't be so bad now."

Grant stood, and Frankie was relieved he seemed to take the

hint. She walked to the door, intending to let him out, but he put a hand on her shoulder. "Wait, there's one more thing."

She turned around, looking up at him. Grant towered over her, and she realized how close he was. So close she could smell his ocean spray scent and hear the roar of the waves in her ear. "What are you ..."

He leaned forward, planting his hands on the door, his arms on either side of her, effectively trapping her. "I think we should talk. About the other night."

She flinched, then sighed. "You remember?"

"I can't forget it." He gave her a wicked smile.

"You were obviously drugged, so it doesn't have to be a ... thing ..." She put her hands on his chest, intending to push him away. She could feel the warmth of his body and his muscles underneath her hands.

"I don't think it was the drugs," he leaned down and whispered in her ear, "and I can definitely remember all of it. You kissed me back, and you enjoyed it. I want to finish what we started." One hand slid down to her waist, and he pressed his lower body to hers.

"Let go of me," she said weakly. Her heart pounded loudly, his scent enveloping her.

"Why?" He nuzzled her neck, and she froze. "Damn, you smell incredible, you know that?"

"Please, Grant ... I ..." She stopped when he trailed kisses up her jawline. Before he could kiss her lips, she turned her head away and pushed him off. "I can't."

"You can't or you won't?" Grant's steely gaze bore into her. "That night, you wanted it, too."

"That's different," she stated. "This won't work."

"What won't work?"

She waved her hand between them. "This. You and me."

He crossed his arms over his chest. "Why not?"

"Well, you're you ... and I'm me!" she stammered. God, his scent was driving her crazy, and she couldn't put a thought together. It was delicious, and she closed her eyes, trying to tamp down a growl coming from within her. It was an instinctive action, like a gut feeling, but she knew where it was coming from.

Yes. Yum.

Her inner wolf, normally so silent and dormant, was somehow reacting to Grant's presence.

"I don't get it," he countered.

"Don't be obtuse, Grant." She ducked under his arm and stood behind him. "You know what I mean, it doesn't work that way." Did he really want her to say it out loud? That she was nowhere near his league? He was Alpha to the world's most powerful Lycan clan and a billionaire CEO. She could barely pay her restaurant suppliers on time and keep her ragtag band of Lycans in check.

He turned around to face her. "What? Two consenting adults doing what they want?"

She threw her hands up in frustration. "Argghh! I mean, you're you and I'm me. Our clans—"

"This isn't about clans," Grant interrupted. "And I'm not asking you for a long-term commitment, just ... go out with me. Dinner. Tomorrow night."

"I'm busy." She brushed him off, and walked over to her desk.

"Then how about the day after that?"

"I'm here all the time; I'm the manager," she retorted as she sat down and turned to her computer. "Now, I still have work to do before we close up."

"Frankie—"

"Don't let me keep you," she said in a cool voice. "And I'll be in touch with Alynna about the mage matter."

Grant stared her down, but she refused to meet his gaze. "Good night, then, Alpha." He gave her a nod and turned to leave.

She kept her eyes on her computer, and, when she heard the door click shut, she let out a deep sigh. Grant's scent lingered on in the small room and she groaned aloud. *Well, hopefully that's the last I see or hear of Grant Anderson.*

CHAPTER EIGHT

The following night, Frankie was in the kitchen, checking to see if the sink was working. The repair guy was there that afternoon and had assured her he fixed it. When she turned the tap on, she didn't realize the nozzle was facing her. Cold water sprayed all over the front of her white shirt.

"Arrggghhhh!" she groaned in frustration. The white fabric stuck to her chest, making it see-through.

"Yo, Frankie," Enzo said as he casually strolled into the kitchen.

"What?" she barked, pulling her shirt away from her chest.

"He's here again."

"Who?" she asked absentmindedly, reaching for a kitchen towel to wipe her face.

"You know, your boyfriend, the New York Alpha."

"He's not my—what?" Her head snapped up so fast, she felt dizzy. "What is he doing here?"

Enzo gave her a grin. "Says he liked the food, wanted to have it for dinner again."

Wanting to see for herself, Frankie pushed the door to the dining room wide open, causing the wood to slam into the concrete wall as she entered the main room. Her eyes zeroed in on Grant Anderson, who was, once again, standing by the host's station. She immediately regretted coming out to the dining room. He saw her, flashed her a smile, and gave her a small wave. Then his eyes moved down to her chest, and she realized he could probably see her pink lacy bra through the wet fabric. Her face flushed, and she stormed back into the kitchen.

"What should I do?" Enzo asked.

"Tell him to go away!" Frankie said angrily.

"Can we really afford to turn away business?" He pointed to the half-empty dining room. "Plus, all the servers are dying to have him seated in their section. You should have seen the tip he left last night, Frankie!"

She sighed, thinking about the bills piling up in her office. "Fine. Seat him, serve him, I don't care."

"Aren't you gonna go and talk to him?" Enzo inquired. "I think it's pretty obvious he's not here two nights in a row because he liked our Osso Bucco." He gave her a knowing grin.

"I don't know what you mean." She tossed her head, shaking the water off.

"Oh, you know what I mean." He thrust his hips in a meaningful way. "Someone's looking to get his dick stroked."

"Oh gross! You're my brother!" She threw a dishrag at him.

"What if he asks for you?"

"Tell him I'm busy! Or unavailable! Or I jumped off a cliff!" She stormed off to her office and slammed the door behind her.

―――――

By the third night in a row that Grant had shown up at Muccino's, Frankie simply had had enough. When she spied him walking through the front door as she was helping the servers get the dining room ready, she squared her shoulders and walked up to the front.

"Let me seat you at your table, *sir*," she said, grabbing the menus from Enzo's hands.

"So formal, Frankie?" Grant asked, his green eyes sparkling with amusement. His gaze swept over her outfit, an off-the-shoulder blue top and skinny jeans. He leaned down and whispered in her ear. "I like what you're wearing now, though I prefer last night's shirt."

She turned red, all the way to the tips of her ears, but continued to walk as he followed behind. "Here you go." She motioned to the table set up for one person. It was right by the kitchen, at the edge of the dining room. At that moment, the door swung open, hitting the single chair in the back.

"I think I'd rather sit over there." He motioned to the many other empty tables in the middle of room.

"Oh, I'm so sorry, sir," she said sweetly, giving him her best smile. "I'm afraid we're fully booked tonight."

"All those tables are reserved?" he asked.

"Yup. All of them. If you're not happy with this table, might I suggest the Denny's ... in the next town over?" She gave him another sugary smile.

"This table is fine." He returned her smile and sat down.

"Here you go," she said as she handed him the menus. "Enjoy your dinner."

"Wait," he put a hand on her hers to stop her from leaving, "what do you recommend for dinner tonight? And a wine to go with it."

"I'm not your server, but let me get him for you," she said, pulling her hand away. She stalked to the kitchen and, as soon as she entered, let out a frustrated scream.

"What's wrong, *mimma*?" Nonna Gianna asked, a frown on her face. The old lady was dressed in her usual hairnet and apron, with a sharp knife in her hand as she chopped up some fresh herbs with scary speed and efficiency.

"Argghhh! He's here again, Nonna." Frankie frowned. "Grant Anderson. The Alpha."

Nonna Gianna put her knife down on the block, digging the tip into the wood so deep the sharp tool stuck straight up. "Is he bothering you?" She took off her apron. "Let me go to talk him."

"Ha!" Frankie said to no one in particular as she watched her great-aunt march into the dining room. *You show him, Nonna,* she thought smugly. If anyone could put Grant Anderson in his place, it was her Nonna Gianna.

She straightened up the serving bowls and plates piled on the side, thinking about how her great-aunt was probably cutting the smug Alpha down to size. Satisfied with her work, she headed out into the dining room, preparing to toss Grant Anderson out of the restaurant and out of her life.

She was surprised to hear, however, feminine giggles instead of shouting and screaming.

"Oh, Mr. Anderson, you're too much!" Nonna Gianna said in a high voice as she blushed. She was sitting in the other chair, across from him.

"Please, call me Grant." The Alpha flashed her a smile and took her hand, giving it a kiss. "You've ruined me, Gianna. I can never eat another Osso Bucco but yours."

Nonna Gianna giggled again.

"Nonna!" Frankie stood by their table, her hands on her hips. "What's going on?"

"Oh Frankie," the older woman practically purred. "You never told me your Grant—"

"He's not my Grant!" Frankie protested.

"Well, you never told me Grant was so ..." she looked over to the man across the table from her, "handsome. And charming."

"And I knew the person making those delicious *ricotta zeppoles* was a talented cook, but I didn't realize she was gorgeous, too." Grant gave the older lady a wink.

Frankie threw her hands up in frustration and turned away, her face turning sour. All the staff watched her as she stormed out of the dining room. As soon as the door to her office closed, she knew they would start gossiping, which only infuriated her even more.

"Urgghhh!" she groaned and sat in her chair. She took out her phone and scrolled through her phone book until she found Alynna's number. She began typing out a text message.

We need to talk about your brother.

The reply came immediately

Grant?

Frankie rolled her eyes and typed back. *Do you have any other stubborn Alpha brothers?*

He's not here right now, came the reply.

She sighed. *I know. He's here. At my restaurant.*

In Jersey?!? Y?

"Damned if I know," she said out loud. With a sigh, she began to type back.

Says he was hungry. He's been here three nights in a row. Can you please do something about him? People are starting to notice. My clan will want to know why I've let a neighboring Alpha have free reign in my territory.

There was a longer pause before Alynna's next reply. This time, however, it was a string of smiley faces and hearts.

Her brows knitted in confusion. *What does that mean? Will you tell him to go home or not?*

Hahaha. It means I'm totally shipping you guys. The end of the message was tagged by a row of smiley faces with hearts in their eyes.

"Shipping?" she asked aloud. She typed again. *What does shipping mean?*

Google it, girl. Sorry, gtg, I need my beauty sleep. TTYL!

Frankie stared at the screen. "What the hell?"

CHAPTER NINE

"Nice dress," Enzo said cheekily as he passed by her office. "Are you expecting anyone special tonight?"

"Oh, get out of here!" She slammed the door in his face. Frankie looked at her herself in the mirror behind the door and sighed. She smoothed down the front of her white floral dress, which clung to her generous curves.

At first glance, the dress looked conservative. The sleeves came up to her elbows, and the skirt fell just below her knees, but the wide sweetheart neckline neck showed off her slender neck, delicate collarbones, and just a hint of cleavage. She wore white pumps, not too high that they were uncomfortable but just enough to add height to her frame and elongate her legs.

It's Friday, she told herself. They were fully booked, according to Enzo. That meant she had to be at the front of house and help out where she could. She definitely did not dress up because she was hoping to see a certain stubborn, smug Alpha.

It was just before seven p.m., which meant the dinner crowd was going to arrive soon. Frankie checked her makeup one last time; smoothed down her long, wavy black hair with her fingers;

and left the office to go to the dining room. She wasn't even halfway across the dining room when she spotted the tall Alpha, waiting at the host's station. His face broke into a smile when he spotted her. She rolled her eyes as she approached him.

"Hey, Frankie!" came a voice from behind Grant.

"Alynna?" Frankie's eyes widened in surprised. "You're here!" Alex was standing right beside her, his arm around his wife. She came over and embraced the younger woman, giving her a kiss on the cheek, while her husband nodded reverently at her, as a sign of respect. She gathered him into her arms for a warm hug.

"Yeah well," Alynna looked at Grant, "I heard the food was so good here, it was worth coming back for. Three nights in a row, in fact."

Frankie let out a huff, her nostrils flaring in anger. "We do our best." She straightened her back and took two sets of menus from the host's station. "Let me get you a table," she said.

"I'm afraid we don't have a reservation," Alex said sheepishly. "And looks like you've got a full house tonight, Lupa." He looked meaningfully at all the people waiting behind them.

"Don't worry about it." She tossed her hair over her shoulders. "And call me Frankie, Alex. We don't do that Lupa-Regal shit over here. I'll take care of it. Go right ahead." She motioned to the dining room, letting Alynna and Alex go ahead of her. When Grant tried to follow along, she stepped in front of him. "I'm sorry, *sir,* do *you* have a reservation?"

"Actually, I do," he looked down, giving her a sweet smile. "I booked it last night."

Frankie looked at the reservation book. "Tsk, tsk," she shook her head and gave him a mock sad smile, "I'm afraid your reservation is at 7 p.m. and it's only 6:54 p.m. You'll have to wait." She shrugged and left him to seat Alynna and Alex.

Grant's eyes remained fixed on Frankie as she walked away from him, her hips swaying as she made her way to the center of the dining room.

He couldn't look away, not after seeing her in that dress, showing off her every curve, with her glorious hair unbound, lips painted red, and anger flashing in her bi-colored eyes. She was magnificent and, seeing her, scenting her, made his blood boil with desire. No other woman had gotten under his skin the way Francesca Muccino did, and to think they hadn't even slept together yet. He knew he had to have her or he would go insane. The other Alpha was proving to be difficult, but Grant Anderson never backed down from a challenge, especially when the prize was worth it.

As soon as Frankie walked away, Enzo came by, gave him a pitiful look, and then led him to one of the tables close to the center. Thankfully, they didn't stick him at the worst table again, but he had made reservations just in case.

"Do you know what you'd like, sir?" His server asked as he finally sat down.

Grant looked up and blinked at the young man in the black shirt, skinny red tie, dark pants and wingtips. The server was almost a carbon copy of Enzo and Matteo, but probably a few years younger. He searched his memory, trying to think of the name Frankie mentioned.

"Rafe, right?" he asked.

The young man nodded. "Yes, sir, I'm Rafe. Rafe Morretti." He paused, then his eyes widened in recognition. "Hey, you're Grant Anderson! CEO of Fenrir Corporation, right?"

Grant nodded, "Yes. I'm sure your sister and brothers have told you about me."

"What? No, they didn't tell me you were dining here

tonight." He shook his head. "Sorry, I mean ... it's an honor to meet you! I'm a student at NJU and we were doing a case study in my Business Management class about your company. I also saw you on the cover of Fortune Magazine." The young man held out his hand, and Grant shook it.

"Oh, so you're studying business?" Grant inquired.

"Yes. Well, double major. Doing my pre-law and business degrees together," he said proudly. "I'm hoping to get into Harvard Law when I graduate."

"Harvard's a great school," Grant said. "I went there for undergrad and MBA."

"I know. I mean, I read about it. Wow, this is really ..." Rafe seemed flustered. "Sir, it's great to meet you!"

"Please, call me Grant," he said with a smile. "And double major, huh? I'm sure Harvard will be lucky to have you in a few years." Grant took out his wallet and gave the young man a white card. "Here's my card. Fenrir is always looking for interns every semester, you know. I'm sure we can find something for you there, if you're interested. Help beef up your resume before you apply to law school."

Rafe's eyes went wide as he took the card from him, carefully tucking it into his front shirt pocket like it was gold. "Th—thank you!"

"Everything, okay, Rafe?" Enzo asked as he passed by the table. "Hey Grant, did you figure out what you want tonight? We have a nice Ruffino Reserva Chianti. It'll pair well with the fish special!"

Grant glanced at the menu and then at Rafe. "You know what, that sounds great. Go ahead and get me the special, the Chianti, and then maybe the calamari salad and the *caccio e peppe* to start?"

Rafe nodded. "Will do! Nice to meet you, Mr.—I mean, Grant." And with that, he left for the kitchen.

Enzo shook his head. "Hope he wasn't botherin' you, Grant. Did he go all fanboy on you? I shoulda warned him you might be here."

Grant chuckled. "Don't worry; it's fine. He's a nice boy. Seems bright too, huh?"

"Yeah, we're pretty proud of him. And Matt, too," he said. "Of course, they must've gotten all the brainy genes, huh?"

"Well, you're all very accomplished; I'm sure your mom would have been proud," Grant said. "And not everyone needs to go to college to be smart, trust me." He thought of his sister, who was street smart and intelligent, despite never having stepped foot in a college classroom.

"Ha, sure, sure." Enzo gave him a good natured pat on the shoulder and went back to his station to seat more guests.

As he relaxed in his chair, Grant glanced over at Alynna and Alex. Frankie had personally taken their orders and was already on her way to the kitchen to get their food. Alynna glanced over at him, raised her water glass, and gave him a knowing smile. The sly young woman had manipulated her way to dinner, of course, though Grant could hardly say no to her.

That afternoon, once the workday was done, Grant had made his way to the garage and, much to his surprise, Alynna and Alex were waiting for him by his town car. Alynna, being her usual pushy self, insisted that they were joining him for dinner, knowing he would never deny her anything she asked. And so he found himself squeezed in the back of the car with his very pregnant sister and her husband.

Grant smirked and raised his own glass to the couple. A few minutes later, Frankie came out of the kitchen with a plate of food and placed it on their table.

As the night went on, his eyes never left Frankie while she worked the dining room. They were packed tonight, which was a stark difference from the last three nights. She was efficient, graceful, and played the perfect hostess, refilling glasses here and there, and asking diners if everything was alright.

The one table she avoided was his, of course, but he didn't mind. He loved watching her move and do her thing. Her smile lit up the room, and he could tell that the patrons appreciated the personal touch. He felt pride, watching her work and caring for her people— not just the diners but her staff, too. Nothing was beneath her, whether it was helping a nervous young server who was carrying a tray of water glasses or the bus boy clearing away plates. This was a woman who knew how to work and took pride in what she did.

When Frankie stopped by a particularly rowdy group of male diners about two tables from him—college kids, most likely —Grant frowned. He didn't like the way the young men looked at Frankie, like they were undressing her with their eyes, their gaze lingering too long on her cleavage and her ass whenever she walked by. His keen ears tuned out the din of the room and focused on what they were saying.

"Say, sweet cheeks," one of the men said, most likely their ringleader. "Tell me, is there anything not on the menu I can have for ... dessert?"

Grant growled softly, catching his meaning.

"Well sir," Frankie replied coolly. "We could make some *affogato* for you and your friends. It's ice cream with espresso and then we can add some whipped cream on top, if you'd like."

The man looked at his companions with a grin. "I know what I'd like with whipped cream on top." His eyes lingered on her breasts.

Grant gripped the table so hard he thought it would break. Something, a gut instinct maybe, screamed at him to go over there and wipe the grin from the man's face.

From their table, Alynna looked at him, a worried look on her face. *Are you okay?* She mouthed.

He nodded but turned his attention back to Frankie and those Neanderthals. She had obviously shot them down, but as she turned to leave, the young man grabbed her arm.

"Hey, sweet cheeks, where're you going? We're not done."

"Oh, I think we're done." Anger blazed in her eyes, and she took his wrist with her other hand and pried it away. "And once you're done with your dessert and pay your bill with a sizable tip, you will leave immediately."

The man's face scrunched up in anger. "Listen here, I'll tell you when I'm done and when I'm going to leave." He grabbed her ass, giving it a squeeze.

Grant stood up so fast, the table nearly knocked over. His chair made a scraping noise across the floor. Before he could get to her, however, a loud cracking sound rang through the dining room.

"You bitch!" the young man spat, clutching his cheek. "I'm gonna have you fired! Don't you know who I am? Where's your manager?"

"I am the manager and the owner, you asshole!" she screamed at him.

The man tried to grab her arm again, but Grant was too fast. He was right beside him, and his large hand wrapped around the man's forearm, pulling it back so far the young man shouted in pain.

"I wouldn't do that, *son*," he growled. The man's companions, two burly, football-player types stood up, ready to defend their friend. A voice inside him growled something, and it sounded like *kill, kill*.

"You're gonna pay for that, you asshole, and your stupid townie bitch, too!" The young man nodded his head at his goons.

By this time, Enzo and Rafe were already standing behind Frankie, their arms crossed over their chests. Dante and Matt, meanwhile, were making their way toward them, still in their kitchen attire. Nonna Gianna followed, a big kitchen knife in her hand.

Grant felt another presence behind him and knew it was Alex, ready to defend his Alpha.

"Are you sure about that?" Grant said smugly. The two burly men looked at each other, and Grant could smell the hesitation and fear coming from the group. "Apologize to her," he said, twisting the man's arm further.

"Oww ... owww! Okay! Jesus!" He looked at Frankie. "I'm sorry! I'm sorry, okay?" Grant let go and the man slunk down to his chair, rubbing his arm.

"Apology NOT accepted!" She turned to her brothers. "Take this piece of garbage out and ban him and his friends from ever coming back!" With that, she left the dining room, storming back to her office.

———

Frankie walked confidently out of the dining room, but her hands began to shake as soon as she was out of sight. *Townie bitch.* The words rang in her ears over and over again.

She got to her office and slammed the door behind her. Walking over to her desk, she placed her hands on the well-worn top, taking a deep breath to try and calm herself.

After all these years ...

She thought she was over it. Over him. Well, what he did to her, anyway.

Jacob James Caldwell. She hadn't even said the name out loud in years.

Jacob James Caldwell was a typical rich college kid who coasted by on his family's money and good looks. He strolled into Muccino's one night and 18-year-old Frankie caught his eye. He and his friends were seated in her section, and he flirted relentlessly with her. Young, pretty, and innocent, Frankie was flattered by the attention. After all, she had grown up sheltered by her family, and she always thought she wasn't as beautiful or popular as some of the girls in her high school, with her awkward mismatched eyes, wiry curly hair, and features that were still growing in, thanks to puberty. After she graduated, though, it was like her body had finally caught up. Her slight frame grew lush curves and her facial features softened, and soon men of all ages were paying attention to her. And Jacob was the most handsome, charming, and richest of them all.

He ate at the restaurant every weekend, bribing the hostess to make sure she seated him in Frankie's section. He asked her out a couple of times. She turned him down of course, especially since her mother and grandmother watched her like a hawk. Finally, one night, after she finished her dinner shift, he was waiting for her outside the restaurant, leaning against the side of his sports car with a dozen roses in his hands. She went out with him right then and there. He took her to an all-night diner where they talked until Frankie's phone started ringing and her mother screamed from the speakers, demanding she come home.

During the next few weeks, she spent all her free time with Jacob. She even went to frat parties with him. All his friends treated her nicely, much to her surprise. It was only much later she realized they were just being nice to her because of Jacob, and they not only gossiped about her when she wasn't around, but quickly turned on her when things went sour with Jacob.

Townie bitch. The words didn't make her cry or become angry anymore, but there was still a dull ache somewhere deep inside her, a part she thought she had buried long ago.

Tears sprang to her eyes. *Men always leave*, her mother's voice echoed in her head. Her father left them when he couldn't take being trapped in their one-horse town. Her stepfather divorced her mother shortly after Rafe was born, when he couldn't accept her mother for who she was.

A knock interrupted her thoughts.

"Go away!" she said, wiping the tears before they fell. *Thank god for waterproof mascara.*

"Frankie, can I come in?"

Urgggghhhh! Grant Anderson. Another rich, handsome man wanting to bully his way into her life. Oh yes, she knew his type. He would drop her like a hot potato once he got what he wanted.

"No!" she said defiantly. The door opened anyway and Grant strode in. "What part of 'go away' don't you understand?" She stood in front of him defiantly, planting her feet firmly on the ground.

"I wanted to see if you were okay." There was concern in his voice.

"As you can see, I'm fine." She crossed her arms over her chest. "What the hell did you think you were doing anyway?"

Grant's scent filled her nose, mixed in with ... anger and jealousy? She shook her head. No, she was imagining things.

He placed his hands on her shoulders gently. "I couldn't just sit there while he pawed at you. Touched you like he owned you." A deep, rumbling sound came from his chest.

She let out a sardonic laugh. "I can protect myself! You think he's the first man to pull that shit on me? I've been dealing with assholes like him for years. I can assure you I can handle myself and he won't be the last man I'll have to put in his place."

"I won't stand for it," he growled.

"Well I've got news for you, Mr. Smug New York Alpha! You don't get a say in it! Or my life!" She struggled to get away from him, but he backed into her until her ass hit the edge of her desk. "What are you—mmmphh!"

She saw Grant's eyes go wild before he grabbed the sides of her face and slanted his lips over hers. Frankie struggled—weakly—before leaning into him. The hard planes of his body felt amazing against her own soft curves; they fit together so perfectly. His hands slid down to her ass, grabbing the generous globes of flesh, and pulled her against him. She gasped into his mouth when she felt his erection pressing against her stomach through his pants. He quickly delved his tongue into her mouth, tasting her. Ocean spray scent and sugary sweetness filed her senses, the roar of waves rang in her ear.

Hmmm yes ... smells so good ...

She growled into his mouth, nipping softly at his lips. Effortlessly, Grant lifted her up and placed her on the table. He dragged his lips to her jaw, trailing a line down her neck, behind her ear. She eagerly exposed her neck, and his teeth grazed the soft skin there, making her whimper.

A hand crept up her thigh, pushing her dress higher and spreading her legs wider. His fingers brushed over the silky fabric of her panties, which had already grown damp from desire. A low rumbling came from his chest, and her heart slammed into her sternum when his fingers pulled her panties aside, baring her pussy to his touch. A thumb found her hardened clit, circling it and teasing it until she was mewling and panting.

Her hand slid down to his waist, her palm pressing down on his hard cock through his pants. Shaking fingers unbuckled his belt and unzipped his pants, then she shoved a hand into his tight briefs. God, he was like silken steel, his cock so wide her fingers barely circled around his shaft. He groaned when she pulled his underwear down and began to stroke him. Her softly callused hand gripped his shaft, moving up and down in a slow, tortuous dance.

"Frankie," he whispered into her ear. "Come for me."

"Grant," she said, his name a prayer on her lips. "I can't ..."

His thumb pressed harder, circling faster on her clit. "Yes, you can." He slid two fingers into her, her wetness coating his digits.

Frankie let go of his cock and then gripped his shoulders, clinging to him. "I ... I ..." She buried her face in his shoulder, muffling her cry as her orgasm hit her hard. Her arms wound around his neck, her body lifted up as waves of pleasure washed over her. He was relentless, pushing his fingers into her, his thumb playing with her clit as her body shook. She collapsed against him, and he held her close, burying his nose in her hair.

"Frankie," he murmured. "So sweet ... so beautiful ..."

She let out a breath, her head spinning as her body wound down. God, had she really let him do that? His naked, hard cock pressed against her stomach insistently. "Grant, I want—"

"Primul?" a voice called from the other side of the door.

"Yes?" They both answered, pulling away from their embrace.

The thick haze of passion dissipated, and Frankie's head suddenly cleared. Grant stepped away from her, zipping up his pants and fixing his belt. She slid from the table, smoothing her dress down over her knees. She sighed as she saw her reflection in the mirror behind the door. Her hair was mussed, lipstick was gone, dress was wrinkled. She didn't bother to fix herself up anymore, since she knew whichever Lycan was out there (Dante, Alex, or possibly Alynna), would smell the sex reeking from her office anyway. She yanked open the door.

"Grant." Alex stood on the other side of the door. He nodded to Frankie, his face not betraying his thoughts, but the slight flare in his nostrils indicated he knew what he had interrupted. "Er, sorry, Lupa," he said apologetically to Frankie. Then he turned to Grant. "Alynna isn't feeling well. She needs to go back to Medical now. Do you want the car to come back for you ... later?"

Grant hesitated for a moment, his face conflicted. "I should go and make sure she's okay." It sounded like a question to Frankie, and he looked at her meaningfully.

"Yes, you should," she said quietly, opening the door wider so he could pass.

"Let's go," he said to Alex. He gave her one last look.

"Your sister needs you, go make sure she's okay," she urged. "And tell her I'm thinking of her and I'll give her a call."

"Of course." He nodded, and then left her office.

Frankie let out a long breath. *Madre de dio,* what the hell was she thinking?

CHAPTER TEN

I t turned out Alynna was having some premature contractions, which, according to Dr. Faulkner, were normal in this late stage of pregnancy. Still, it was a good thing they came back to The Enclave as Dr. Faulkner prescribed bed rest until the baby was born.

Grant wanted to go back to Muccino's again, but he could feel how hesitant and skittish Frankie had been when he left. It had been a week since that night, and it took all his willpower not to go back. He didn't mean for the events of that night to go that far, but jealousy and anger had gotten the best of him. Seeing that asshole touch Frankie ... something snapped inside of him. He wanted to see him suffer, wanted to make her forget and cover her with his scent until she could only smell and taste of him. Frankly, it wasn't just the New Jersey Alpha who was on edge over what happened in her office. He had never lost control like that, and, if Alex hadn't interrupted them, he would have taken her right then and there, consequences be damned. He had to stay away to give them both time to breathe. But, finally, he decided that they had both had enough space and he began to put a plan into action to get her alone again.

"Alpha? Grant, did you hear what I said?"

"Hmmm?" Grant's head snapped back to the man sitting across from him. Rodrigo Baeles, one of the members of the Lycan High Council, gave him a strange look. Grant glanced at his watch.

At the very last moment, the High Council requested a meeting with him and this was the only available slot in his schedule this week. Grant didn't really want to have this meeting, not when everything was set up to go perfectly tonight, but he had no choice. When the Lycan High Council "requested" something, one didn't say no.

"Sorry, go ahead Rodrigo," Grant said.

The older Lycan nodded. "Right, so you're sure it was the mages who kidnapped you?" Rodrigo had flown into town as soon as the High Council was informed of Grant's kidnapping.

"Pretty sure," Grant confirmed. "I was hit with a blue potion before I lost consciousness. Then I shifted, escaped my captors, and found myself in the New Jersey Alpha's territory."

"Good thing you weren't too far off," the Lycan next to Rodrigo said. Grayson Charles, the Connecticut Alpha, was also invited to the meeting. He was Grant's closest neighbor and leader of one of the bigger clans on the East Coast. "What did they want?"

"Who knows?" Grant said. "But they must be getting bolder." He turned to Rodrigo. "The High Council needs to do something. We must move forward on the talks with the Witch Assembly and begin to work together. If we put our knowledge and resources together, we can defeat the mages."

The council member's nostrils flared. "If only it were that easy. The witches are being stubborn."

"That's what they're saying about us, too," Grant retorted. "Look, I know the two councils need to sort these things out, but if you would let me and Vivianne Chatraine attend the meetings, then maybe we can come to some understanding."

"Grant, we've told you many times," Rodrigo began. "Let us handle this. This is what the Lycan High Council is for. We can't just let an Alpha join in such delicate negotiations like this. We would be accused of favoritism by other clans."

He sighed in frustration. "Then let them join too, and let everyone know about the threat of the mages." Grant felt like a broken record. He kept bringing up the same argument with the Council, and their answer was the same each time. Let them handle it.

"Grant," Grayson Charles began. "I know you're frustrated and so am I. Might I suggest, that we—the clans, I mean—we should do what we can amongst ourselves. Tighten our borders and most importantly, secure our own alliances."

"Do we really need to do that?" Grant asked. "I mean, as neighbors, you and I have always had good relations."

"Of course, but, you know, we can always use stronger bonds, so our people will feel more united," Grayson continued.

Grant wanted to tear his hair out in frustration. It was like talking to a brick wall. "If you're not going to do anything more to proceed with talks with the witches, then I'm not quite sure these meetings are productive," he said to Rodrigo.

"Look, Grant," the older Lycan put his hands on the desk, "I sense your frustration. I know it. But it's not just us. Their side is not giving us an inch either. But," he looked Grant straight in the eyes, "with news of your kidnapping, perhaps I can get the council to take action."

"That's all I ask," Grant said. "Just let me know what I can do."

"Of course." Rodrigo looked at his watch. "Well, gentlemen, it's nearly five o'clock. Shall we talk more over dinner?"

"I'm up for it," Grayson nodded.

Grant shook his head. "Apologies gentlemen, I already made plans," he said. "If you'd like recommendations or want to make reservations, stop by my admin's desk. He can probably get you a table at any restaurant in New York, even last minute."

"Are you sure you can't join us, Grant?" Grayson sounded disappointed. "I dropped Vanessa Bennet off at Saks before I came here," he said, referring to his vivacious Lycan cousin. "She'll be disappointed you won't be able to join us."

Grant groaned inwardly, but kept a straight face. Vanessa had been doggedly pursuing him for months. "Do give my apologies to Ms. Bennet. Maybe next time." He stood up, hinting that they should leave. "I do have to make one more stop and then head out to dinner, so I should get going."

The two men shook hands with Grant, and he led them out of his office. As he passed by Jared's desk, he gave his admin instructions to assist the two Lycans in securing a dinner reservation for the evening. After bidding them goodbye, he headed to the set of private elevators, away from the main room. The doors opened and he stepped in. Pressing his palm to the security sensor under the buttons, he touched the button for the 33rd floor.

———

The 33rd floor of Fenrir Corp's headquarters was accessible only via the private elevator, and the special security protocols only allowed certain people in. When the elevator car reached its destination, the doors opened, revealing a small room with another set of secured doors. Grant peered into the retinal scanner by the door. After the scanner verified his identity, the doors opened automatically, letting him in.

The main laboratory took about half the floor. It was sleek, modern, and outfitted with the most modern pieces of science tech available (and not yet available). Holographic panels were located on different corners of the room. Two people in lab coats —one Lycan, one human—sat in opposite corners, typing away on their computers. In the middle was a raised platform with a set of stairs leading up to the inner lab and office of Dr. Jade Cross.

Dr. Cross was a Lycan scientist Grant had hired to study magic. Born in New York, Jade moved to England when her American father and British mother divorced. Jade was a gifted scientist, graduating from Cambridge at eighteen years of age with a degree in Physics and Biology. She then finished her Ph.D. in Biochemistry and Bioengineering two years later at Oxford. It was actually Cady who brought her to Grant's attention. When he realized the talent she had, he offered her a position as their chief magical expert right after she finished her studies. He gave her a generous salary, but she seemed more interested in the idea of running her own research lab and studying magic than the money. Dr. Cross was brilliant, if somewhat flighty and a little naive when it came to human interaction. But, she was one of the best in her field (and a Lycan to boot), and Grant was lucky to have her.

As he made his way up to the platform, he could hear the speakers blasting loudly through the doors. Dr. Cross had an eclectic taste in music. Sometimes when he came to visit, opera would be blaring through the speakers, and other times it would be classic rock, African drums, or the blues. Today, it was Bruno Mars' latest upbeat hit.

"Dr. Cross?" he called as he entered her inner lab. He wasn't even surprised by what he saw.

Jade Cross was standing next to a large, cylindrical glass case in the middle of the lab. Inside was another person—a redhead that Grant recognized as Lara Chatraine, Cady's witch cousin. Dr. Cross was holding a tablet in one hand with her safety glasses perched on her nose.

"Ready, Lara?" she asked.

"Ready," the redhead replied.

"Okay, in three ... two ... one ..." She gave the other woman a thumbs up.

Lara closed her eyes and raised her hands. Nothing happened for the first few seconds, but then bits of paper began to float around her. They flitted around weakly at first, but as the witch's face scrunched up in concentration, the pieces of paper began to fly wildly.

"Oh, motherfluffer!" The brunette scientist frowned and stamped her foot in disappointment. Grant suppressed a smile at Dr. Cross' creative use of language. It seemed the prim and proper lady in her, raised by her English mother, didn't allow her to use crude language, so she made up some colorful phrases of her own.

"Sorry Jade," Lara said as she exited the glass chamber.

"Ah, not your fault. I told you to do your best to break the dampening field." Jade sighed and looked at her tablet. "Back to the drawing board."

Grant cleared his throat, which made both women look at him.

"Primul," Jade greeted.

"Alpha," Lara nodded.

"Hello Dr. Cross, Lara," Grant greeted back. "What's the latest?"

Jade sighed again. "Sorry about that. We were testing this special magic dampening bracelet I've been working on." Lara raised her hand and showed off a thick silver bangle wrapped around her delicate wrist. "It works based on the biochemical signals that witches produce as they give off energy—"

"English, please, Dr. Cross," Grant reminded her.

The brunette blushed. "Right. Basically, I'm trying to develop something that will stop witches—or mages—from using their powers, especially blessed witches," she said, referring to the type of witch born with extra powers beyond just activating potions and spells. Lara was one such type of witch, as she could control wind currents. During their first encounter with the mages, Vivianne, Lara's mother, had told them that Stefan and Daric also had these extra powers, though they couldn't say what they were exactly. For sure they had seen both Stefan and Daric not only move things with their minds but also teleport themselves and others.

"That's actually not a bad idea," Grant commented.

"Well, I only have this one prototype, and it's not working right," she confessed.

"It did, for a bit." Lara patted the other woman on the shoulder. "I could definitely feel my powers being suppressed, but Jade told me to do my best to fight it off."

Since neither the Witch Assembly nor the Lycan High Council seemed inclined to prepare to defend themselves against the mages, Grant and Vivianne Chatraine decided to take matters into their own hands, at least discreetly. Grant had directed Dr. Cross to put all her resources and efforts into defensive tactics and technologies, and Vivianne had gladly given permission for her daughter, Lara, to assist them, with the understanding she wouldn't be harmed and that all knowledge gained through the research would belong to both sides equally. Grant was happy to agree to such an arrangement. Seeing as she was Cady's cousin, it was easy enough to explain Lara's sudden appearance and she became an official Fenrir employee, working as a "lab intern" for Dr. Cross, who was supposedly working in their Food R and D division. Lara was also set up in her own apartment not far from Fenrir, and she would go home every weekend to her coven upstate. According to Cady, Jade and Lara had also become fast friends, since they were about the same age and now worked together closely.

"Off to a great start then," Grant commended.

"Thank you, Alpha," Jade replied. "Now, was there anything in particular you needed?"

"Ah, yes," Grant said, remembering what he had come in for. "The blood sample Dr. Faulkner sent to you? Did you find out anything?"

Dr. Cross put her safety glasses away. "Yes. I tested the sample, but I'm afraid the traces were too degraded for me to figure out definitively what it was. I do have some theories, though." She tapped on her pad, then gestured to one of the screens. "It's definitely magical, based on your description. Lara helped me identify some of the ingredients."

"I'm not the best in potion making, Alpha," Lara interjected. "But, I can tell you it's like some bastardized version of a confusion potion."

"And that's what worries me." Jade's brows were knitted.

"Why?" Grant asked.

The two women looked at each other, and Lara nodded. Jade turned back to Grant. "Well, from what Lara's been teaching me about potions, they often have to be measured and portioned based on the target. If this potion affected you, that means it was mixed specifically for Lycan physiology."

Lara continued. "And the only way to do that ..."

"Would be to have a Lycan subject to test it on," Jade finished and tapped on her pad. "They might possibly have a Lycan subject or subjects to test on. Of course, they can't test for every variable. Your weight, height, metabolic rate, activity level are all things to consider. If they had an expert potions-maker and had the right tools, they could get a potion near perfect enough to make sure you couldn't metabolize it until they got you somewhere they could secure you."

"Still the fact that they could knock you out and bring you what ... thirty miles or so before you woke up? That's pretty close," Lara supplied. "I mean, witches haven't had to create potions that would work on Lycans for a long time, so there's no definitive recipe that can ensure it will last against your enhanced metabolism."

Grant sighed. "I'll have Nick or Alynna check and see if any of our people are missing." He shook his head. The mages had to be stopped, especially if they were bold enough to actually capture Lycans to experiment on.

"Good." Jade nodded. "I'll let you know if I find anything else."

"Excellent," Grant said. "Now, if you ladies will excuse me, I'm headed out to dinner. Have a good weekend, and say hello to your mother for me, Lara." With that, he left the lab.

CHAPTER ELEVEN

Frankie pulled up to her spot in the back of Muccino's, then shifted the car into park. With a long sigh, she gripped the steering wheel and stared at the back door leading into the restaurant.

It had been seven days since Grant had last come to Muccino's. Part of her was glad he didn't come back. She shivered, remembering what had happened—almost happened, she corrected herself mentally—in her office. Her body had been on fire, wanting him so bad. And it scared her. She had never felt like that, not with anyone else and, even until now, her traitorous body was humming with desire and craving Grant's touch. She shook her head, trying to forget. Still, every night since then she'd dressed up a little bit, just in case he did come back. But a whole week passed and no sign of Grant.

Tonight, however, she was dressed carefully in a white blazer and lace top, white pencil-cut skirt, and matching pumps. Her makeup was applied lightly to enhance her features, and her thick black was hair pinned up in a French twist. She wanted to look nice but also professional.

Enzo had gotten a tip from a friend in New York that there

was going to be some important food critic from a major national newspaper visiting tonight. She initially wanted to come to Muccino's early, but her brothers assured her they would make sure everything was perfect at the restaurant. Still, she had to do her part to prepare. They sent her tons of articles and materials to study and read at home, to make sure she could answer any question the critic might throw at her. She trusted her brothers to take care of things at the restaurant, so she did her part and read through all the materials they sent her.

Frankie entered the back door and headed to her office. However, as she was about to enter, she realized the hallway going to the dining room was completely dark.

What's going on? Frankie frowned and walked towards the dining room.

It wasn't pitch black, but only the lights in the middle of the room were on. A single table was set up, lit by three candles.

"Enzo? Dante?" she called out. "Matty? Rafe? Nonna?"

The kitchen door swung open, and her heart thudded in her chest when she saw who it was.

"Grant?"

He grinned at her, his face turning devilishly handsome. His hair was slicked back, his jaw was cleanly shaven. He was wearing a black suit, white shirt, and no tie—just the collar left open, exposing the tanned skin of his throat. "Hello, Frankie." He was also holding a bottle of their best red wine and two glasses.

"What are you doing here? You can't be here; we have an important critic coming tonight!"

He gave her a sheepish look and walked towards her, placing the bottle and glasses on the table. "Yeah, about that ..."

Grant didn't have to finish his sentence. Frankie felt her cheeks grow hot as anger rose in her. "There's no critic, is there?"

"I'm afraid not."

Frankie let out a string of Italian curses, and then turned to leave. A warm hand wrapped around her forearm, and she stopped as a zing of electricity shot up her arm, causing desire to sweep through her body. She swallowed a gulp and closed her eyes.

"Don't go. Please, Frankie. I'm sorry ... for making your brothers lie to you."

"Of course, they were in on this!" She slapped her hand on her forehead, then turned around. "What did you do?"

"Nothing, I swear," he said. "Well, I mean ... I told them I just wanted to take you out to dinner, but you kept saying you were busy running the restaurant. So, I said I'd buy out every table tonight and give all your staff double what they would have made in tips."

Her eyes went round as saucers. "What?"

"Frankie, the other night ... things went too far too fast," he admitted. "But I don't regret it. I want you, and I know you want me, too."

Her nostrils flared. "We can't always have what we want."

"But there's nothing stopping us from trying," he countered. Frankie crossed her arms over her chest, and he let out a sigh. "Look, what's the harm in having dinner with me? Here in your own restaurant. Nonna Gianna even made your favorite dish and showed me how to serve it to you."

"My favorite dish?"

"Yeah, veal involtini."

Her keen senses picked up the smell of the veal, cheese, and garlic from the kitchen. Involtini or braciola was her favorite dish in the whole world. It was made by wrapping thin slices of veal around cheese and herbs, then baking in the oven with a little bit of olive oil. Her grandmother, and now Nonna Gianna, only made it on her birthday. Her stomach growled loudly, and she realized she hadn't eaten since breakfast. Grant stifled a laugh, and she cursed her tummy.

"Fine," she said with a defeated sigh.

He pulled out a chair for her, and she sat down. His hand brushed over her shoulder. "Good, now just sit back. You don't have to do a thing."

She gave him a smirk as he filled her glass.

True to his word, Grant took care of everything. The salad was already on the table, as well as the starters, so all he had to do was take out the veal after he cleared their plates. Of course, Nonna Gianna and Dante probably prepared the food, but Grant was attentive, refilling her glass when she was running low and making sure she didn't even need to stand up to get more bread.

"This food really is amazing," Grant said as he took a bite of the veal. "All the food you serve is from family recipes?"

She nodded, her eyes closed as she savored the flavors of the veal, cheese, garlic and olive oil. "Mmm hmm. Nonna Guilia immigrated here from Positano in Italy. The previous Alpha was a cousin of hers, who didn't have children of her own, which is why she was chosen to take over. My mother was only seven when they moved here. My grandmother and grandfather started the restaurant."

"The American dream." He raised his glass. "To your grandparents."

She clinked her glass to his. "To my grandparents."

"And now? What are your plans?"

Frankie blinked in confusion. "What do you mean plans?"

"Well, your business ... do you want to expand? Maybe branch out? Or you could go into food manufacturing and bottle up your sauce. I think a Muccino-branded tomato sauce would fly off the shelves."

"Well, I'd like to keep running the restaurant but—" She

stopped herself and frowned, thinking of the dipping profits and their bills.

"But what?" he cocked his head.

"Nothing." She sipped her wine. "Now, tell me how you got my brothers and Nonna Gianna to agree to this," she asked, quickly changing the subject.

"Oh, they were on board from the beginning. Enzo especially," Grant quipped.

"Enzo?" she asked, her voice rising at the end. It wasn't that she and Enzo hated each other—of course they didn't—but she and her middle brother often clashed, which Dante attributed to them having such similar and passionate personalities.

"Yeah. He said, 'Frankie needs to get some, then maybe she'd get that stick out of her ass and stop meddling in our lives.'"

Frankie snorted. "Of course. But that still doesn't answer my question."

"Well, I called Dante and asked him what it would take to get you out of the restaurant for a night and go out with me," he explained. "He basically said that there was no way you would take a day off and you even go in on Mondays to do bookkeeping and admin stuff. So, I said, if the mountain won't come to Muhammad ..."

"I see," she took a sip of the wine. It was an excellent vintage, and she'd had one glass of it herself from a bottle they had a few years ago. "So, you decide to bribe my family and pay off my staff."

Grant put down his fork and reached over to grab her hand. She was so surprised that she didn't have time to pull away. "I decided to come to the mountain," he said softly. His thumb made circles on her palm, sending heat through her entire body. She lowered her lashes as desire pooled in her belly, her arousal so strong she could feel the dampness between her legs. He must have scented it too, as his nostrils flared and his eyes glowed into deep green pools.

God, one touch was all it took to make her melt. The air between them began to feel heavy, and she knew one spark was all it would take. "I ... I can't ..." She pulled her hand away.

He huffed, his eyes returning to normal. "Why are you fighting this, Frankie?" he asked.

"Because ..." She didn't know the answer. It wasn't wrong, but her head was screaming at her, telling her it wouldn't work out. That she would be hurt again when he decided she wasn't good enough for him. It was suffocating, and the air was thick. *Men always leave.*

Out ... out ...

And there it was. Her inner Alpha wolf, struggling to get free, trying to protect her from the hurt the memories were conjuring up again.

She stood up and tossed her napkin on the table, running out of the restaurant.

———

Grant sat for a moment, dumbfounded. *What did I do wrong?*

Without another thought, he stood up and followed Frankie outside.

The other Alpha was standing in the empty parking lot, her arms wrapped around herself, breathing heavily.

"Frankie, please ..."

She turned around and her eyes were glowing, one a bright green sphere, the other an icy blue pool. "I'm sorry, I didn't mean ..." She took a deep breath. "I need to ... get out of here ... out of this skin ..."

"It's my fault." What Grant didn't tell Frankie was the strange warning he got from Dante. Though the other Lycan supported Grant's pursuit of his sister, he had told her that wooing Frankie would not be easy. He had alluded that she'd been hurt too many times and since then, had never let anyone in. Frankie was like a wounded animal, skittish and guarded, and she could bolt any moment. And, in this moment, he could feel that she was ready to run.

"I'm sorry for taking things too fast." He shook his head. He didn't want to scare her away, not when he had seen some of the iciness being chipped away from her. It pained him to take things so slow, when all he wanted was to make her his. He sighed and turned to leave.

"Grant, wait," she called. Her voice was shaky but strong.

Hope blossomed in his chest. "Yes?"

"Shift with me."

He was dumbstruck. "What?"

"I need to change. I can feel it. To shift. To run in the woods and just feel the earth under my paws and the wind in my fur." Her brows furrowed when he gave her a strange look. "Don't you get that urge? To just let your inner Lycan free? I get antsy if it's been too long."

Grant frowned. "You know we can't just do that."

She gave him a sardonic smile. "I know you city Lycans can't just run down Fifth Avenue and chase around tourists, but we're a little looser out here in the country. Have you never visited clans that don't live in the city?"

He opened his mouth and stopped. Searching his memories, Grant realized that, aside from a few trips to the countryside with his folks, Blood Moon shifts, and, of course, rescuing Cady a few months ago, he didn't just let his wolf free. The actual rule stated that Lycans couldn't just shift in front of humans for no reason. Since he lived in one of the densest cities in the world, he was always surrounded by humans.

Something deep growled within him, an inner voice urging

him. Urging him to let it out, wanting to break free. Wanting to roam the woods with Frankie's wolf.

She must have sensed it, as a deep rumbling sound came from her chest. God, it was sexy, and made him want to march over to her and nip her all over her luscious body, especially on the neck. All his life, he was expected to be in control, to be the Alpha. It came with a lot of privileges but also so many responsibilities. No one would understand, except another Alpha.

"Come with me," she said. "I want to show you something."

Grant followed her to the back of the restaurant, then climbed into the passenger seat of her ancient Honda. She revved up the engine, pulled out of the parking lot, and headed down Main Street toward her house.

A few minutes later, she pulled into the driveway of her home, but, instead of parking her car out front, she maneuvered it to the back of the house.

"We own about two acres of land," she explained, turning the engine off. "Plus, most of the adjacent properties are owned by other Lycans. I know where to go, so just stick with me."

It had grown dark, the nearly full moon was rising in the distance, and the air was crisp and cool. Frankie opened her door and stepped out, and he did the same, closing the passenger door behind him and following her to a clearing.

"Turn around," she ordered. "And don't even think about peeking!" she warned as she reached behind her to unzip her skirt.

"I wouldn't dream of it." He winked at her, turning to face the house. He couldn't help it, though, and snuck a glance. He saw a glimpse of smooth skin and full, round buttocks that sent blood straight to his cock. He quickly turned away and began to undress. After removing his jacket, shirt, and pants, he folded them neatly on the cool grass.

Frankie may have been prudish about her naked body, but he wasn't. He turned around, fully naked, his cock half-hard, and faced her.

His breath caught in his throat when he saw her wolf. The she-wolf before him wasn't as large as his, but it was certainly impressive. Ink-black fur covered the animal's lean body, except for patches of dark and light brown on her snout, face, and paws. The tips of her ears were standing at alert, and her dark bushy tail was wagging behind her. The wolf looked at him with keen blue-green eyes, urging his own animal to come out and play.

The change came quickly, so he barely felt the usual tension and pain that came with a shift. Soon, his own wolf stood proud and tall in the moonlight, and he let out a loud howl, the sound piercing through the still air. She joined him and their dual howls rang through the tranquil spring night.

Frankie's wolf came to him, warily at first, sniffing the air around him. Grant got down on his front legs, leaving his hind legs unbent in a play bow position. She moved closer, rubbing the sides of her body against him in affection, and he licked her face. His wolf growled in approval, a low rumble in his chest, as warmth spread through him.

Yes, let's play, his wolf said.

In an instant, she sprinted toward the woods at the edge of the property.

Catch her, the wolf pressed, and he needed no more urging.

He quickly followed, his longer and more powerful legs quickly catching up with her, but she was surprisingly fast. Plus, she had the advantage of familiarity with the woods, dashing here and there to avoid obstacles a second faster than him.

They charged through the woods, the wind blew through his fur and the feel, scent, and sights of the woods and the damp earth filled his senses. Frankie's wolf, right beside him, lead him through her territory. They ran as fast as they could, jumping over felled logs and sprinting through the trees.

Grant had never felt so ... free and wild. The wolf in him felt the same, as if he'd been caged for years and was only now allowed to roam. Nostrils flared and warmth spread throughout his Lycan body each time he got close enough to sniff the she-wolf's delicious scent. His inner wolf itched with desire as he pushed his body to keep up with her.

They roamed the woods, racing each other through the trees. He wasn't sure how long they were out, but, eventually, they circled around the property and were headed back to the house.

They ran side by side, racing to the back porch. Grant's more powerful legs spurred him forward, but, to his surprise, Frankie lunged at him, her front paws digging playfully into his fleshy rump and sending them sprawling across the lawn, landing near where they started. Grant quickly changed back, his limbs tangling with furry legs and a tail, forcing her to shift into her human form so as not to crush him.

After rolling around for a few feet, they finally stopped, Grant lying on his back on the grass, Frankie sprawled on top of him, giggling and laughing.

Her laughter was the most beautiful sound he'd ever heard. Full, rich, and sincere. She sounded relaxed and happy, and his inner wolf was appeased. So was he, especially with her soft, naked curves pressed against him.

She sighed, melting into his arms and moving her head up so she looked at him. Her chin dug into his chest; her wild, dark hair spilled over her shoulders. Her bi-colored eyes burned and glowed in the moonlight. It felt so right, having her in his arms, and he pulled her tighter against him, trying to ignore the way his fully erect cock was pressing against her stomach and her full breasts flattened up against him. Frankie also seemed more relaxed; the tension from dinner had all but left her body.

"You never just ... shift and let the wolf take over?" she asked, cocking her head to the side.

"No," Grant confessed. "Not lately, I mean. When I was younger and learning to shift, of course I had to learn to change back and forth. I was in training summer camp with other Lycans my age, and we went upstate so we had a safe place. It was fun, and we got to roam around, but since then it's always been about following the rules. No shifting unless absolutely necessary."

Frankie wrinkled her nose. "I couldn't imagine not letting my wolf out. Sure, Nonna and Ma taught me and Dante how to shift when we started going through puberty. But then, when we mastered controlling the shift, we'd have nights like this, when the moon was full and bright and we'd go out and just run and play. Even my human brothers got to tag along."

As a smile lit up her face, Grant thought she looked even more beautiful. He placed a hand on her cheek, caressing it gently. A satisfied growl came from her chest, and he impulsively shoved his fingers through her hair and pulled her down for a kiss.

She nipped at his lips playfully, but let him slant his lips on hers. His tongue snaked out, dragging along the seam of her lips. Eagerly, she opened her mouth to him, letting him taste her.

Grant groaned into her mouth when she adjusted her hips so his aroused cock lay right under her sex, the neatly trimmed hair tickling his shaft. Her arousal was unmistakable—the smell of almond cookies and her excitement were teasing his senses. He only had to move lower, maneuver himself in the right direction, and he could bury himself inside her. She moaned, rubbing her core against his shaft, and she took a deep breath, reaching between them to wrap her hands around his cock and guide him to her entrance. His heart was beating so loud he could feel it slamming against his ribcage.

"Frankie," he ripped his lips away from hers, "I—"

A loud, piercing sound rang through the air—an unmistakable sound that sent Grant's blood cooling.

"Fuck," he cursed, closing his eyes. He grabbed the back of her head and pressed their foreheads together. "That's my phone."

Frankie froze and then let go of him. "Is that important?" she whined, the need in her voice evident.

"Yes. Goddammnit." That was Nick's ringtone, a special tone that would ring his phone even if it was on silent mode. It'd also switch the phone on if it happened to be off. But it only did that in extreme emergencies. His first thought was that there was another mage attack.

She sighed. "Go and answer it then." She rolled off him and began to gather her discarded clothes.

Grant cursed again as he watched her curvy, luscious body move away from him, her buttocks jiggling enticingly as she shrugged into her tight skirt.

His inner wolf snarled at him, as if blaming him. *Why are you just letting her go?*

Oh shut up, he thought. Years of training and learning control snapped back into place, and the wolf was silenced. Following the sound of the rings, he found his pants and fished his phone out of the pocket.

"Nick," he said as he began to dress. "What's wrong? Is it the mages?"

There was an amused laugh on the other end. "No, not at all. Sorry to, er, interrupt." Nick knew where he would be tonight. "It's Alynna. She's in labor, and I thought you would want to be here when the baby comes."

"Right." He glanced over at Frankie, who was already fully

dressed with her hair falling over her shoulders like a pitch-black waterfall. She gave him a weak smile, nodded her head toward the back porch, and began walking. "I'm on my way." He pressed the red button on the phone and then dialed another number. "Hello, Patrick? Yes, I went to Ms. Muccino's house. Can you pick me up, please? We need to head back to New York. Two minutes. Great." He put the phone in his pocket and walked toward the back porch. Frankie was on top of the steps, leaning against one of the railings.

"I have to go," he said, looking up at her. He shrugged on his shirt on but left it unbuttoned, then slung his jacket over one arm. "It's Alynna. She's having the baby now."

Her eyes lit up. "Oh wow! That's amazing ... I mean, congratulations!"

"Come with me," he urged, climbing the steps. He wrapped his arms around her waist and pulled her close, nuzzling her hair to breathe in her scent.

"I can't," she replied, but snuggled against him, her hands slipping into his open shirt and wrapping around his middle. "This is a special moment for your family. I can't—don't want—to intrude."

He nodded and kissed her forehead. "Alright, but give me your phone number," he said, fishing his phone out of his pocket. Handing her the phone, he watched as she tapped her number into the device. She handed it back to him, and, before he took it, he kissed her palm. "I'll text you."

"Sure." She stepped back. "Your ride should be here any moment."

They walked around to the front porch, and, sure enough, Patrick was already holding the door of the town car open.

"Have a safe drive and tell Alynna I said congratulations."

"I will," he said and walked toward the car. He fought the urge to grab her and kiss her senseless; he torn between wanting to stay and needing to get back as soon as he could. The birth of Alynna's child, the first True Mate child for this generation, was a big deal, and he had to make sure his clan was safe. As the car pulled away, his eyes never left the front porch of the house, looking at Frankie standing there, watching him leave.

CHAPTER TWELVE

G rant entered the private room at The Enclave's medical wing, and his eyes were immediately drawn toward the figure on the bed. Alynna was lying down, looking exhausted but happy, holding a small bundle in a pink blanket in her arms. Alex was sitting in the chair beside the bed, watching his wife and baby with the biggest grin in the world, looking like he couldn't stop smiling even if he tried. When he saw Grant, he quickly stood and strode over to the Alpha.

The drive back from New Jersey took less than an hour. Still, the baby came quickly, and, by the time he arrived, it was all over.

"Congratulations." He clapped his brother-in-law on the shoulder, but Alex pulled him in for a hug. Grant hugged him right back.

"Thank you," he replied as he let go, his face beaming. "Now, go meet your niece!"

"Grant," Alynna called and motioned for him to come over. He walked toward his sister, and she moved her arms to show him her bundle. "Say hi to your niece. Michalina Jean Westbrooke. Mika, meet your Uncle Grant."

Mika was barely awake, her tiny features scrunched up in a yawn. She was still all pink and wrinkly but looked healthy. Grant felt love and pride swell up inside him as he watched the perfect, tiny face. He leaned down and pressed a kiss to Mika's forehead. The scent of daisies and earthy rain marked her as pure Lycan.

"She's beautiful," he said to his sister. "I'm proud of you."

"Yeah, well, I did push a life out of my hoo-ha, so thanks!" she joked.

Grant laughed and pressed a kiss to her forehead. "How did the delivery go? Sorry I missed it."

"Not bad," she answered. "It went much better and quicker than we thought."

"Alynna only threatened to have me castrated about half a dozen times," Alex quipped. "And only tried to reach for a scalpel to do it herself once."

"Yeah, well next time, you can carry the baby," she retorted, pulling her daughter close. "But she was worth it." She snuggled Mika closer.

"Knock knock!" A bright voice came from the doorway. Cady entered with Nick behind her. "How's everything? How is the baby?"

"She's beautiful, healthy, and perfect," Alex said proudly.

The other couple walked in, and Cady hugged Alex while Nick shook the new father's hand.

"Oohhh, she's beautiful!" Cady cooed as she stared at the bundle in Alynna's arms. Her hand instinctively went to her own belly.

"Congratulations," Nick said to Alynna.

"Come say hi, Uncle Nicky!" Alynna teased, lifting up Mika.

Nick laughed and came closer, giving Alynna an affectionate hair ruffle and looking down at the baby. "Beautiful, just beautiful," he proclaimed as his large hand brushed gently over the baby's tiny cheek.

"Yours will be just as perfect," Alynna said. "I know it's difficult not knowing, but see? She's fine and you'll have one just as healthy. Let's just hope he or she takes after Cady in the looks and brains department and not you, right?"

Nick gave Alynna a mock dirty look and then laughed. "I'd be just fine with that." He looked at Cady with pure adoration and love, and she came to him, snuggling against his side.

Grant glanced at all the people around him, including the newest addition to his family. As Alpha, the protective instinct rose in him, and he knew he was going to do whatever it took to keep them all safe. However, a hollow feeling in the pit of his stomach formed, and he suddenly felt a longing ache as he watched the two happy couples.

Want ... this ...

Grant was startled. His inner wolf had never talked to him this much, especially not while he was fully in human form. He frowned and gave a soft growl.

Mika fussed at the sound and let out a cry. "Aww, don't worry Mika, Uncle Grant will forgive you, even though you cock-blocked him," Alynna joked, her eyes sparkling knowingly.

"Shouldn't you watch your language now that you have a baby?" Grant countered.

"She's two hours old." Alynna rolled her eyes. "I doubt hearing 'cock' will harm her development. Judging by the way you're all wound up, I suppose you didn't get any bow-chika-wow-wow tonight?"

"I think it's time for you and my niece to get some rest."

"So you're not going to talk about your sex life?" Alynna joked.

"Not in front of the baby," he said as the corners of his mouth twitched up into a slight smile.

"Okay, but you have to promise you'll tell me about your grand plan to make Frankie fall for you." Alynna yawned. "Because I wanna keep her."

So do I, Grant thought to himself. A soft, contented sound rumbled in his chest, as if to agree.

CHAPTER THIRTEEN

The anteroom lay in shambles. The curtains had been ripped out and shredded, the chairs and tables smashed against the walls, paintings torn down, and the precious vases shattered on the floor.

Daric winced as he heard another loud crash, but he remained rooted in his spot. Stefan stood in the middle of the room, his hands fisted at his sides.

"Lord Stefan," an unfamiliar voice greeted him as he entered the room.

"Come in!" he roared.

Daric turned around and looked at the newcomer. If he was surprised by who it was, he didn't show it. Victoria, who stood next to him, opened her mouth to protest but shut it quickly when Stefan sent her a warning look.

"You've heard the news?" Stefan asked the stranger. "The child has come."

"Y—y—yes," he stammered.

"And what are you going to do about it?"

"Lord Stefan, I swear ... things are moving along," he began.

"We are looking to get into Grant's good graces, and we've already planned to ingrain ourselves—"

"I don't care to hear your plans!" Stefan roared. "I need action! Now. And you will deliver Grant to me once you have secured his legacy or you will not get New York."

"Of course." The man cowered slightly. "But these things take time."

"I can be patient," the mage said. "But do not try me. And do not fail. You know the consequences."

"We won't, Lord Stefan."

CHAPTER FOURTEEN

"Hello." Frankie picked up her mobile phone absentmindedly as she was looking through all the purchase orders on her desk.

"Frankie!" a bright voice greeted her. "How are you?"

"Alynna! How are you? And the baby, how is she? Thank you for sending me that picture." Frankie grinned, remembering the picture Alynna had sent the day after she gave birth. It was Grant holding little Mika, which was quite sneaky of her, as it definitely sent her hormones into overdrive. Butterflies didn't flutter as much as start a revolution in her stomach when she saw him holding a baby, his strong forearms gently cradling the pink bundle. That was a week ago and her ovaries were still threatening to explode. And, of course, she glanced at the photo at least once a day.

"I'm great, and you?"

"Oh you know, just busy," she said with a sigh. "Did you get the package we sent?"

"Oh my God, yes!" Alynna gushed. "Thank you, it was amazing."

"Glad you liked it, but it was mostly Dante and Nonna Gianna who put it together."

As soon as they found out that Alynna had had the baby, her brother and great-aunt put together a food basket, filled with various homemade goodies like cookies, jars of their special sauce, freshly-made bread, fresh buffalo mozzarella, and two casseroles they didn't even serve at the restaurant. Enzo himself delivered the basket to the New York Lycan headquarters on the Upper West side.

"I finished all of it," she admitted without shame. "I was hoping my appetite would slow down once I give birth, but now with breastfeeding and stuff, my body's still trying to eat its weight in pizza."

Frankie laughed. "Thank God for that Lycan metabolism, huh?"

"Yeah, well, at least there's that," she said. "So, how are things? I mean ... with you and Grant?"

"Grant?" she asked innocently. She was glad Alynna wasn't there to see her cheeks grow hot. "Uhm, I haven't seen him since ... the night you gave birth."

They had, however, been exchanging brief text messages. She blushed each time she thought of the messages from Grant. She would get them first thing in the morning, as soon as she got up.

Good morning, sexy.

I miss your scent.

Thinking about you.

He also apologized for not coming out to see her. With the birth of his heir apparent and running the company and the clan, he just couldn't get away. The stakes were too high and he was securing his territory, after all, making sure they were safe from the mages. But he promised he would come to Jersey as soon as he could manage. She shivered, not knowing what would happen when they did meet again.

"Yeah, sorry about that," Alynna said sheepishly. "And I know Grant hasn't had time to come to Jersey, but let me make it up to you."

"How?" she asked, biting her lip.

"Come to New York on Monday. I'm throwing a party at The Plaza. Muccino's is closed on Mondays, right?"

"A party?" she echoed. "What type of party?"

"Just a little get together. It's a celebration, and I'll be bringing Mika. You can see her, but we'll probably duck out early. Grant will be there, too."

"I don't know ..." she hesitated. It was one thing to flirt over text message and another to see Grant face to face again. God, she didn't know what had gotten into her, inviting him to shift with her. She had never done that with anyone except her Nonna, Ma, and her brothers. It was too intimate, too familiar and her brain was telling her to pull away. But afterwards, as she lay on the grass in his arms, it felt so right and her she-wolf was pleased.

"Please, Frankie?" she pleaded. "I can't bring the baby into New Jersey, not until after her welcoming ceremony." Frankie wouldn't care about the rules of course, but bringing a Lycan pup outside his or her clan's territory was risky if he or she had yet to be formally welcomed into the clan and introduced to the Lycan world.

"Alright," she relented. "Text me the details. I'll be there."

———

Frankie sighed and looked at the two outfits on her bed. One was a drab gray pantsuit, all business but still appropriate for a dinner party in the city. The other was a red, off-the-shoulder gown that had a mermaid skirt and a small train. It was vintage Valentino and was actually her mother's dress, though she could only remember Adrianna wearing it once before. When she died, Frankie couldn't bear to wear it or get rid of it, so she left it in the back of her walk-in closet instead.

The gray pantsuit was like armor, something that was cool and standoffish and would never be mistaken as anything but an outfit. The red gown, on the other hand, was meant to tempt and tease and there were consequences to wearing it, a bridge she couldn't uncross.

Grant was sexy, handsome, and set her blood on fire. She was an adult, a woman with desires, and she longed for him as much as he did for her. God, she was a mess, her past finally catching up with her.

She flopped down on the bed facedown, between the two outfits, and let out a frustrated cry into the comforter. Why was the decision so hard?

Jacob. That's why. He was the reason she never let anyone close. *Townie bitch.* The hurt threatened to spring up in her again, but, years later, it was more of a dull ache. Still, some days, like today, she allowed herself to look back and play it all in her mind again.

Jacob had been pursuing her all summer and she fell for him, hard. He was charming, funny, and so handsome that every girl in town was green with envy when they saw her in the passenger seat of his sports car, riding with the top down. She went to parties with him, met all his friends, the whole nine yards. After two weeks, she knew Jacob was planning something special, so she snuck out with him, after she went home from her shift at the restaurant.

He took her to the shore, driving for a couple of hours until they got to the ocean. There, on a beach blanket, he lay out on the sand and told her he loved her. Frankie gave him her virginity and fell even deeper in love with him. She came home the next morning and her mother was screaming like a banshee, threatening to ground her, but she didn't care. She and Jacob were in love.

Of course, the calls and text messages became shorter and farther in between after that. And soon, they stopped altogether. It wasn't until much later, when she saw Jacob riding in his sports car with another girl, that she realized she had been played. Her Italian temper got the best of her, of course, and she confronted him while he was with his new girlfriend and his friends, walking along Main Street.

She screamed at him, calling him a cheat and liar, but Jacob merely sneered at her and said, "You thought I was going to make a little townie like you my girlfriend? Don't you know who I am? I'm going to be CEO of a major media company in ten years! You're just a piece of ass I wanted to have some fun with —just be glad I even lowered my standards to be with you."

Tears stung her eyes and her inner wolf had screamed to be let out, to rip Jacob into little pieces. His new girlfriend and friends laughed at her, muttering "townie bitch" and "pathetic slut" as she walked away.

She cried for days, and her mother and grandmother consoled her, but she saw the look in her mother's eyes, one she'd seen before. It was the same sad look she got when Frankie or Dante would ask about their father or when she thought her daughter wasn't looking and she stared at a blank wall or into the distance. Her mother also wore the same look for weeks after the divorce papers from her second husband arrived.

Her mother was right. *Men always leave*, she had warned her. And after Jacob, she understood. That day, she decided that she'd never fall in love with a man. She put herself on birth control, just in case, as she didn't want to end up being a single parent either, like her mother.

With another frustrated groan, Frankie got up from the bed and grabbed the two outfits, holding them next to her in front of the full-length mirror. She should really just say fuck 'em all and stay home. Going to some fancy dinner party with snooty New York Lycans who could probably smell her working-class upbringing a mile away wasn't her idea of fun. What would they have in common? She should just cancel. Yeah, that's what she should do, just call Alynna and tell her she was sick or busy. Putting down the outfits, she reached for the phone on her dresser. There were already two messages waiting in her inbox.

The first one was a picture from Alynna. It was baby Mika, dressed up in her first fancy dress, green and silver with ruffles, and the caption read "Hello Auntie Frankie!"

The next was a simple text message from Grant. *Can't wait to see you tonight.*

"Unnghhhh!" she groaned again. She looked back at the two dresses. She would wear her armor, wear it proudly, but she would protect herself and her heart. Frankie would give in to her own desires, give in to Grant and offer her body, but nothing else.

CHAPTER FIFTEEN

"Alynna," Frankie whispered urgently as she sat next to the brunette. The younger woman was sitting on one of the couches just outside The Palm Court restaurant. "When you invited me to this get-together, you didn't say Grant's mother would be here."

When she had arrived, Frankie parked her car in the garage of The Plaza Hotel (she didn't dare drive her 10-year-old Honda to the valet station) and made her way to the restaurant.

As soon as she entered, she saw Grant, looking devastatingly handsome in his tux, standing next to a beautiful older woman. As someone jostled her from behind, she overheard them talking about how good the Alpha's mother looked, especially at her age. Frankie retreated, making her way back to the elevator but had been spotted by Alynna before she could get away.

"Hey Frankie! Glad you could make it!" Alynna smiled at her friend. She shoved a small bundle at her. "Look Mika! Auntie Frankie's here!"

Frankie's frown disappeared as soon as she saw the beautiful little baby, who looked up at her with interested eyes. "Oh my God! She's gorgeous!" She traced a finger down the chubby little cheek and then leaned down for a quick kiss. Mika's lips twitched into a smile. "Hey, no fair!" Frankie playfully slapped Alynna on the arm. "Stop using your adorable daughter to distract me. Now, why didn't you tell me Grant's mom was here?"

"Well, it's her birthday and her party; of course she's here," Alynna said in an innocent voice. When Frankie gave her a steely glare, she held up the baby in front of her like a shield.

The other woman crossed her arms over her chest, unmoved. "And you left out that piece of information because ..."

"Well, if I told you who the party was for, would you have come?" the younger woman asked as she pulled Mika back to her chest.

"Of course not!"

"Then that's why!"

Frankie slapped her forehead. "*Madre de dio*, I'm not ready for this ..."

"Callista is a lovely lady," Alynna declared. "You have nothing to worry about."

"I didn't even bring a present." Frankie shook her head. "This was a mistake. I can't do this. I'm sorry, but I'm going home."

"No, don't!" Alynna pleaded. "You can't!"

"And why not? You tricked me into coming here!" Frankie stood up and spun around but nearly toppled over when she hit a brick wall. At least she thought it was a brick wall; it was actually a solid chest. "Ommphh!" Strong arms caught her before she hit the floor.

"Frankie ..." Grant's voice was a low rumble that sent heat through her body. He pulled her close and brushed his lips over her hair. "You look ..."

"Amazing? Stunning? Spectacular?" Alynna quipped as she

looked up at them. "Woohoo, girl, you're on fire!" The younger woman, who had put down her baby in the carrier, fanned herself with her hand.

"She's definitely all those things ... and more." Grant's eyes roamed over her body, and she felt her cheeks grow hot.

"Grant?" a voice from behind them said.

"Mother," Grant said with a nod to the older lady. He let go of Frankie but pulled her to his side. "May I present Ms. Francesca Muccino. Alpha of the New Jersey clan. Frankie, this is my mother, Callista Mayfair."

"H—how do you do, ma'am?" Frankie stammered and looked at the floor. "Thank you for, er, having me here. Happy Birthday."

"Lupa, please." The older woman, dressed in a gorgeous floor-length silver dress, gave her a slight bow. "You honor me with your presence here. And call me Callista." She leaned over and gave her a kiss on the cheek. "Oh my, is that vintage Valentino?"

She nodded, her hands smoothing down the silky red fabric of her gown. She was nearly out the door in her gray pantsuit when something just tugged her back, and she decided on a last-minute switch to the gown instead.

"It's gorgeous." Callista's gaze flew from Frankie to Grant, her eyes sparkling.

"Thank you, Callista," she said. "It was my mother's. She had great taste in clothes."

Callista's brows knitted. "A—Ana? Adrianna! That's your mother, right? I remember meeting her once or twice, when Michael was still alive. She always wore the most elegant gowns. And her eyes, just like yours!" Her beautiful face fell. "Oh my, since you're Alpha now ... I'm sorry, my dear. How long ago?"

"I'm afraid she passed on two years ago," Frankie relayed.

The older woman took her hand. "I'm so sorry, Lupa. She is

... was a beautiful woman and wonderful person, from what I remember."

"Thank you." Frankie gave her a sad smile. "She was. And please, call me Frankie."

"Well now," Callista looked towards the restaurant, "I think we should start dinner soon." She looked at Alynna and to the carrier. "How's my darling girl? All settled?"

Alynna nodded. "Yes, she's good. She's down for a nap, but she'll probably be up in another hour. I'm gonna put her in our room. The night nanny should be there already, but she'll call me if Mika wakes up and needs a feeding." She gave Frankie's hand a squeeze. "I'll join you in a bit."

Frankie looked lost, trapped between Grant and his mother. "Er ... where do I sit? For dinner?" she asked Alynna.

"You'll sit with us, of course," Callista declared. "I won't have it any other way."

"Is that okay?" She knew dinner parties had seating arrangements and did not want to mess up anyone's work.

"It's my birthday and everyone has to follow what I want, right, Grant?"

Grant smiled. "Of course, mother. I'm sure we can find a seat for Frankie."

"Excellent." Callista linked her arms with Frankie. "Shall we?"

———

"How is your wine, dear?" Callista asked, leaning toward Frankie.

"It's great." Frankie took a delicate sip. "Full-bodied, not too bitter. I think it pairs well with the main course."

"I didn't realize you knew so much about wines," the older woman remarked.

"Frankie owns a restaurant," Grant supplied. "They have a great cellar."

"My family owns it," she clarified. "I mean, my grandmother and grandfather started it after they moved here from Italy. But my brothers and I run it now."

Frankie looked around the room, smiling in spite of herself. There was a bit of a kerfuffle with the seating arrangements in the beginning, as the event coordinator had already put the name cards on each place setting, seeing as the New York clan booked the entire restaurant for them and their 100 guests. Originally, Callista was going to be seated with her husband Jean-Luc, Grant, Nick, Cady, Alex, Alynna, as well as Grayson Charles, his wife Caroline, and Vanessa Bennet.

Frankie, on the other hand, had a seat at one of the tables in the back. Of course, Callista wanted Frankie to sit with them, but the coordinator was insistent they keep the place settings. There was a heated argument, but in the end, Callista won, making all the other people in their table scoot over to make way for Frankie. She was now squished between Grant and Nick, and, though it was a little hard to maneuver her elbows, she didn't quite mind. Grant was attentive, asking her if everything was okay as he kept his eyes fixed on her. If he wasn't talking to her, he was always touching her, brushing his hand on her arm or shoulder, or threading his fingers through hers under the table, which made her blush. Nick, his Beta, was also polite and asked her intelligent questions, though she mostly enjoyed talking to his gorgeous wife, Cady.

Frankie felt a burning shame. She thought all of the New York shifters were snooty and haughty, but they were warm and kind to her. If anything, she was the one who was prejudiced, judging them all without getting to know them. Of course, she could have done without Vanessa Bennet's dagger eyes on her all night from across the table, but nothing could ruin her good mood. Why the other woman acted like Frankie had the plague, she didn't know. Maybe she had some type of OCD and didn't like that the table now had an uneven number of place settings. But as the night wore on, she realized why she might have ticked her off, if the way she constantly batted her eyes at Grant was any indication.

"What type of food do you serve?" Vanessa asked, her voice grating Frankie's ears.

Speaking of the she-devil. "Italian, home-style," Frankie said proudly.

"Oh how ... quaint," the other Lycan said, her voice dripping with sarcasm. "Do you have that kitschy stuff on the walls, too? And red and white checkered tablecloths?"

"Of course," Frankie said proudly, refusing to back down. No one would make her ashamed of her background. "It's the same as it's been for three generations."

"Sounds like those touristy restaurants in Rome," Vanessa sneered. "When I went to Italy, we only ate at Michelin-starred restaurants. Mother wouldn't have it any other way."

"My cousin tends to be a food snob," Grayson Charles explained, trying to lighten the mood. "I'm sure your restaurant has fine food, Lupa."

"It's the best," Grant said. "The food is delicious."

"You've been there, Grant?" his mother asked.

"Of course, I've been a couples of time."

Callista said nothing but raised a delicate brow at him, sipped her wine, and then looked at Frankie. "Really? That's interesting."

"He went four nights in a row," Frankie declared. She cheered silently when she saw Vanessa's face turn sour, the vein in her neck threatening to pop.

"It must really be delicious, then," Callista said. "We must try it some time, Jean-Luc," she said to her husband.

"Of course, *ma-cher*," the older Lycan man replied, smiling at his wife.

"Please, come anytime," Frankie said. "You're most welcome."

"Excuse me." Vanessa Bennet whipped her napkin off her lap and stood up, causing her chair to scrape against the floor loudly. Grayson and his wife looked embarrassed at their companion's behavior, but no one made a comment about Ms. Bennet's departure.

"You look beautiful tonight," Grant whispered as he bent his head down to Frankie's ear, his lips barely brushing her lobe. "Have I told you that?"

"Only about a dozen times," she said wryly. "Are you fishing for a compliment?"

"Well, I did dress up tonight," he said, his eyes sparkling in amusement.

"Uhmmm ... well, Grant Anderson ... you ... you clean up nice." She pursed her lips, trying not to laugh.

"I'm hurt," he said in a joking tone. "I went through all this effort, primping and fixing myself up, and that's all I get? That's not fair."

"Suck it up, Alpha." She jabbed him in the ribs with her elbow playfully. "Life isn't fair."

"Ow! Nick, she's hurting me," Grant called. "You have to avenge my honor. Challenge her to a duel or something."

"I wouldn't take her on if I were you, Nick," Cady quipped and gave Frankie a wink. "Frankie looks tough. And I heard she was willing to take on four Lycans for saying the wrong thing."

Nick laughed. "Well, Ms. Muccino *is* an Alpha and I'm only a Beta."

"I can take it easy on you for the first few rounds," Frankie joked.

"I'm doomed," Grant groaned. "I'm just going to roll over and let you take over my territory."

"Oh, no way." Frankie shook her head. "That sounds like a terrible idea. I don't want your responsibilities."

"How about we switch?" Grant asked. "I'll be Alpha of Jersey and you be New York Alpha and see how you like it."

"I don't know ... how are you with trailer park disputes?" Her eyes sparkled with mirth. "Do you know what to do when one of your people puts feral opossums in his neighbor's pickup truck?"

"That didn't really happen!" Alynna interjected in an incredulous voice.

The Lupa nodded. "Oh yeah. That was just last month. There's also the time one of my cousins thought it would be fun to steal one of the monster trucks at this show that rolled into town ..." She flushed when she realized that everyone at the table was looking at her. "Er, never mind."

"No please," Callista urged. "Go on."

"Well, Denny, one of my Lycan cousins, thought it would be hilarious to get drunk and sneak into the Monster Truck show ..."

CHAPTER SIXTEEN

G rant watched Frankie as she relayed her story. Fierce pride surged through him as she charmed his family and clan.

His heart had slammed into his chest and desire had pooled in his middle the moment he spied her outside the restaurant in that dress. The red silky fabric clung to her every curve and left her shoulders exposed. He wanted to run up to her, kiss her collarbones, drag his lips across the tops of her breasts, and make his way up the slender column of her neck to claim her luscious mouth.

"Grant?" Frankie asked, her mismatched eyes blinking. "Are you okay?"

"Yes," he said. "I'm just thinking ..."

"Of what?" she asked.

"I'll tell you later," he replied in a low voice. "How about some dessert?"

The rest of the dinner passed quickly, though for Grant it seemed like a lifetime before things were finally winding down. After dessert, guests slowly started to call it a night. Alex and his sister retired to their hotel room, and Cady and Nick seemed eager to do the same. Soon Callista declared she was ready to retire, too, so the remaining party stood up and made their way out of the restaurant. Cady needed to use the ladies' room, and Frankie offered to go with her, in case she needed help.

"Grant," Vanessa Bennet purred as she cozied up to him by the doorway. She dug her hands into his bicep and leaned forward, brushing her breasts against him. "Are you going back to The Enclave so soon? It's only midnight, and there are probably lots of clubs that are still open. I've never even been to Blood Moon. I was hoping you'd take me ..." Her voice trailed off, giving a double meaning to her words.

Grant pried the young woman's fingers off gently. "I'm afraid I have an early meeting tomorrow, Vanessa," he said.

"Oh," the young woman pouted, "rain check then?"

"Uh, sure," Grant said absentmindedly.

Vanessa sidled up next to him, placed a hand over his chest, and slipped a piece of paper into his jacket pocket. "Here's my number, then." She leaned over and whispered into his ear. "Call me any time."

Someone clearing their throat made Vanessa jump back. Frankie stood there, eyes blazing, her arms crossed under her chest. "Excuse me," she said as she breezed past them and went toward Callista. Grant could have sworn he heard a low growl as she walked by the other woman.

"Well, bye then, Vanessa." Grant nodded to the young woman.

"Bye, Grant." She batted her eyelashes at him as she walked away to join Grayson and his wife after they had said their goodbyes.

Grant let out a relieved breath once Vanessa was out of his sight, then turned to his mother and Frankie.

"I had a lovely time," Frankie said to Callista in a warm voice. "Thank you for having me."

Callista leaned over and gave the young woman a kiss on each cheek. "Thank you for coming." She looked at Grant meaningfully. "It's been … an interesting night, and I hope to see you again."

"We'll see," Frankie said in a tight voice. She looked at Grant. "Alpha, thank you for letting me into your territory," she said in a cold tone. "It was an honor celebrating this joyous occasion with you." After saying goodbye to Cady and Nick, she turned and headed for the elevators.

"Grant," Callista had a hard time keeping a smile from her face, "she's lovely."

"I know." Grant's brows furrowed at Frankie's puzzling treatment.

"So? What are you waiting for?" His mother's eyes were filled with amusement. "Go get her before she escapes and the last thing she remembers is that hussy rubbing herself against you like a cat in heat."

"Oh, fuck me." Grant slapped his palm over his eyes. "Sorry, Mother, I know, language." He gave his mother a kiss on the cheek. "I'll see you before you fly back home to Paris," he said as he sprinted toward the elevators.

Frankie was pacing in front of the set of elevators, her arms stiff at her sides. One of the doors opened, and she stepped inside.

Grant barely made it, his hand slapping the door before it closed. "Frankie," he called.

The other Alpha turned around, and her eyes grew wide in surprise as Grant pushed his way into the elevator car and cornered her against the wall. "What the hell are you doing?"

"Something I've wanted to do the whole night," he said before he swooped in and pressed his lips to hers.

She made a small sound of protest and pushed him back

with unnatural strength. "Maybe you should go and find Vanessa instead."

Grant moved closer, his hands on either side of her, trapping her against the wall. "I don't want her; I want you." He pressed his lower body against her. "I've had a damn hard-on from the moment I saw you." He ground his erection against her, making her gasp.

She opened her mouth to protest, but he silenced her by slanting his lips against hers. He grabbed her waist and pressed their bodies together.

"You can't wear a dress like that and expect me to just let you go," he whispered as he trailed kissed from her jaw to her ear.

"Grant," she moaned as he pressed his lips to the soft spot under her neck. He licked her there and sucked back at the skin. Her knees buckled and he held her against the door. Her heady scent filled his nostrils, mixed with her arousal. A low growl emanated from his chest.

"Fuck, I bet your panties are soaked through," he said, lifting her dress up.

A soft ding sounded from the elevator, and the doors opened.

"Find another damn elevator!" Grant snarled as he spun around and jammed his finger on the close button. Nick's face as the door shut was one of confusion, but Cady's expression was amused. He jabbed his finger on the button for the 18th floor.

Grant turned to face Frankie, who was leaning against the opposite wall. "Where are we going?" she asked with a frown.

He moved closer and took her hand, kissing the soft palm. "Come back to my room with me," he pulled her into his arms and looked into her eyes, "please."

Her facial expression changed. "Yes."

When Grant asked her to come up to his room, she didn't expect that said room was actually a 1,500 square-foot suite on the top floor of The Plaza Hotel. Her eyes widened as they entered the main living room, richly appointed in grays and blues. "Don't you live on the Upper West side?" she asked, dumbfounded.

"Yes, but this was easier," he said as he closed the door behind him.

"Easier for what?"

"To convince you to stay with me tonight," he said in a serious tone. "And I can't take you back with me to The Enclave; we have protocols in place for visitors."

"You what?" she asked, her voice raising slightly. "You planned to ..." She shook her head.

"Frankie," he growled, grabbing her by the waist before she could protest. "Yes, I planned to bring you up here tonight. But I would never force you to do anything you don't want. Just say no and I'll walk you to your car. Hell, say yes now, but anytime you change your mind, just tell me and you can leave. I won't have you unwilling. But this push and pull between us has to stop. You have to either give in or tell me to leave you alone forever because you're driving me crazy."

She looked up into his eyes; the expression on his face was sincere. Ocean spray, sugary sweetness, and the roaring in her ears were back again, making her feel dizzy and lightheaded. "I ... I ..." She took a deep breath. She wanted this, wanted Grant. "I want this, Grant. Yes."

Yes. A soft growl agreed with her, urging her on, and then went quiet.

He leaned down and slotted his lips against hers, pulling her closer to his body. His kisses were soft but made her knees buckle, causing her to melt against him. She grabbed onto his shoulders for support.

Grant's hand slipped up her back, finding the zipper on her dress. He pulled it down, exposing the smooth skin as his fingertips traced a line down her back. Once the zipper opened all the way, a gentle tug was all it took to send the dress to the floor, pooling around her feet like a hot lava.

On instinct, Frankie put her hands over her chest to cover herself.

"No," Grant growled, his hands tugging at hers. "You don't have to hide yourself, not from me." His eyes roamed over her body appreciatively.

She lowered her hands and stood in front of him in nothing but her matching black lace bra, panties, and garter belt with stockings.

"Fucking hell, Frankie," he cursed as he realized what she was wearing. "Are you trying to kill me or something?"

Her cheeks burned at the way his eyes blazed over her body. "It's a vintage dress, so I thought this would match. Do you like it?"

Grant's fingers ghosted over the scrap of black lace around her hips, tracing down to the straps that held the stockings up. Slipping his finger under one of the garters, he snapped it back gently. "I fucking love it," he said, before he backed her up against the plush blue-gray couch.

"Ooomph," she panted as she fell down on the soft cushions. Grant got on his knees, his eyes hungry as he looked up at her. "What are you ... oh!" She moaned as his fingers yanked her panties aside and began to massage her damp nether lips. "Grant!" She arched her back as he slipped a finger inside of her.

"You're so wet," he said, pushing one more finger inside. "So ready for me ..." He reached down, unzipped his pants, and took out his cock. He gripped the shaft, fisting it tight.

"Please, Grant ..." Frankie moaned, her body tightening as his thumb brushed over her clit. "I need you inside me now. I'm on birth control."

"Patience," he soothed, as he slowed down his fingers and leaned his head between her knees. "We have all night."

A soft rip tore through the air, and her panties were nothing but scraps of lace in Grant's fingers. Before she could protest, she let out a gasp as his tongue licked at her damp core. He laid his tongue over her pussy lips, tasting her and savoring her as he ran it along her seam.

"Grant! Fuck!" Her hips bucked up to meet him, but his hand steadied her, pushing her down as his tongue relentlessly lashed at her in a torturous dance. He lapped at her, teasing her entrance, and then slid his tongue into her, while his thumb found her clit, drawing circles around the nub.

Frankie lost all thought as white heat spread through her like a burst of flame; pleasure shook her body as an orgasm ripped through her. Grant was unrelenting and continued worshipping her with his tongue, teasing another orgasm from her body.

"Grant." She lost her words, his name the only thing on her mind and on her lips. Closing her eyes, she let her body sink back into the couch, boneless and sated. For now.

She let out a small whoop of surprise as Grant picked her up, carrying her bridal-style into the bedroom as if she weighed nothing at all. He walked into the other room, then laid her down on the luxurious bed. As he stepped back, he began to remove his clothes, shucking off his jacket and then unbuttoning his shirt.

Frankie's eyes never left him as he gave her a private strip show. She'd seen it before, seen him naked, but now, as he stood there in the low lamplight of the plush hotel room, it was somehow different. His shoulder muscles ripped as he shrugged off his shirt, the triceps on his muscular arms flexing with the movement. Her eyes trailed down the defined muscles of his pecs to the rippling six-pack abs to the narrow, defined hips that made the rest of him look bigger to the delicious indentation on his hips. The happy trail of dark hair disappeared under his pants, much to her disappointment. As if reading her mind, he hooked his thumbs in the waistband of his trousers and shucked them down, along with his underwear, to unsheathe his throbbing dick, the thick shaft jutting out between his powerful legs. For a moment, she wondered how this would work. She had only been with one man, one time, and he was nowhere near as big as Grant.

He got on the bed with her, crawling over her slowly. "Frankie," he whispered. "So beautiful ... sexy ..." Leaning down, he pressed his lips on her knee and moved up, tracing a path over her thighs, hips, and stopping just under her breasts. With a quick motion, he unhooked her bra and tossed it away. "Perfect." His eyes glossed over as he looked at her breasts.

Large, warm hands cupped over the mounds, filling his hands as he stroked her soft, pink nipples into hard nubs.

"Unnnghhhh," she moaned, arching her back, pushing her breasts against his palms.

"So eager, my little Alpha," he teased. "What do you want?"

"I want you, Grant," she panted. "On me, inside me."

"I'm going to make you come over and over again," he promised. He bent down and took a nipple into his mouth, sucking hard. He spread her knees and shifted his hips, rocking his raging hard-on over the slick lips of her pussy.

Frankie cried out as the underside of his shaft connected with her clit, sending small shocks of pleasure through her. She spread her legs, arching her hips into him, begging him to take her. He continued to tease her, rubbing his cock against her.

She smirked up at him, her eyes sparkling with mischief as she reached down and grabbed his shaft. Gripping him tight in her small hands, Frankie stroked his cock, sliding up and down. This time, it was Grant who groaned. He rocked his hips against her fist, his head rolling back in pleasure.

"Tease," he groaned as she swiped the drop of moisture from his tip with her fingers.

"You're the tease," she said with a grin, sticking her finger in her mouth and sucking it dry.

"Fuck, Frankie!" he moaned, pushing his hips at her.

She sucked in a breath and pointed the tip of his cock right at her hot, wet entrance.

"Are you sure?" he asked, his voice tender.

"Yes." She rocked her hips up at him, teasing him. "I want you inside me, Grant." She pulled him down for another kiss, nipping at his bottom lip and holding it between her teeth. With a soft growl, he slid into her slowly.

Frankie gasped and let go of his lips. God, he was big and he was filling her up. He stopped suddenly.

"Frankie ... are you a ...?"

"No." She shook her head. Well, technically she wasn't a virgin. "It's just ... it's been a long time." *A very long time.*

"I'll be gentle." Grant cradled her, wrapping his arms around her back. A sexy, soft growl rumbled from his chest as he moved in slowly, pushing and burying himself inside of her. He eased out halfway and then pushed in again.

"Oh!" she moaned, her breath coming in small gasps.

Grant started a slow gentle rhythm, sliding into her until she expanded to accommodate him. But his control slipped, and he gripped her tighter as he thrust into her, in and out, faster and faster. His hips bucked forward, ramming her down onto the mattress. Hands, lips were everywhere, touching her, teasing her, heating her with small bursts of flame. Grant angled his hips, changing it so he bumped her clit just right to send shockwaves of pleasure through her.

"Grant! Oh yes! Yes!" she called as her orgasm exploded through her body. He buried his face in her neck, calling out her name before he sank his teeth into her skin. It wasn't deep enough to draw blood, but she yelped. The pain was brief, but it sent her into dizzying heights, enhancing her pleasure, and another orgasm shook her body. Her fingers dug into his back, nails scraping down the skin, leaving claw marks.

"Fuck, Frankie!" Grant groaned. He bucked into her faster, and then his back stiffened. A feral growl escaped his lips, his cock throbbed inside her, and shot after shot of wet warmth pulsed through her. He murmured her name, burying his face against her neck, taking in a deep breath as he slowed down.

Frankie lay under him for what seemed like forever, her heartbeat slowing as they both came down from their orgasms. With a groan, he slipped out of her and rolled over. His feet hit the carpeting, and soft footsteps lead to the bathroom.

And there it was. Her heart constricted in her chest. She didn't have to worry about getting too close to Grant after all, not when he was the one running away. She sighed, slipped off the bed, and began to search for her discarded bra.

"What are you doing?" Grant's voice boomed throughout the room.

Frankie looked back toward the bathroom door as she was hooking her bra back into place. "Getting dressed."

He frowned and lifted a washcloth in his hands. "I wanted to help clean you up. You were bleeding."

Her brows knitted, and she sniffed. Her enhanced sense of smell picked up the scent of iron. "Oh."

Grant walked over to her and took her hand, dragging her

back to bed. Spreading her legs, he pressed the warm, wet washcloth over her.

"Does it hurt?" he asked, concern in his voice.

"I didn't notice it," she replied.

"I'm sorry."

"For hurting me with your titan dong?" she quipped.

He threw his head back and let out a laugh. The sound warmed her heart, and it was infectious. She laughed along with him.

"I thought you said you weren't a virgin," Grant asked as he put the cloth aside.

"I'm not, but it's been a while," she confessed. "Ten years."

"Ten years?" he asked incredulously.

"Yeah and it was only ... well, just the one time." She buried her face in the pillows, her cheeks burning like someone had put gasoline on her and lit it up. "Are you disappointed?" Oh God, she was probably a terrible lay.

"Disappointed? Frankie, look at me." He gathered her into his arms, pressing his face into her neck. "No, of course not."

"But were you ... satisfied?"

He smiled against her skin. "Very."

She said nothing but nestled against him.

"Stay with me." He nuzzled her neck.

"I don't have to be in the restaurant 'till twelve," she said with a frown. "But don't you have work tomorrow?"

He released her, reached for the phone on the bedside table, and then tapped out a quick message. "I just cancelled all my morning meetings," he declared. "Now, will you stay?"

Her lips curved into a smile. "Yes."

"Good." Grant shifted, rolling her under him. He leaned up on his elbows so he could drink her lips softly, sipping at her. His hands were all over her as if he wanted to mark and memorize every inch of her skin. Her eyes fluttered closed, and she moved to his side, cuddling up against him. She settled in his arms easily, and he threw an arm over her. When she drifted off to sleep, the last thing she remembered was the soft sound of the ocean in her ears and the smell of the saltwater spray.

Mine. Mine.

Grant was startled from his sleepy state by the low growl. He looked down at Frankie, sleeping deeply in his arms, her face buried in his chest. She looked so peaceful and beautiful and soft. His inner wolf seemed to approve, and he felt the animal settle in contentment.

He couldn't get enough of her luscious body, and sex with Frankie was a hundred times better than in his imagination. She didn't seem to mind at first, and was just as eager as him. After the first time, they napped for a bit, sated for the moment. However, he woke up an hour or two later with Frankie's soft ass pressed up against him, and he was instantly erect.

She wiggled her butt against him, sighing softly, and he thought she was still asleep. When she grabbed his hand and placed it between her legs, he knew she was as awake and eager as he was. It was easy enough to slip into her from behind and rock into her, gently at first. But soon, she was begging for more, and he pounded his cock into her until she came twice. He flipped her over, so she was on top and guided her hips down. Her face looked so damn sexy, surprised and confused at first. Then she found her rhythm and was eagerly rocking her hips against his, her full breasts bouncing as she slid up and down his shaft. Her face twisted into pure pleasure, and he shot his warmth deep inside her.

Grant coaxed her into a late night shower, but, really, it was just an excuse to see her body slick and sudsy. The little minx, however, shoved him against the wall, got down on her knees, and eagerly sucked on his cock. He almost came in her mouth, but he took control, bending her over the side of the bathtub and screwing her until she was screaming his name. Then, he brought her back to bed, teasing her with his tongue and making her ride his face until she came. He wanted her again, but she protested that she was sleepy and sore, so he relented. She settled into his arms, and he watched her, feeling her breathing and making sure it was steady and even before he closed his eyes.

This was certainly new to him. He couldn't remember the last time he had woken up next to a woman, much less slept beside one. Usually, he was eager to leave after the deed was done and, once or twice, it was the woman who actually left first. But it was different with Frankie. He didn't want to be away from her, from her soft skin and almond cookie scent. God, he probably smelled like her and she smelled like him. A wave of possessive pride swept over him, knowing she'd be covered in his scent all day.

"Grant?" she asked sleepily, her blue eye opening. "What time is it?"

"Time to go back to sleep," he teased, giving her nose a kiss.

She snorted prettily. "Seriously?"

He touched her cheek with his thumb. "It's only eight a.m. I don't have my first meeting until one."

"Hmmm ..." She snuggled deeper into his arms, rubbing her soft cheek on his chest.

"How are you feeling?"

Dark lashes fluttered open. "I'm good," she purred, rubbing her body against his. Arousal and almond cookie scent made the air thick with desire. She growled softly as his erection rubbed against her stomach.

Frankie opened up easily to him, spreading her legs to

accommodate him as he slipped into her already wet opening. Grant hooked his hands under her arms and gripped her shoulders. Her small hands went up his chest; her eyes sparkled and her mouth opened as he thrust into her, bearing her down on his cock.

"Grant," she moaned, which only made him fuck into her faster and harder. Her narrow passage squeezed tight around him, signaling her orgasm. One, two, three more thrusts and she fell apart, gasping his name over and over again. He didn't last much longer. He pulsed into her, his orgasm tearing quickly through him, and continued to thrust into her as she writhed in pleasure.

"Hmmmm," she sighed in a contented voice and leaned her forehead on his shoulder. "What a nice way to wake up."

"You'll be the death of me, woman," he joked, kissing her forehead.

"Hey, I wasn't the one who wanted bathroom sex in the middle of the night," she teased.

"And I suppose it's my fault you were rubbing that sweet, pert ass of yours on my dick before that?" He nibbled on her ear.

"Your dick was already half hard," she countered, then gave him a playful nip on his chest.

A loud gurgle interrupted their conversation, and she blushed. "Sorry, I haven't had anything to eat since last night. I'm famished."

He grinned down at her. "Well good thing there's room service." Reluctantly, he disentangled from her and reached for the phone. "What do you want?" He dialed the number for room service.

"Hmmm ... pancakes," she said thoughtfully. "And bacon or sausage. Or both! And then hash browns, two eggs, and coffee."

"Anything else?" he asked with a raised brow.

"Well, what are you having?" she asked seriously.

He laughed and repeated the order into the receiver. "Hope that's enough," he teased when he put the phone down.

"I'm a healthy eater," she declared. "Always have been, especially as a Lycan and with four brothers, plus growing up around cooks. Good thing we have that Lycan metabolism, though I don't think mine is fast enough to get rid of all the carbs I eat." She frowned, looking down at the soft, slight curve of her belly and hips.

"You're perfect," he growled. When she tried to cover herself, he yanked her hands away.

"I could lose ten pounds," she protested. "I'm ... soft ... too soft."

"You're just right." He moved his hands up from her thighs to her hips, curling around her bottom. "Your ass is the perfect heart shape." He leaned down and kissed her hip. "Your hips are made for me to grip while I slide into you." His fingers dug into her hip, making her gasp. "And this ..." he dipped his head down and licked her belly, making her squeal, "this is so cute."

"Cute?" she asked.

"And sexy." He nipped right below her belly button, which sent her into a fit of giggles.

"Don't ever think you're less than perfect, Frankie." He looked up at her, worshipping her with his eyes. Her mouth formed a perfect O shape, and she pulled him up for a kiss.

Grant thought that one time, one night with Frankie Muccino would slake his thirst, but he was wrong. It only sparked the flame, and one night wouldn't be enough.

———

"I had a good time," Frankie murmured as she stepped into his arms. They were standing by her car, as Grant insisted on walking her to the garage. She felt a little better, not having to do the walk of shame in her red dress by herself, though Grant assured her there was nothing to be ashamed of.

After breakfast, they lounged around in bed, watched some TV, and just enjoyed each other's company.

As she watched him shave and get dressed, she had this dreaded feeling in the pit of her stomach. She wanted to touch him, kiss him, and drag him back to bed. But this was it. The beginning of the end. She was fooling herself if she thought what had happened between them was anything more than what it was. Grant got what he wanted, and he would grow tired of her. This time, however, she was smarter.

"Me, too." He kissed her hair.

"Um, thanks," she said awkwardly as her back stiffened. She pulled back and turned to her car. "So, I guess I'll see you around." She opened the car door, but his hand slammed it shut.

"See you around?" he asked. "What does that mean?"

"Grant," she put her hands into fists at her side and turned towards him, "I meant what I said, that I had a good time last night. But—"

"I'll come to Jersey tonight," he interrupted. "After dinner service. Or I can take some paperwork with me and I'll work while I eat."

"You don't have to say things you don't mean." She frowned. "Really, you don't. I'm a big girl, I know where this is leading."

"Oh yeah?" He crossed his arms over his chest and leaned on the side of the car. "Do you now?"

"Of course. This was a one-night thing," she said with a shrug. "We both got what we wanted, scratched the itch, and neither of us has to pretend it's more than it is." As she said those words, a vice-like grip tightened around her chest.

No, a growl said from inside her. *Don't leave*, it whined.

Shutting her she-wolf down, she bit her lip and fisted her

hands, her nails digging deep into her palms. "Bye, Grant," she said flippantly, getting into her car.

Turning the key in the ignition, she started the car and pulled out of her spot. She didn't even look back. It took all her energy, but she did it. She put up walls around her heart, locked it away so no one would hurt her. But why did she get that sick feeling in her stomach?

Lies, lies, the she-wolf taunted.

She barely got past the entrance to the Jersey Turnpike before she had to pull over and lose her breakfast on the side of the highway.

CHAPTER SEVENTEEN

"What news do you have for me?" Stefan asked the other man as he entered the dining room. "Is your plan underway?" He was sitting alone, having his breakfast. "Leave us!" he said to his servant, and the man scampered away, his head bowed.

The visitor approached him slowly. "I'm afraid there have been some ... complications."

"What complications?" Stefan's voice boomed across the room.

"Well, it seems the Alpha isn't interested in what they have to offer," Daric said. He was sitting in the shadows, as he always did.

"What?" Stefan looked at his protégé.

"Tell him." Daric smirked, looking at the other man.

"Lord Stefan, please, we are working on him," the man said, his voice shaking. "We need time."

"I don't have time!" Stefan slammed his fist on the table, sending the plates and cutlery bouncing on the wooden surface. "What happened?"

The man remained quiet, so Daric continued. "The Alpha has chosen someone else."

Stefan stood up quickly, eyes blazing in anger, his fingers pointing at the man. "Get rid of her, now."

CHAPTER EIGHTEEN

Frankie went about her day normally, trying to push all thoughts of Grant and the night before aside. After a quick nap, then shower, she got dressed and headed to Muccino's to start her day. Since Spring Break was over, they would begin serving lunch.

She drove to the restaurant, and, as she pulled into her spot, the hairs on the back of her neck prickled. "What the hell?" She scratched at her neck, and, as she slid out of the car, a dreaded feeling came over her. It was like she was being watched, but she looked around her and the parking lot was empty.

Must be imagining things, she thought with a shrug, trying to push that strange feeling to the back of her mind.

As she entered her office, the scent of roses hit her nose.

"Your boyfriend sent those," Enzo quipped as he popped up behind her. Frankie jumped back in surprise, but she really should have expected it. He was the only human who could creep up on her.

"He's not my boyfriend," she stated dryly.

"Well, he probably wants to be. Those are Ecuadorian roses,

Frankie." He pointed to the two vases of pink roses on her desk. "Do you know how much those cost?"

"Ah, *cazzo*," she cursed as she approached the desk. Taking one of the vases in her hand, she handed them to Enzo. "Make yourself useful and take these out. I can't work with these in here."

"Aren't you going to read the card?" he asked as he took the vase.

"Why don't you tell me what it says?" She smirked at him, knowing what a snoop he was.

"*You're perfect.*" He smirked back, making kissy faces at her. "Frankie and Grant, sitting in a tree," he sing-songed, "K-I-S-S—"

"Shut up! It did not say that."

"Go and take a look." He shrugged, leaving her office with the vase of flowers.

With trembling hands, she took the card from the remaining vase of flowers and opened it. Just as Enzo had said, those two words were scrawled on the white, expensive-looking paper. Her heart thudded in her chest. What was he thinking, sending roses to her? She sighed and shoved the vase to the edge of her desk, trying to make room on the already cluttered surface.

As she worked, Frankie tried not to look at the roses, but her eyes were drawn to the perfect, pink petals every time she had a free thought. The sight of them sent the butterflies in her stomach fluttering. God, she was pathetic. Grant probably sent roses to every girl he slept with. She wasn't special. *Probably had the florist on speed dial and bought in bulk*, she told herself bitterly. He would soon forget about her.

———

"Where do you want these, Frankie?" Matt asked as he entered her office.

"Just put them in the dining room, next to the other flowers." She sighed as she saw the large bouquet in his hands. This one had all sorts of exotic flowers; half of them Frankie didn't know the name of nor had she seen them in real life.

"Maybe we should start a flower shop," her brother teased.

"Oh don't start with me, please," she begged, rubbing the area between her brows, hoping to soothe away the headache plaguing her.

"C'mon, Frankie." He tried to place the bouquet on the table next to the door, but it was already overflowing with boxes of chocolate. They had run out of room in the kitchen for them, so they started serving them to the guests. "What's going on with you and Grant Anderson?"

"No—"

"Don't say nothing." He gestured to the gifts stacked all over her office. Flowers, stuffed animals, and boxes of treats were slowly taking over the already crowded room. "This is not nothing. What does he want?"

"I don't know!" She threw up her hands.

She really didn't know. Frankie had made it clear it was a one-night thing, but obviously Grant didn't understand.

After the first set of roses, more followed, each delivery bigger than the last. Their dining room was filled with flowers of all kinds and, though she was tempted to toss them all away, she instructed the staff to place as many as they could on the tables, in the bathroom, even out front, and give the rest to their patrons. She also came home to gifts on her porch, including two, six-foot-tall stuffed wolves guarding her front door, which she would never admit made her smile.

Frankie tried ignoring his gifts and the text messages and emails (how did he get her personal email anyway?). Her brothers and Nonna Gianna teased her relentlessly and kept asking when Grant would come for a visit.

Maybe ignoring him was the wrong tactic because, as the week passed, she was bombarded with more gifts.

"Delivery for Ms. Muccino!" Enzo joked as he barged into her office.

"Arggghhh!" she cried out in frustration. "What is it this time?"

"It's a small one," he said, slipping a box wrapped in blue paper on her table. "Maybe he's giving up!" he teased as he and Matt left the office.

She stared at the box, contemplating chucking it in the trash bin. Of course, curiosity got the best of her and she ripped open the paper. Frankie gasped when she opened the box. Inside was a necklace with a pendant, shaped like a wolf. The wolf itself was the size of her palm, and its body was covered in black and brown diamonds, while one green and one blue stone made up the eyes. She quickly shut the box and grabbed her phone.

"Did you get my last gift?" Grant's voice was amused when he picked up after the first ring.

"This is ridiculous, Grant." She shook her head as if he could see her. "I'm sending this back." She eyed the box again. "This is too much."

"Not for you," he drawled, his low baritone sending heat straight between her legs.

God, she missed that voice. "It is! This must have cost a fortune! And where did you find it?"

"I had it made, of course," he stated matter-of-factly, as if having jewelry custom made in less than a week was something everyone did. "You're a magnificent she-wolf."

"You don't have to send me gifts, you know." She bit her lip.

"Why not? Did you like them?"

"Yes," she admitted. "But that's not the point."

"I think that's the point of gifts, Frankie," he stated. "I want you to like them. I want to make you happy."

"You have to stop," she said. "I'm running out of room for your gifts, and everyone is talking."

Word had gotten out to her relatives and clan members, of course, since Enzo couldn't keep his big mouth shut about the New York Alpha courting Frankie. They all wanted to know when they would meet the big shot Alpha or when he would come to the restaurant.

"Let them talk."

"What do you want? When are you going to stop sending these gifts?"

"When you let me come over," he said.

"You can come eat at Muccino's anytime; I didn't rescind your invitation," she shot back.

"I mean, come over. To your house. Or you can come to New York and stay with me," Grant replied, his voice serious. "I miss you."

Frankie went silent at his declaration; hope fluttered in her heart. She quickly squashed it. "Stop. Just stop." *Don't make me hope for something that won't last,* she added silently.

"Frankie, I want you. Just you."

Tears threatened to spill down her cheeks. "For now," she said, clearing her throat. "Goodbye, Grant." She hung up.

CHAPTER NINETEEN

The gifts stopped coming, which made Frankie sigh in relief, though a small part of her was definitely disappointed. It was Sunday, and she was looking forward to closing up the restaurant and taking a day off tomorrow. She thought about lounging around at home and watching TV all day.

"Frankie, I need you out here!" Nonna Gianna's voice rang through the hallway connecting the kitchen and her office. "Come to the dining room!"

"Give me a minute!" She shut down her computer and walked out toward the main room.

"What is it?" she asked, then stopped suddenly. Her heart slammed in her chest.

Grant stood in the middle of the dining room, looking even more handsome than she remembered.

Mmmmm, her she-wolf growled happily as soon as she locked eyes on him.

"Hello, Frankie," he greeted, coming closer to her.

"Grant," she whispered. "What are you doing here?"

"I wanted to see you," he said matter-of-factly.

"You could have come any other day," she said with a frown.

"I know, but I wanted to give you some space," he said, his hand tracing a line up her arm. "Time to think."

"And now?"

"Well, I was hoping you'd change your mind."

"About what?" Her brows furrowed.

"About us being a one-time thing," he declared.

"You don't ... that's not what you want?" Her face was a mask of confusion. "I thought you just wanted sex."

"I do," he soothed. "But I want more. I want you."

"That's what you keep saying," she said. "But I don't understand." She shook her head, taking a step back. "What do you want from me?"

"I want to spend time with you, to get to know you more and, yes, to have more mind-blowing sex with you," he said with a grin.

She was confused. Men like Grant always left. Men always left. If not now, then later. "It won't work."

"Not if you don't give it a chance." He held his hand out to her. "Please, Frankie?"

"I ..." She stared at his open hand. God, she was torn. Her chest tightened, and she couldn't breathe. Her brain was telling her no, reminding her of the hurt that came with falling for a man like Grant. But something else inside her was telling her that Grant wouldn't be like other men. "Can we just take it one day at a time, please?"

He nodded. "Whatever you want. Now, will you come with me, please? I want to show you something."

———

Frankie had thought he was going to take her to some fancy restaurant, but, to her surprise, his town car had pulled into a private airstrip. Dante, Matt, Enzo, and Rafe were already waiting for her at the foot of the staircase leading up to a sleek jet.

"What are you guys doing here?" she asked, a confused look on her face. Enzo handed her a carry-on suitcase, and Matt gave her an envelope that contained her passport.

"You have the next four days off," Dante declared. "Uh uh." He shook his head when she tried to protest. "You've never taken a vacation, not since you took over for Ma," he said. "Now, we're making you take a break."

Her brothers stood there, their arms crossed, as if they were making a stand.

"We've talked about it, and Rafe and Matt will be around to help out at the restaurant. Don't even think about saying no, not when we went through all this trouble."

"I ..." She didn't know what to say, so, instead, she hugged her brothers one by one.

"Take care of her, man," Matt said, as he shook Grant's hand.

"I will," he declared in a serious voice. "I promise."

"Hurt her and we'll kill you, yada yada. We'll consider this the shovel talk." Enzo clapped him on the shoulder, and Frankie snorted.

"Have fun," Rafe said in a bright voice. They all hugged Frankie again and stood back as Frankie and Grant walked up the stairs.

"Where are we going?"

"I don't want to ruin the surprise." He winked at her. "Besides, you look like you're curious enough that you won't run."

"I doubt I can run away at 50,000 feet," she replied, looking up at his plane. She followed him inside, following his lead as they sat in the plush chairs of the private jet. "This isn't what I meant when I said we should take it one day at a time, Grant," she said, annoyed.

"I can't believe you're still mad at me," Grant replied in an amused voice. "You've already fastened your seatbelt."

"Well, it's the strong feminist raised by matriarchs in me," she snorted. "I felt like I had to give just one last protest. Where are we going again?"

"It's a secret." His eyes sparkled.

The flight steward introduced himself as James to Frankie and greeted Grant as they sat down. James served them drinks and handed them each a menu. They took off and, once the plane was at cruising altitude, James came back to serve them appetizers and champagne.

Dinner was divine, making her growling stomach happy. Grant, as usual, was attentive and asked her about the restaurant, her brothers, Nonna Gianna and how her week went. When they finished dinner, James told them that he had already turned down the bed and that they had another nine hours before they reached their destination.

"There's a bedroom?" Frankie asked incredulously.

"Of course," Grant said, then winked at her. "So, want to join the mile-high club?"

———

"Wake up, sleepyhead." Grant gave Frankie a kiss on the cheek.

"Five more minutes," she protested, pulling the covers over her head.

"C'mon, grumpy, we're almost there."

"Wait, what?" She shot up in bed. Grant stifled a laugh as she looked around. Her hair was sticking out at odd angles, her lips were swollen, and her eyes were still half-closed as she struggled to wake up. She looked adorable. "Good morning, sex hair," he joked, pulling her in for a kiss.

"Mmmph, no!" She shut her lips and hopped off the bed. "I've got morning breath!" She sauntered to the bathroom. "And I'm totally rocking this sex hair," she declared as she shut the door.

Grant leaned back on the headboard, clasping his hands behind his head. God, he could spend every morning like this, sated and happy after a night with Frankie. She was a little hellcat in bed, scratching and biting and giving as good as she got. Thinking of her luscious, curvy body made him hard again, despite the fact that they'd had sex two times the night before. Turns out, she also had a filthy mouth, both in English and Italian, and it made him even hotter thinking about the dirty things she said while he had her every which way. Could he get enough? He doubted it.

The door opened, and Frankie came out, naked as the day she was born. She skipped over to him, her tits bouncing delightfully as she hopped on the bed and cuddled up to him. He immediately rolled her under his body, his erection rubbing against her thighs, then took a nipple into his mouth.

"Mr. Anderson? Ms. Muccino?" James' voice rang through the intercom. Grant muttered a silent curse as he lifted his head from her breasts. "We're going to land in 20 minutes. The captain asked if you could please take your seats. I can serve breakfast as soon as we land, while waiting for immigration formalities."

"Thank you, James," Grant replied as he pressed the intercom button beside the bed.

"When am I going to find out where we're going?" Frankie asked as she rolled off the bed.

"Get dressed and you'll see." He rose up and headed to the closet where he kept his extra clothes.

"Fine," she grumbled and went to her suitcase, zipping it open.

Grant opened the closet and contemplated what to wear, when Frankie let out an expletive.

"Son of bitch!" Frankie cursed. "What the fuck, Enzo?"

"What's wrong?" Grant frowned and walked over to where she was standing over her suitcase.

"Enzo! That asshole!" She held up a see-through purple negligee. "See! Did you tell him to do this?"

He was confused, and, frankly, aroused, thinking of Frankie wearing the negligee. "It's sexy," he said with a grin. "So, he packed you some sexy lingerie. He's a man too, you know."

"Well, lingerie was the only thing he packed!" Frankie flung out a couple of pieces from the suitcase, all lacy, see-through pieces of fabric. "It's not funny!" she cried as he was trying to stifle a laugh. "Are you taking me to a private sex island with no one else around? Cause that's the only place where these are appropriate!" She flung a red thong at his face, which he easily caught.

"I'm sorry," he said, his smile wide. "We'll get you some clothes, I promise. Why don't you wear your jeans from last night?"

"You ripped the buttons off them!" she reminded him. "Can I borrow a shirt?" she asked. "Maybe I can fashion some type of dress from one of them?"

"Go ahead." He gestured to his closet. "Whatever you want. Then we can go shopping."

She stomped over to his closet, muttering something about murdering her brother.

CHAPTER TWENTY

As soon as the immigration officer stepped on board, Frankie knew where they were.

"*Buongiorno, Signore, Signorina,*" the tall, severe-looking man in a blue uniform greeted them.

"We're in Italy?" Frankie looked at Grant, her eyes wide. He nodded. "Oh my God!" She babbled excitedly, greeting the officer in fluent Italian. The immigration official's stern face softened when he realized Frankie was speaking to him in his language, and they talked animatedly as he stamped their passports and welcomed them to Italy.

"I haven't been here in years!" she said as they descended the steps of the jet. "But we're not in Rome, are we?" She looked around, trying to find any signboard that declared where they were.

Grant shook his head. "No, we're still getting permission from the Alpha of Rome to come visit, so we had to land in neutral territory."

"I haven't been here in so long!" Her grandmother was insistent that she and her brothers get to know and learn about their Italian heritage, so she set aside her money so that when they all turned nineteen, they could go to Italy. Even with her Nonna gone nine years now, she left money in her will for all of them to go for at least a month. Rafe was the last one, and he went the previous year.

She saw the sports car waiting for them at the bottom of the steps. "Where are we?"

"We're in Salerno," he said, referring to a city in southwest Italy. "I rented a villa near Positano."

"That's where my grandmother grew up!" Her eyes went wide. "Oh my God, Grant, I don't know what to say ..."

He gathered her in her arms. "Are you happy?"

She nodded. "Yes."

"Then you don't have to say anything."

———

The drive to Positano from Salerno was pleasant, especially in the spring weather with the top down. They took the longer route, going through the small towns of the Amalfi Coast. The drive along the cliffs was amazing, if heart-stopping, as their car squeezed against the side of the road to let the giant buses pass. The sea shimmered like diamonds, and quaint little seaside towns dotted the coast.

It was a little chilly, and Frankie felt goosebumps over her exposed legs. She had managed to fashion a makeshift dress from one of Grant's shirts by rolling up the sleeves and wrapping one of his belts around her waist. He had looked at her with hungry eyes when she stepped out of the bedroom wearing his clothes and her sexy stiletto heels (one of the few non-lingerie items Enzo packed). Grant's eyes had raked over her with approval.

After navigating the twists and turns of the Amalfi Coast, they arrived to the mountainside villa Grant had rented. It was gorgeous and huge—five bedrooms spread over three floors. The outside was done in the classic Italian style, with huge outdoor terraces and wrought-iron railings. The inside, however, was sleek and modern with all the amenities, and there was a large infinity pool facing the ocean. There was also a butler, Gio, and personal chef, Carlo, on-site, who welcomed them as they arrived.

It was past lunchtime when they arrived, so the chef had food ready for them: a delicious, freshly-prepared classic Italian meal with an antipasto, pasta, and a veal main course, served in the dining room with a view of the infinity pool.

Frankie moaned as she took a third serving of tiramisu. "Oh my God, do you think Carlo would give me the recipe for this?"

"I think Carlo would give you his left arm, if you asked," Grant quipped. "You do sound so sexy when you talk in Italian."

She winked at him as she spooned a creamy bite into her mouth. "*Mille grazie, bello.*"

"What do you want to do now?" Grant asked.

"Hmm ... how about we go for a swim?" She gave him a cat-like smile.

"Did Enzo pack you a swimsuit?"

Frankie stood up and started to unbutton the shirt. Flashing him another naughty smile, she disappeared out onto the terrace but not before tossing his shirt back into the dining room.

"Fuck," Grant cursed as he practically ran after her, shucking his own clothes along the way.

———

After a leisurely afternoon spent frolicking naked in the pool, Grant drove them into town for dinner. They stopped by a couple of shops, and Frankie bought some clothes, though she still couldn't find anything appropriate for their dinner with the Alpha of Rome the following night.

One of the shops they went into sold beautiful Italian linen dresses, and she wore one of the pieces—a white linen dress with eyelet detailing around the collar—right out of the shop and to dinner.

Grant took her to the highest point over Positano at one of the cliffside restaurants. The town and the sea glittered under them as the sun started fading, painting the sky with gorgeous shades of red, pink, and purple. After a sumptuous dinner (and three desserts, since she couldn't make up her mind), they walked down to the beach and took a leisurely stroll along the shore.

At the end of the evening, they drove back to the villa and Gio had coffee ready for them on the terrace.

Frankie was still buzzing from excitement, telling him she didn't know how she'd be able sleep that night. Grant pulled her into the bedroom, declaring he had the cure to jet lag in his pants.

The next day, they packed up early; said goodbye to Gio and Carlo, who had put together a to-go breakfast of freshly baked pastries for her; and made their way to Rome. Frankie was sad to leave Positano, as she felt connected to the place; however, she knew that they had to meet with Alessandro, Rome's Alpha, as it would be considered an insult if they were so close and the two Alphas didn't pay their respects.

They arrived in Rome around 10 a.m. and checked into their luxurious suite at the St. Regis. Frankie was still not used to all the luxuries Grant could afford. When she came for her Italian trip, she mostly stayed in hostels and cheap hotels.

Frankie flung herself on the plush, king-sized bed, flopping down with arms outstretched like a starfish.

"Okay, okay, I'll get on it," Grant said with a frown as he

entered the room, his phone pressed up to his ear. "I'll hop on the call with London; it shouldn't take too long. Thanks." He sighed and sat on the bed next to Frankie. He traced a hand up her leg.

"Everything okay?" she asked, turning her head to face him.

"I was hoping I could go sightseeing with you this morning," he said, "but I have an emergency at the London office. I need to be on this conference call in twenty minutes."

"Oh," she rolled on her back, "I can wait."

He shook his head. "I don't want you to miss out on Rome." He leaned down and kissed her languidly. "Besides, I have a surprise for you."

She sat up. "More surprises?"

He nodded. "The driver's waiting for you in the lobby; go ahead and I'll meet you for a late lunch."

CHAPTER TWENTY-ONE

Frankie sat in the plush salon of the well-known designer brand at the end of Via Condotti, Rome's most famous (and expensive) shopping district. When she got into the Mercedes driven by the nice, older driver, she didn't expect to be going on another shopping spree.

She should be grateful, surrounded by all the nice things. Plus, everyone was being polite and attentive to her. But, she'd never even stepped into one of these stores before. Except for the vintage designer pieces handed down to her by her mother and grandmother, she never spent more than $200 on clothes, and even then it seemed like such a splurge. Her heart stopped when she inspected one of the price tags on a little black dress, her eyes going wide at all the zeroes.

"*Signorina*," the lovely sales assistant Valeria said, catching her attention. "Would you like to see anything?" She gestured to the purses behind her in the glass case. "*Signore* Anderson's assistant said that you should please feel free to choose any item in the store and we'll have it delivered to your hotel."

Frankie wondered if that was rich-person code for 'your

sugar daddy will pick up the bill' and she suddenly had a sick feeling in her stomach.

"Are you alright?" Valeria asked, concerned. "We also have some items from the new collection, which won't be available to the public until next week, but I'm happy to let you have them now, especially since *Signore* Anderson is such a loyal client."

"Loyal client?" She looked around at all the beautiful things. Dresses, purses, shoes. The pit in her stomach grew bigger. "Actually, I'm feeling ill," she declared. "Can I have some still water, please?" She felt dizzy, and it was suddenly hard to breathe, like the walls were closing in her.

"Of course." Valeria turned to another sales assistant standing behind them. "Antonia, can you please bring *Signorina* Richardson some water, *per favore?*"

"It's Muccino," she corrected. "My name is Francesca Muccino."

Valeria's brows knitted. "No, Mr. Anderson's assistant was quite explicit in his instructions. He said we were to assist a Miss ..." She looked at the piece of paper in her hand. "Miss Katherine Richardson. That's you, isn't it?"

The edges of Frankie's vision seemed to blur, and anger rose in her, just as her cheeks burned in mortification. She stood up and grabbed her purse. "No, it is not," she said before she walked out, leaving Valeria to stare after her, slack-jawed.

Frankie pushed at the heavy glass and metal doors with all her might, wishing she could fling it open and smash it into a million pieces. There was only one other time she'd been humiliated worse than this in her entire life, and she thought she would have been smarter. Of course, this is what he did. He sent his women off on shopping sprees, buying off their affection. She wondered if Katherine Richardson was off in the boutique next door, and Grant had mixed up their names.

She stalked down Via Condotti, ignoring the calls of her

driver. Grant Anderson could go to hell; she would not take another cent from him.

The walk back to the St. Regis was long, but Frankie bit her pride and went on foot all the way back. The blisters on her feet would probably kill her in the morning, but she didn't care. Tears threatened to spill from her eyes, but she swallowed them and instead channeled the hurt into rage. She stormed into the suite, flung her carry-on onto the bed, and began to pack her meager things.

Oh God, did she have enough money to get a one-way ticket home? Who cares. She had her credit card with her; she could always put it on that. It was going to cost a fortune to get home last minute, but what was she supposed to do? She would rather be in debt than stay here another minute. Angrily, she shut the carry-on, and hoisted it off the bed. She would find a way home and forget that Grant Anderson ever existed.

"Frankie, I'm back early," Grant called as he entered the suite.

Speak of the devil.

"What are you doing?" he asked as he walked into their room, staring at her carry-on in her hand.

"I'm going home!" she screamed at him.

"Home? What happened?"

"What happened?" She stopped in front of him. "*What happened?* You lying, cheating scumbag!" She let out a string of curses in Italian as she whipped past him, but she never made it more than a foot away. Grant's strong arm caught her by the waist and held her back.

"What the hell? Frankie, stop it!" He raised his voice but struggled to keep her firmly planted next to him as she tried to wiggle away. "For God's sake, talk to me! What did I do?"

Rage burned through Frankie. She spun around and slapped at his hands, then backed away. "You thought you could hide all your other women from me! Well, apparently you can't juggle all of us! Your assistant must have mixed us up because the store your driver took me to was expecting Katherine Richardson instead!"

"What are you talking about? And why would they be expecting Katherine?"

"So you *do* know her! Is she your side piece? Or ... oh my God, am *I* the side piece?" She grabbed the first thing she could —a mantel clock—and flung it at Grant. He easily ducked out of the way, but the piece smashed against the wall behind him.

Grant's eyes blazed with anger and he stalked towards her, his face determined. He grabbed her wrists and forced her to sit down on the couch next time him. "For Christ's sake, Frankie, talk to me! What's gotten you so angry?"

"You!"

"What did I do?" he asked, confused.

"You sent me to that boutique, why? To buy me off? To pay me for sleeping with you? And then they started calling me Ms. Richardson and talking about what a loyal client you are! Tell me Grant, just how many women do you bring to Rome on shopping sprees? Because it sounds like you have a fucking loyalty card that gets stamped each time one of your women walks through their doors!"

Grant's brows furrowed, and then his eyes widened. "Fuck. Dammit, Jared." He shook his head and rubbed his face with his hands. "I ... I know this looks bad, Frankie, but please." He took her hands in his. "There's only you, okay? It's only been you! I haven't even slept with another woman since I met you! Hell, I couldn't even look at another woman since I scented you at Alynna's ball. I couldn't, not when all I wanted was you."

"What?" Frankie's heart slammed into her chest. "What are you saying?"

"Look ... I'll admit it, I've sent some women I've been with on shopping sprees before. It was just easier to break things off that way. Some even expected it," he said bitterly. "But that's not what I was trying to do here. I just ... I asked my admin, Jared, to take care of you and make sure you were able to pick up something to wear for the dinner tonight with Alessandro. Then I asked him to schedule a meeting with my lawyer, Katherine Richardson, as soon as possible. It was about 3 a.m. in New York when I called him." His eyes widened in realization. "Shit. I woke him up in the middle of the night and he ... he probably mixed up his emails or something. I'm sorry, Frankie," he said with a sigh. "But I swear to you, there's no one else. No one."

Frankie could hear the sincerity and truth in Grant's voice and read it in his eyes. If anything, she was shocked by his earlier confession, that even though they hadn't met face-to-face, he wanted only her. "I ... I'm sorry, too." She put her hands on her face. "I should have asked you first."

"I understand," Grant soothed, pulling her into his arms. "I would never do that to you."

She buried her face in his chest, inhaling his scent as her anger dissipated. "I ... it's okay."

"Look, I'm sorry for having to leave you alone. This wouldn't have happened if I had just stayed with you. Let me make it up to you." He kissed the top of her head. "I'll take you out now. We'll do whatever you want, okay?"

Frankie looked up at him. "Whatever I want?"

"Yes." He gave her nose a quick peck. "Anything you want to do."

———

Grant thought there were very few things that could frighten him, especially in his adult life; however, sitting behind Frankie as she navigated the Vespa through the streets of Rome truly terrified him.

She cackled with delight as she zoomed past cars and trucks, winding around the narrow streets of the Eternal City. The little minx probably did it on purpose so he would cling to her tighter and so she could scent the terror from him.

Frankie wanted to go sightseeing, but they were going to do it her way. She told him about her month-long trip to Italy when she was nineteen, including the two weeks she spent in Rome. She wanted to show him all her favorite spots, so they rented a Vespa. Grant confessed he had never toured Rome despite having visited several times. So, she took him around, going to the Colosseum, Pantheon, Trevi Fountain, Spanish Steps, and the Vatican City.

She also wanted to go shopping, so they walked around Via Del Corso, and Frankie haggled like a pro to get various trinkets and souvenirs for her family. Grant wanted to buy her something nice at one of the shops, but she insisted she only wanted a kitschy little keychain that read "Caesar is my Rome Boy," which she also haggled down to an acceptable price before she even let him open his wallet. She strapped the keychain to her set of house keys, gave him a kiss, and said she'd treasure it forever. She did allow him one splurge—a beautiful wool coat for Nonna Gianna, which would certainly make the old lady love Grant even more.

"Where are we?" Grant asked as they pulled up to a small side street not far from the Vatican City. It was a busy pedestrian street with restaurants and shops lining the sides. People were walking from shop to shop, others were sitting and having lunch, just enjoying the beautiful spring day.

"This is where I stayed when I was here." Frankie parked the Vespa on the side of the street and hopped off. "I was running out of money, but I had two more weeks before I had to go home. I was contemplating going home, but I met this nice Italian man, Angelo, who owned a bakery. I went into his shop because it was raining and I had nowhere else to go."

She took Grant's hand, laced her fingers through his, and led him down the cobblestoned street as she continued her story. "I must have looked really terrible because he asked me if I was okay and I broke down and told him I didn't have a place to stay. He was really nice and offered me a spare room in the apartment above his bakery. I helped him make bread in the morning in exchange for room and a couple meals."

Her eyes scanned the street as they approached the other side. "There it is!" She pointed to the unassuming shop near the corner. The old, wooden signboard above the door read "Panifico," and there was a slight, white-haired old man outside, wearing an apron and sweeping the front. He was frowning at the cafe tables set up outside the restaurant next door and at another man standing next to them.

The broad, dark-haired man wore a suit and was holding menus and calling out to tourists walking by, enticing them to come and eat at his restaurant. The white-haired man dropped his broom and walked over to the man, pointing his fingers at the table. The man in the suit started pointing back at the white-haired man, and, soon, they were shouting at each other in Italian.

Frankie rolled her eyes and picked up her pace, approaching the two men. Grant's protective instincts kicked in, trying to block Frankie, but she pushed him gently aside, put her fingers to her lips, and let out a loud whistle.

"Angelo! Massimo!" she shouted and then began to speak in rapid-fast Italian.

The two men stopped fighting and looked toward Frankie. Their faces changed from anger to recognition to finally shock.

"Francesca?" the white-haired man said.

Frankie ran over to both men, and they took turns hugging and kissing her on the cheeks. It seemed they had forgotten their fight and, instead, welcomed her warmly.

Grant stood and watched them for a few minutes as the three of them spoke in Italian, gesturing and laughing. Finally, Frankie called him over.

The two men looked at him curiously. The dark-haired man said something to Frankie, and she blushed. "Grant, I want to introduce you to Angelo and Massimo." She then turned to the two men and said something in Italian, which caused them to break into smiles.

Grant held out his hand and introduced himself, but both men kissed him on the cheeks and pulled him into a hug while talking with gusto, even though Grant didn't speak a word of Italian.

"Sorry, they don't speak a lot of English," Frankie explained. "But I'll do my best to translate, okay? Massimo wants us to have some wine at his restaurant, and Angelo will bring us some bread."

"Thank you ... uh, *grazie*," he said to the two men, who nodded and enthusiastically clapped him on his back. Massimo led them to one of the cafe tables and called over a waiter to serve them some water.

The two men disappeared into their respective establishments, and Frankie shook her head. "Sorry about that, but those two will never change. Every day Angelo fights Massimo over the placement of his tables, claiming they're blocking the door to his bakery, and Massimo says its payback because Angelo overcharges him for bread and that he'll never order from him again." She took a sip of her water. "And then by evening time, they're best friends again."

"So, you lived here for two weeks?" Grant asked.

She nodded and pointed her chin at the apartment above

the bakery. The wooden shutters were open, and, on the windowsill, were pots of brightly-colored flowers. "Right there. It was basically a closet but cozy. And Angelo was very kind to me. Massimo took a liking to me, too, and would offer me meals from his kitchen."

Massimo came out of the restaurant, brandishing a plate of Caprese salad and a bottle of wine, talking animatedly on the phone. He looked at Frankie, chatting with her and into the phone at the same time. Her eyes danced with laughter and she nodded at something he said.

"What is it?" Grant asked, taking a sip of the wine.

"Oh! That was Massimo's son, Andrea, on the phone. Massimo called him up and told him I was here, and he wanted to know if it was okay if he stopped by since he lives about a block away." Frankie avoided his eyes. "I said yes. He's a ... friend."

"A friend?" Grant asked, and he felt a strange pang of jealousy at the way she said the word.

Frankie blushed. "Okay, full disclosure ... I had a big crush on him, okay? Don't laugh!"

"I'm not laughing." Grant frowned, not really looking forward to meeting a man who made her blush so prettily.

"No, I mean ... it's silly!" She put a hand over his soothingly. "I was nineteen and he was like this typical Italian guy who would tease and flirt with me. I swear, nothing happened between us!"

Grant gritted his teeth but then relaxed and took Frankie's hand. "If you say so."

"Look, there he is!" Frankie pointed behind him to the approaching Vespa. The motorcycle stopped right in front of them, and the man hopped off the seat with ease.

"Francesca!" His voice boomed as he called to Frankie. He was tall, broad-shouldered, and handsome in that typical Italian way. Perfect white teeth, tanned skin, and probably shampoo-commercial-worthy hair under his helmet. She laughed and stood up, then walked over to greet the man.

Grant clenched his fists, fighting the urge to stand up and shove his handsome face into the cobblestones. He stopped short, however, when he looked down at what was strapped to the man's chest.

"Andrea ... *madre de dio!*" Frankie laughed as she looked at his "package" and giggled. "Is this yours?"

"Ah yes, my beautiful *bambino!*" Andrea unstrapped the blonde-haired, rosy-cheeked baby from the carrier on his chest. He raised it up, making the baby giggle, and kissed him on the cheek. "Frankie, this is my son, Piero." He handed the baby to Frankie, and she eagerly took him, her eyes wide with surprise. She kissed the baby's cheek and, in return, small fists wrapped in her hair, tugging as he laughed.

Grant felt a different pang: not jealousy, but longing. Watching Frankie hold and cuddle the baby made something in his heart swell, and he imagined her doing the same to a baby with dark hair and green eyes.

Frankie suddenly looked at him, her head cocked as she placed the baby on her hip. "Are you okay?" she asked as she approached him.

"Yes, sorry, was thinking of something." He stood up to greet Andrea.

Frankie introduced them, and the other man greeted him warmly, kissing both cheeks and clapping him on the back. "Finally, I get to meet your boyfriend!"

"He's not my boyfriend ... he's a friend," Frankie said, swatting him playfully on the arm.

Andrea winked at him knowingly. "Nice to meet you, not-boyfriend of Francesca." He held out his hand. "Andrea Ricci."

Grant shook it, squeezing a tad stronger than he meant to

(he chalked it up to Lycan strength), and introduced himself. "Grant Anderson."

All three sat down, and Massimo and even Angelo joined them as they talked and laughed, with Frankie or Andrea doing their best to include Grant in the conversation by translating here and there. They drank more wine, or at least the men did. Frankie had coffee instead, since she was driving them back to the hotel.

"We really must go," Frankie declared. "We have an appointment tonight; I really wish we could stay."

Andrea shook his head. "That's too bad. And you're leaving tomorrow?" Frankie nodded. "Ah, you won't be able to meet my Graziella," he said, referring to his wife.

"Next time, I promise," she said. "I have your email now, and I'll send you a message next time I'm in town."

Their goodbyes took longer than expected, but, finally, they were on their way back to the hotel. As Grant held on tightly to Frankie's waist and buried his nose in her hair to breathe in her scent, there was a feeling in his middle that he had never felt before. He was pretty sure it wasn't the wine.

———

"Thank you for inviting us to dinner, Alpha," Grant greeted as they entered Count Alessandro di Cavour's splendid villa just outside the main city center. He placed a hand on Frankie's lower back as he guided her inside.

"Of course, Grant. I was glad you both could make it, despite your tight schedule." Alessandro shook his hand and then turned to Frankie. "Ah, Francesca! I think you've only grown more beautiful these last years!"

"Oh, Alessandro." Frankie gave him a kiss on each cheek. "I can't believe you still remember me!"

"Of course! I know I didn't have much time for you on your visit here." He led them to the dining room where there were other people waiting for them, standing around and chatting.

"I went to his office and we chatted for a few minutes," Frankie explained to Grant. "He is the Alpha, after all."

"And you were going to be Alpha as well," Alessandro said.

"But his wife took me to tea afterwards; we had a lovely time," she said with a frown. "I'm sorry about your loss, Alpha." She put a hand on his arm. "I was very sad to hear of Elia's passing."

A small hint of sadness passed through the older man's eyes. "Thank you," he said somberly. "Now, let me introduce you to the rest of the clan."

Alessandro walked them around and made the necessary introductions. They were mostly members of the Rome clan, including his Beta, Antonio. The Alpha didn't have children of his own and his clan was even smaller than New Jersey, so most of them were here tonight.

The butler announced that dinner was served, and they all sat down in the magnificent dining room, with Grant and Frankie taking the place of honor on Alessandro's right and left sides. After dinner, they all went to the terrace for coffee, where they had an amazing view of Rome at night, as well as the stars in the clear sky.

Frankie was chatting in Italian with the women in one corner, her voice carrying over the wind, and Grant smiled as he watched her.

"She's a beautiful woman," Alessandro remarked as he came up behind Grant.

"She is," Grant responded and took a sip from the wine glass in his hand.

"You know, I remember her from long ago. Her mother asked for permission for her to come to Rome and, of course, I gave it. Back then, she seemed somewhat broken and sad. So different from now."

The other Alpha's eyes roamed over Frankie, and Grant didn't miss the desire there. He stifled a growl that was threatening to come out, not wanting to offend the other Alpha with his jealous tendencies.

"I've thought about taking another mate, another wife," Alessandro continued. "Francesca would make a good match. I'm still young; we could try for pups and I could have an heir apparent."

Grant gripped the glass in his hand so hard the stem broke. "Christ," he cursed as the glass fell on the ground and shattered. At least it was just the stem. The cup was still whole in his hand. Blood dripped from where the broken glass had cut his fingers.

"Here." Alessandro handed him a white handkerchief. He gestured to one of the wait staff to take the broken wine glass.

"Thanks." Grant took the piece of cloth and pressed it against the cut. It would completely heal in an hour or so, but he appreciated the gesture.

Grant watched Frankie again, and, this time, she probably felt his eyes on her as she turned to them and flashed him a bright smile. He smiled back and gave her a two-fingered wave.

"So," Alessandro chuckled as he looked at Frankie, then at him, "do you mean to make her yours?"

"I don't think anyone can own her, Alessandro," Grant said. "She's definitely her own woman."

CHAPTER TWENTY-TWO

The trip home was uneventful, and, soon, they were in the town car, driving back to Frankie's house. Clouds loomed overhead, and fat raindrops began to fall and pelt the car as they drove along the highway.

When they reached her house, Grant helped her out of the car with his umbrella in hand to make sure she didn't get wet.

"Well, here we are," he said as they stood in front of her door.

"Yeah, here we are," she said quietly. There was a strange fluttering in the pit of her stomach.

Grant dropped the umbrella on the porch and then wrapped his arms around her waist, pulling her up for a kiss. Frankie felt breathless as his lips moved over hers in an urgent rhythm. She opened up to him, her lips parting to let his tongue taste her.

Finally, he pulled back and let her go, and she had to brace herself against the front door to stop her from melting into a puddle on the floor. No matter how many times they kissed or had sex, he still had that effect on her.

"Wow," she said in a befuddled voice. "Some goodbye kiss," she joked.

"That wasn't goodbye," he said, his voice low and rough.

"Oh yeah, what kind of kiss was that?"

"That was an 'I love you' kiss."

Frankie's jaw dropped so fast and so low she thought she would have to pick it up off the floor. Grant smiled down at her, seemingly enjoying her reaction.

"What?" She blinked.

"I mean it. I love you, Frankie." He swooped down and gave her another kiss.

Her heart was beating so fast she thought she'd expire right then and there. She put her hands on his chest and pushed him away gently. "You don't mean that," she said with a frown.

"I do," he insisted. "Look, you don't have to say it back, not if you don't feel it now."

Love. Was she in love with Grant? Frankie shook her head mentally. She wasn't sure. But the last time she thought she was in love with someone, she got badly hurt.

"I mean it, no pressure." He kissed her knuckles. "One day at a time."

"Right," she agreed, but she could tell he was disappointed that she didn't say it back. "I ... I think ... I'm not sure ..." She buried her face in her hands. "It's all too fast. Can you give me some time, please?"

"Of course." He kissed the top of her head. "Look, I'll call you later, and we'll make plans for tomorrow, okay? I just want to spend more time with you. As much as you can give me. I'm a patient man."

She nodded. "Okay, well ... bye then." She unlocked the door and went inside the house. Leaning against the door, she closed her eyes and listened to Grant's steps as they faded away while her heart slammed into her chest. *One day at a time.*

"Graaaannnnnnt! Fraaaaannkie!" Alynna sing-songed as she barged into Grant's apartment, pushing a stroller through the door. Grant had given her a copy of the key while he was away, just in case, and she used the opportunity to visit as soon as she heard they were back from Italy. "Put your pants on and stop boinking!"

Her brother was sitting by the window, watching the rain fall outside, sipping from a glass of amber liquid.

"Hey," he greeted and stood up to give her a kiss on the cheek. Then he picked up Mika from her stroller. The baby was awake and smiling, obviously happy she was getting some attention from her uncle. "Hey, sweetie, did you miss me?" he cooed and cradled her to his chest.

"Grant Horace Anderson!" Alynna frowned.

"Not my name," he said absentmindedly as he sat down on the couch.

"Where is Frankie? I thought you would have swept her off her feet by now!" She put her hands on her hips. "I was hoping she'd come back here with you."

"She had stuff to do." Grant shrugged and stared at Mika.

Alynna sat next to him, took Mika gently from him, then placed her back into the stroller. "Now what happened? I thought for sure you'd be riding off into the sunset together or whatever it is Lycan Alphas do!"

"Nothing happened." He scratched the day-old scruff on his jaw. "And that's the problem."

"What did you do?"

"Something stupid."

"What?" Alynna's eyes widened.

"I told her I loved her."

Alynna squealed in delight but stopped when Grant frowned. "Wait, she doesn't feel the same way?"

"Not exactly. I mean, she said she needed time," Grant said with a sigh.

"Well, that's not a rejection!" Alynna reasoned. "C'mon, you're just gonna have to work harder and not give up!"

He gave his sister a smile. "I'm not going to give up; I'm just going to give her some space and some time, like she asked."

"Wow, you must really love her, then," she declared.

"I do. I really do."

"Good boy." She ruffled his hair. "Now, what did you bring me and Mika back from Italy?"

CHAPTER TWENTY-THREE

F ourteen hours, thirty-seven minutes, twenty seconds.
That was how long it had been since Grant left.
Since he said he loved her.
Since she didn't say it back.

What the heck is wrong with me? Frankie thought with a sigh. She couldn't sleep. She tossed and turned in bed, trying to get comfortable. Soon, it was early morning and, seeing as it was futile to try and get any sleep, she showered, got dressed, and then headed into the restaurant to catch up on some paperwork.

Now, it was past eight and she was busying herself, looking over the accounts, checking on the emails she missed, and trying to forget what had happened. She let out a long sigh. Two hours after she rolled into the office and she was done. *Hmmm ... maybe I could go to the kitchen and straighten out the cabinets.*

A soft noise interrupted her thoughts, and her sensitive ears perked up. The hairs on the back of her neck stood on end, like they did that day she left for Italy. A warning. After straining to hear, she figured out it was coming from the kitchen.

Go! her she-wolf said, and Frankie bolted for the door. Her inner wolf was never wrong.

She ran to the kitchen, reaching there in record time. Her nose burned with the smell of smoke.

"What the hell?" There was smoke coming from one of the stoves. "Cazzo!"

She looked around; the fire extinguishers they kept were nowhere in sight. There was something definitely wrong here as they always kept extra ones in the kitchen just in case.

The fire grew and spread quickly, and the scent of burning gas filled the air. Flames licked up the walls, consuming the curtains and the wallpaper.

Run!

Frankie turned and headed toward the back door. As soon as she reached it, she pushed, but it didn't budge.

"Help!" she cried as she slammed her palms on the door. The knob wasn't locked, but it was like something was blocking the door.

"Oh God!" She turned around, toward the dining room, but the flames blocked her way and the thick smoke was slowly filling the hallway.

Looking at the blocked door, she realized she would have to break it down. With a deep breath, she let the wolf take over her body. Her muscles elongated and ripped through her clothes; fur sprouted all over. Shaking her wolf head, she padded back, giving herself as much room as possible. Her Lycan body barreled into the door, knocking it off its hinges.

As she blasted outside, she rolled to the ground, landing a few feet away. Pain shot through her shoulders, and she remained on the ground.

"Fucking hell!" a voice said. "Is that ..."

"The Alpha!" another voice answered. "I told you we should have just shot her first and made it look like a gas explosion! The fire would have gotten rid of the body."

Opening one eye, Frankie saw three men slowly

surrounding her. She lay low, letting them think she was down. Adrenaline pumped through her veins and, when they got closer, she pounced on the closest one.

"Damn bitch!" the man under her screamed, and she could smell his fear and his scent, thick and sweet like cloves and cinnamons.

He's a Lycan! She bit down on his arm, blood pouring into her mouth as the man howled in pain. She just hoped it was enough to stop him from shifting.

"Get off him!"

Frankie turned to the other man and snarled. She pulled up to her full height and bristled her pelt to appear even larger. Baring her teeth and gums, she stalked him, but he seemed hesitant. He would be vulnerable during the change, and that was when she would pounce. He was talking his time, backing away slowly, but she followed him.

"Get outta there; I got him!"

She swung her head around. *No!* She howled.

The third accomplice had gotten their injured man into a vehicle and was already pulling out of the parking lot. She ran after the car, as fast as her four legs could carry her, but it was too late. The unmarked van was already speeding down Main Street. The adrenaline was slowly seeping out of her system and her shoulder began to throb. Turning back, she limped toward the remaining Lycan, but all she saw was hind legs and a bushy gray tail disappearing into the trees. From faraway, the sirens of the Barnsville fire trucks screamed their impending arrival.

The restaurant!

Still in wolf form, she looked back at Muccino's, her beloved second home and her life, as flames licked and surrounded it. She broke down in a whimper.

———

Dante, Rafe, and Matt found her as she limped toward the back porch of the house, howling and calling them. Her shoulder was dislocated and she was in intense pain, which was why she couldn't shift back. Matt held onto her tightly and Dante apologized as he popped the bone back into place. She howled in pain, but soon it was over and she changed back into human form. She cried, tears pouring down her cheeks, and she buried her face in Dante's shoulders as he carried her back to the house before anyone saw them.

The fire department came knocking on their door to tell them what they already knew. They were able to put the fire out before it demolished the entire restaurant, but the inside was a mess.

Dante went to inspect the building with them and to make a statement to the police while Matt and Rafe put Frankie to bed. They didn't believe her when she said her shoulder felt fine, so they put ice on her and placed her arm into a makeshift sling.

Enzo arrived not much later, still in his clothes from the previous night, having stayed out all night partying. He paled when he saw Frankie and smashed his fist into the wall of her bedroom in anger.

"What happened, Frankie?" Dante asked when he came back a few hours later. They were all standing around Frankie's bed.

"The restaurant?" she asked.

"We'll worry about that later. We have insurance, don't worry," Dante said. "And, for now, we're going to let the fire chief and the police think it was a gas explosion."

Frankie frowned. They did have insurance but only the bare minimum. It was one of the costs she had to cut when things started going down. "I ... I couldn't sleep ... jet lag," she said with a sigh. She told them the rest of the story, up until she tried chasing the other Lycan into the woods. Not finding a trace of him, she decided to walk home before the authorities saw a giant wolf or naked woman lurking about.

"Other Lycans?" Rafe's brows knitted. "But why?"

"Who knows?" Frankie frowned. She searched her brain, trying to figure out who would want to hurt them. Grant had warned her about the mages but not other Lycans.

"Does someone want our territory?" Dante asked.

"There's nothing here. I mean, nothing of value." Frankie frowned again. "Why would they want to hurt us?"

"How about Grant?" Enzo suggested. "Does someone want to hurt Grant and maybe is trying to do it through you?"

"No," Frankie shook her head, "I mean ..." She looked up at her brothers. "There is but not other Lycans. There's some trouble with witches. Or he called them mages."

"It doesn't make sense though," Dante said. "Witches hate Lycans."

"I know." She bit her lip. "It's weird ... last week while I was going into work, I thought ... well, this is silly, but I thought someone was watching me."

"Fuck! Why didn't you say anything, Frankie?" Enzo gritted his teeth. "You need to tell us these things!"

"I wasn't sure what it was, just a strange feeling!"

"If someone is after you, then we have to protect you," Matt said in a quiet voice. "I'm going to stay here tonight. We all are. And I'm taking the rest of the week off."

"Don't be silly!" Frankie shot up in bed. She'd never dislocated her shoulder before, but it felt like it was never even injured. So she removed the makeshift sling and tossed it away. "I can take care of myself. I'm fine!"

"Jesus, Frankie, someone set fire to the restaurant, locked you in, and then threatened to shoot you! You're not fine!" Enzo shouted, then turned to walk out of the room.

"Where are you going?" she screamed at his retreating back.

"Enzo, what are you going to do?" The look in Enzo's eyes, wild and unpredictable, made her worry. "Don't you dare try to find them by yourself!" Enzo would never survive against one, much less three Lycans.

"I won't!" he called back. "I'm just gonna make a phone call!"

"Dante, take care of him," she pleaded. "Don't let him do anything stupid!"

"Frankie, stop worrying about him; he'll be okay," Dante soothed. "Let us take care of you this time, okay?"

She slumped back into bed and pouted. "Make sure everyone at the restaurant knows, okay? And Nonna Gianna! Matty, can you please go to her and make sure she's okay? Those sirens woke up everyone; I'm sure she's up and worried sick by now."

"Just get some rest, Frankie," Rafe urged. "We will take care of everything.

CHAPTER TWENTY-FOUR

"**Y**our incompetence is astounding!" Stefan roared.

"Lord Stefan, please—"

"Silence!" Stefan pointed a finger at the man, his eyes ablaze.

"Master," Daric said in a calm voice. "It's not over yet."

"You dare, Daric?" Stefan turned to him.

The tall, broad-shouldered man shook his head. "Forgive me, Master. I don't mean to be impertinent, but we shouldn't put this plan aside. I've thought much about it, and it's a good plan and a viable one still."

"Yes, we still have a chance!" the other man pleaded. "I can still kill her."

Daric turned back to the other man. "No, Grayson Charles, you will not kill her."

"What?" Grayson's eyes widened in surprise. "I mean, Lord Stefan, I thought that was the plan?"

"It was, but we cannot wait any longer. We must accelerate our plan," Stefan stated.

"But how?"

"Kill Grant Anderson. Or kill them both. I don't care, as long as Grant Anderson is dead."

Grayson frowned. "But the plan was to scare Grant! I already lent you some of my clan members as guinea pigs so you could make potions that would work on Lycans!"

"True," Stefan said, but remained unmoved. "But you still need to work on the second part of the plan. How goes the lovely Ms. Bennet's seduction?"

"We are working on it," Grayson said, his tone changing. "Once he realizes he needs an alliance with us, we'll offer Vanessa, make sure she gets pregnant to secure his heir, and then kill him once he's no longer needed."

"And how long will that take, seeing as she hasn't even drawn him into her bed?" Stefan's cold, steely eyes bore into him.

"But, but ..."

"Grayson, I suggest you choose your next words carefully," Daric said. "But, like I said, the plan isn't lost yet. You want the New York territory. That was the plan, right? Turning Grant's heir into your ward and then controlling the territory from within?"

Grayson nodded.

"Well, we can just skip over the whole heir part. Kill Grant Anderson, and, once the New York clan is thrown into chaos, we will pick them off one by one, starting from his heir presumptive, his sister, then the Beta and both their mates. New York will be vulnerable, and you can take over."

"I can't kill all of them; I don't have those kinds of resources," Grayson said. "They are still well protected and, if the Council found out I killed them, they would act swiftly."

"We have magic, Grayson, powerful magic," Daric explained. "With us behind you, working in the shadows, suspicion will never fall to you or your clan. The High Council already knows about us, and they will just see it as another attack by the mages."

"Hmmm. I suppose I could petition the High Council to appoint me temporarily as steward of New York," Grayson said thoughtfully. "And the New Jersey Alpha?"

"We will take her as ... payment for our services. Draw her in, but don't kill her yet," Daric said. "We will take care of her."

"Fine. It will be my pleasure to kill Grant Anderson," Grayson said with relish. "I'll take my leave Lord Stefan and put our plan into action." With that, the Lycan left.

Once he was gone, Stefan turned to Daric. "What are you thinking, my protégé?"

"It was a good plan," Daric said. "It would have bought us more time to turn more witches into mages, while destroying the strongest Lycan clan from within."

"And once we gained control of the clan and strengthened our forces, it would have been easy enough to kill Grayson and then the heir," Stefan said. "But now?"

"A minor setback. Grayson will get rid of Grant Anderson for us, and, even if he doesn't take control of New York, losing their Alpha will weaken them and create a vacuum of power," Daric added.

"You forget one thing, Daric." Stefan raised a brow at his protégé. "How can we take control of New York without Ms. Bennet bearing his pup?"

"Well, we might not need Ms. Bennet to secure Grant's heir after all."

CHAPTER TWENTY-FIVE

G rant went back to work the day after arriving home from Italy. He had a lot of catching up to do and a slew of meetings to attend. He told Jared to hold all his calls, except important ones, and got to work. It was around noon when he felt the familiar buzz in his pocket.

He checked the caller ID and frowned, not recognizing the number. "Hello?" he answered.

"Grant! It's Enzo," the voice on the other line said. "Listen, sorry for bothering you, man, but you gotta come to Jersey!"

The Alpha shot to his feet. A growl escaped from deep in his chest, and his blood went cold. "What's wrong? Is it Frankie?"

"Yes," Enzo confirmed. "She's been hurt. Someone set fire to Muccino's and locked her inside."

The growl turned into an angry snarl. *Must ... protect ... mine ... ours ...*

"I'm on my way." Grant took a deep breath in an attempt to control of his wolf. "Thank you for letting me know. I'll call you when I'm close by."

After leaving his office, he barked an order to Jared to get his driver and car ready, and then called Nick. He explained to his Beta what had happened and where he was going.

The forty-five-minute drive to Jersey felt like the longest of his life. His inner wolf was screaming to get out, to get revenge on the people who tried to hurt Frankie. Tate Miller was nervous, probably feeling the anxiety and anger coming off his Alpha in waves, and he drove as fast as he could to Barnsville. Grant practically leaped out of the car and made a mad dash to the house as soon as the car stopped.

Dante had probably heard his approach, as he was already opening the door by the time Grant was walking up the front steps.

"She's alright," Dante assured him. "Enzo told me he called you."

Grant nodded. "He did, and I'm glad."

"She doesn't know that you're coming," the other Lycan warned as he ascended the steps.

"I told you—I'm fine, stop hovering!" Frankie's voice rang out from her bedroom.

"You dislocated your shoulder." Enzo's voice was louder. "Now shut up and let me help you."

"It doesn't even hurt, and I don't need that sling anymore. Stop! *Basta!*"

Grant walked through the door, his eyes zeroing in on Frankie lying in bed in her pajamas. "Why didn't you call me?" he yelled as he rushed to her side. He gathered her into his arms and pulled her to him tight. His heart finally stopped slamming into his chest, and his wolf seemed to calm down once he touched Frankie.

"I'm fine!" she insisted, pulling away from him. "I dislocated my shoulder trying to get out of the restaurant."

"Fuck! Goddammit, Frankie." Grant ran this fingers

through his hair in frustration. "You could have been ... you might have ..."

"I'm here, aren't I?" she retorted. "Look, I didn't want to worry you."

"Not calling me and having to find out from your brother that someone tried to kill you and that you're hurt? How can I not be worried?" He gave her a stern look.

Frankie looked at Enzo with daggers in her eyes. "Did you call him?"

"Of course, I did," Enzo replied. "We need his help. Someone is trying to hurt you, and we can't protect you by ourselves."

"We'll be fine." Frankie crossed her arms over her chest.

"Well, we're not! I'm not!" Enzo slammed his fist against the wall. "Dammit, Frankie, if we had lost you—" He stopped short, threw his hands in the air, and left the room.

Frankie stared after her brother, slack-jawed. "*Cazzo*," she cursed and slunk back into the bed.

"You know, he loves you," Grant said, moving up beside her. "He may not show it, but he does."

"I know." Frankie looked down at her lap. "I just ... I don't know what to do and how this all works. I'm supposed to protect them! Not put them in danger and not destroy our ..." She choked up and began to cry softly.

Grant quickly pulled her into a fierce hug. "Shh ... it's okay ..."

"I ... the restaurant ... Ma and Nonna ..." She hiccupped through the tears.

"Frankie ... it's okay. Don't worry, I'll take care of you."

CHAPTER TWENTY-SIX

F rankie followed Grant as he exited the car and walked to the elevators leading to his penthouse. Things had been tense when she was leaving, but her brothers promised to take care of everything while she was away. The ride had been silent with Frankie squeezing herself all the way to the other end of the car, far away from Grant. It was late by the time they got back to New York.

Grant carried her duffel bag, and Frankie was too tired to protest. He pressed the button to the top floor and, when they reached the hallway to his penthouse, there was a tall, broad-shouldered Lycan standing outside the elevator. He eyed Frankie warily.

"Ms. Muccino will be staying with us for a while, Pearson," Grant explained. "The Beta has been informed and will be briefing the security team in the morning."

"Yes, Primul." He nodded and resumed his post by the door.

They entered Grant's massive penthouse, and Frankie held her breath. It was probably bigger than the entire ground floor of her home, richly decorated in warm and masculine browns and dark grays. The living room had a big entertainment area with one wall that was just a large flat screen TV. Paintings and sculptures graced the other walls and corners. As they walked in, she spied a modern-looking kitchen with shiny, stainless steel appliances.

"Wow." She could hardly stop herself from whistling. "This is your home?"

"Yes, it's quite cozy." He chuckled as he opened one of the doors and disappeared inside.

"Right." She raised a brow at his retreating back. She looked toward the large windows with views of the Hudson River and, right across from them, New Jersey. At least she could see her territory from here.

"Is this where you grew up, too?" she asked when he reappeared.

"Yes," he replied. "I mean, this is the Alpha's penthouse, so anyone who becomes New York's Alpha lives here."

"Nice." She traced her fingers along one of the glossy wooden console tables.

"So," he cleared his throat, "I've put your things in the guest bedroom." He pointed to the door he came from.

"Oh, okay." *Guest bedroom?* A stab of hurt went through her. *Right.* She was a guest, after all. A guest of the New York Alpha.

"Are you hungry? Thirsty? Do you want—"

"No." She breezed past him and walked toward the guest bedroom. "I'm not." And then she shut the door behind her.

The mattress in the guest bedroom was the softest and most luxurious thing she'd ever slept on, and the sheets were silky soft against her skin. But, still, Frankie couldn't sleep. God, she was starving, but pride prevented her from leaving the guest bedroom and raiding the kitchen.

Was Grant still mad at her? Punishing her for not saying those three little words back to him? Or maybe he realized it was a mistake, and he didn't love her at all. Despite her protests, a small part of her was secretly happy to see him. Despite all that had happened, she felt so safe with Grant.

And now he was pushing her away, and it was all her fault. This was charity, offering her protection because she couldn't protect herself from whoever was out to get her. This was all a mistake. She was determined to go back to Jersey tomorrow and figure this out on her own.

Her stomach gurgled noisily. *Madre de dio*, she thought. She had had dinner before she left the house. Dante had cooked a massive meal, enough for all of them, yet she was starving again. It was barely past midnight. Frankie got up, wrapped herself in her silk robe, and slowly opened the door. She hoped Grant was in bed.

"Couldn't sleep?"

Cazzo.

And then her stomach answered for her with a loud gurgle.

Fuck.

Grant stood from the couch. "You should have told me you were hungry." He was wearing pale blue pajama pants and nothing else. Her eyes traced down from the strong muscles of his shoulders to the defined pecs to his sexy six-pack abs. She swallowed a gulp and turned away, embarrassed.

"I wasn't until now," she lied.

With a sigh, he took her hand and led her to the kitchen. "Sit." He motioned to the chairs around the breakfast nook.

Grant opened the refrigerator; began to take out some bread, cheese, and fruit; and laid it out in front of her. He took a knife and a wooden cutting board from another cabinet and began to slice up the food for her on a small plate.

"Thanks," she murmured as she bit into a piece of bread. It took all her might not to devour all the food he prepared for her.

Grant ate with her in silence, pushing more food her way as she nibbled on the food. She ate just enough to sate her protesting stomach and, when she was done, she pushed the plate away.

"Done?"

"Yes," she said, hopping off the chair. "Thank you," she said before turning back toward the living room.

"Wait," Grant called.

She froze in her spot and waited for him to say something else. But he was silent.

"I hate this," she finally said, not looking at him.

"Hate what?" he asked.

Closing her eyes, she took a deep breath. "You treating me like a stranger. Putting me up in your extra bedroom like I'm just your guest and—" She stopped as a warm hand closed around her upper arm and spun her around. Big, strong arms wrapped around her and pulled her close. God, she missed this, missed his wonderful scent enveloping her.

"What do you need, Frankie?" He buried his nose into her hair.

"You. I just need you," she confessed. "And I hate that, too."

"You hate it?" he asked, pulling away and looking down at her with those thoughtful green eyes.

"I hate that I need you to help me and protect me. I'm an Alpha, and I'm supposed to be the one protecting my clan and my family. And I failed and I'm weak and—"

Warm lips cut her off. She sighed into his mouth and melted into his arms. His mouth pressed gently against hers, his warm hands moved up to cup her jaw.

"You're not weak, Frankie," he said against her mouth. "You're strong. So very strong. All these years, keeping everyone together. Supporting your brothers, helping them to succeed and achieve what they want, sacrificing your own freedom and wants. You're a good Alpha and a good sister."

"But—"

"But nothing. You haven't failed anyone." He swept her up into his arms and carried her out of the kitchen.

"Where are you taking me?" she asked.

"Where you belong, where I should have put you in the first place." He walked toward the opposite end of the penthouse, away from the guest bedroom. "With me."

They entered his bedroom, and Grant laid her reverently on the bed. Then, he pulled back the covers so she could slip in between them. He joined her, spooning her from behind.

She settled into his arms, the tension leaving her body.

"Did you ... did you research my father?" she began. "Those records are available from the High Council."

"No. I was curious, but didn't want to pry." He brushed the hair from her neck and pressed his lips to the soft skin under her ear.

"He was a Lone Wolf," she stated.

"I didn't know."

Lone Wolves were Lycans who didn't have a clan or associate with one. There were many reasons why some Lycans turned rogue, and usually it was not of their own choosing. Their clan might have banished them, or their family might have died out and they didn't want to join any other clan. The High Council allowed some Lycans such a status as long as they registered and carried a mark somewhere on their body so they could easily be identified in case they wandered into some clan's territory.

"He met my mother while he was on a road trip across the

country. Actually," she laughed, "he apparently hadn't even been on the road for a month when he met her. Then, they had me and he decided to stay in Jersey."

"He's also Dante's father?"

She nodded. "He stayed long enough to get my mother pregnant again, but after that ..." she trailed off. "Well, he couldn't stay put. He couldn't help it, my mother said, it was his nature to want to roam. So, he left us."

"I'm sorry. Is he still alive?" He held her tighter.

"No. I mean, I don't know." She sighed. "I think ... I would feel it if he was. My mom was sad when he left, of course, but I was too young when it happened. I don't even remember him. She remarried a year later, had the twins, but they divorced after Rafe was born. He just couldn't accept her for who she was."

"A Lycan?"

"And the next Alpha of our clan. He wanted her to stop working at the restaurant, give up the position, and stay at home and raise us. When she refused, he filed for divorce and moved across the country." She turned in his arms and faced him. She touched his jaw with her fingers, tracing the stubble.

"Frankie, I ..."

She pushed up against him and kissed him. She didn't want his pity. "Men always leave. That's what my mom said." She turned away, but he wrapped his arms around her.

"I'm never going to leave you," he whispered.

"You don't have to say things you don't mean." God, she was tired and, finally, she felt sleepy.

"Grant ..." she said with a yawn.

"We can just sleep," he said, as if reading her mind. "Don't worry, I'll be here."

And so she slipped into a dreamless sleep.

CHAPTER TWENTY-SEVEN

F rankie was bored. She stared outside, looking at the fantastic views of Central Park from Grant's office. There was a pile of books on the table, a laptop computer, and some new magazines, but none of them appealed to her. She looked at Grant, sitting at his desk, talking on the phone, and tapping the keys on his computer. Her eyes watched him hungrily. It was strange, but he looked sexy and powerful, like a king commanding his kingdom from his throne.

The New York Lycans couldn't spare the extra manpower to guard both her and her family back in Jersey. So, she asked Grant to send one of his security guys to Barnsville, just in case. That meant she either had to stay in The Enclave or follow Grant to the office. She chose the latter.

If the Fenrir employees were surprised by her appearance, they didn't show it. She met Jared, who seemed apprehensive about meeting her and apologized over the mix-up in Rome.

Of course, she quickly forgave him, stating she herself had made many mistakes before her first cup of coffee in the morning.

It wasn't even lunchtime and she was already bored. And

horny. It was nice sleeping next to Grant, but that was all they had done. She went ten years without ever wanting to sleep with another man and, here she was, craving Grant so badly she could burst. From the boner poking at her ass this morning, she knew it wasn't because he didn't want her. She started rubbing up against him, but he quickly rolled over and went to the bathroom. He was probably trying to be sensitive, with what had happened to the restaurant, her near-death experience, and her confession from the night before. But, dammit, she wanted him so bad.

"I'm bored," she called out from the couch. She was lying on it now, her legs kicked up on the arm.

"Sorry, I'm not done yet. We'll have lunch soon," he promised, as he picked up the phone again. "Jared, get me Marino's office."

Frankie blew a stray hair away from her face and huffed. Grant continued to ignore her, talking on the phone about this or that deal. *Whatever.*

She looked at the clock again. Only five minutes had passed since she last checked the time. *Dammit.*

Frankie was done waiting. She was going to take a page from Grant's book. *If Muhammad won't come to the mountain ...*

She opened the top three buttons of her black blouse, exposing a generous amount of cleavage and just a bit of her lacy pink bra. Sauntering over to him, she walked slow and graceful like a cat.

"Grant," she called.

He looked up at her from his computer, his brow raising. "Frankie?"

"I said I'm bored." She moved around his desk, swiveling his chair toward her. She slid her skirt up her thighs and straddled his lap. Leaning down, she moved in for a kiss, but she let out a yelp of surprise when his strong hands wrapped around her waist, twisting her around so she sat on his lap. His thick erection pressed up at her ass.

"Oooh, Grant," she squirmed around, grinding on his cock, "you're hard already."

"Of course I'm hard." He gritted his teeth. "I've been sporting this hard-on since we woke up."

"Let's go back to your place, Grant," she teased. "I want you inside me."

"I told you, I'm not done with work yet." He nipped at her earlobe. "But, if you're bored, we can stay here at my desk ..."

Frankie gasped as his hand snaked between her thighs.

"So wet already ..." His fingers teased the front of her damp panties, tracing the seam of her pussy. "Naughty girl ... trying to disturb me while I work. I should spank you."

Her breath hitched, his words exciting her.

"You like? Maybe later." His fingers yanked her panties aside and easily slipped into her wetness. "Maybe I'll punish you another way."

"H—h—how?" she gasped as his thumb found her swollen clit.

"Well ..." He pushed her up on his desk, then bent her over. Grant unzipped her skirt, letting it fall to the floor. Her panties came next. He lifted her legs so she could step out of her clothes. Excitement filled her, thinking about him fucking her on his desk. But, he had other plans.

Strong hands grabbed her hips; fingers dug into her soft flesh as he pulled her onto his lap. His cock was swollen and ready, the tip piercing her entrance as she came down on him.

"Grant," she gasped as he impaled her on his dick. He filled her slowly, dragging his shaft against her, making her shudder. She held onto the desk as she sank down, engulfing him completely.

He finished unbuttoning her blouse, exposing her skin to the cool air. Yanking the cups of her bra down, he cupped a breast with one hand, rolling the hardened nipple between his fingers.

"Is this what you want?"

"Y—yes," she panted.

"Do you want to come?" He licked at her neck and then grazed his teeth on the soft skin.

She couldn't speak, so she nodded instead.

"Go, then." He relaxed back into his chair. "Take what you want."

Frankie grabbed the edge of the desk to brace herself and then planted her feet on the ground. Slowly, she raised her ass, moving just until the tip of his cock was inside of her, and then sank back down.

"Fuck, Frankie, you look so good."

She moved slowly—up and down—letting him fill her up and then withdrawing. It took some time, but she adjusted, and, soon, she was bouncing on his cock enthusiastically.

One of his hands moved between her legs, found her clit, and rubbed circles around it. Frankie moaned and continued to move up and down his shaft.

"Come, baby, come for me," he encouraged, his fingers moving faster on her clit.

"Grant!" She gripped the table and then sank down on him one last time before her body jerked and shook as her orgasm ripped through her. Her legs were like jelly, and Grant snaked an arm around her waist to steady her. She was still floating back down from her orgasm when Grant stood up, pushed her against the desk, and proceeded to thrust his cock into her.

"Frankie ... Frankie ..." he moaned over and over again as he pushed deeper and deeper into her. He cried out her name one last time before his strokes became uneven and he came undone. Frantically, he drove deep into her and spilled his sticky warmth inside her. She clenched down on him as he pushed her over the edge again. White-hot heat exploded in her veins. Panting, he braced his hands on the desk so as not to crush her. He leaned down, pushed her hair aside, and gave her shoulder a playful nip, then licked her down her spine. She laughed and squirmed underneath him, and he withdrew from her.

After helping her up, he twisted her around and captured her mouth in a soul-searing kiss.

"Fuck, that was fantastic," he said, nibbling at her lips. "I hope you're bored like this everyday."

"Oh, ha ha," she said with a smirk and pushed him away. "*Merda*, I'm glad you didn't rip up my panties this time," she said as she picked up the scrap of pink lace, then slipped it on. She adjusted her bra and started to button up her blouse. She heard a zip and turned around. "Jeez, Grant, did you just unzip and whip out your dick?"

He sank back down on his chair, a big smile on his face. "I couldn't wait to get inside you." He grabbed her hand and pulled her down, making her straddle his lap. "You little minx."

"Hmmmm ... well maybe I should come to your office more often."

"Oh, you'll be coming in this office a lot."

She squealed when he smacked his palm playfully on her ass. "Why you—"

A frantic knocking interrupted them, and Frankie jumped off his lap in surprise. "Grant!" It was Alynna, and she sounded pissed. "Grant! Frankie! Open this door, now!"

"Shit!" Frankie quickly grabbed her skirt and shimmied into it. She tried to put her hair back into some semblance of order, but it was no use. *Sex hair it is.*

Frankie walked to the door and opened it. "Alynna, what's wrong?"

The younger woman burst through the doorway, her husband following behind. "What's wrong? *What's wrong?* Why don't you tell me what's wrong?"

Frankie's brows knitted. "Are you hurt?" She studied Alynna from head to toe. The buttons on her blouse weren't matched up properly and her hair was disheveled. Alynna's sex hair was rivaling her own. She glanced at Alex, who had a look of embarrassment on his face, and his fly was undone.

"Alynna, Alex, what's the matter?" Grant asked as he stood up from his chair. "Are you ..." His eyes widened when he sniffed the air. "Oh my God, why the hell would you barge in here after you've had an office quickie?"

"You mean, right after *you've* had an office quickie?" Alynna raised a brow.

Frankie turned as red as a tomato. "How did you ... I mean ..."

Alynna laughed. "I guess we know what happens when two Alphas have sex near other Lycans. Your pheromones were off the charts, and you triggered the whole floor into a sex frenzy!"

"The whole floor?" Grant repeated.

"Yes, the whole floor." Alynna rolled her eyes. "Oh my God, I had to walk by Cady's office on the way here, and I think I'm gonna be scarred for life. I wish I could erase the memory of what Nick Vrost sounds like mid-orgasm." She gagged. "This is revenge, isn't it? For all the times you had to know about my sex life, and now you broadcast yours! I had to send poor Jared home; he was crawling up the walls! Good thing Patrick was off duty today!"

"Sorry, I—What?" Grant looked floored. "Jared and ... John Patrick?"

Alynna laughed. "Oh yeah, they've been going steady for weeks. It's sickeningly cute seeing them canoodling."

"Going steady? Are you like, twelve?" Frankie asked.

"Well what should I call it? Playing hide the pickle? Waxing each other's bananas? Locking legs and swapping gravy? Making the—"

"Alright, alright!" Grant waved his hand. "You know lots of sex euphemisms, we get it."

"And you!" Alynna wagged a finger at Frankie. "You've been opening the gates to Mordor for Grant!" Frankie hid her face in her hands.

"I think we've embarrassed poor Frankie enough." Grant slapped his hand on his forehead.

"You're not embarrassed?" Frankie put her hands on her hips.

"Of course he's not," Alynna interjected. "Look at that smile on his face; he wants everyone to know he got to torpedo the eel into the cave."

"You guys should go get ready, we have a meeting coming up." Grant gently took Alynna by the arm and ushered her out of his office with Alex and Frankie following them from behind.

"Sorry, Primul," Alex said, as he took Alynna's elbow.

"You two really need to be careful next time," Alynna said in playful manner. "At least, you know, wait until everyone goes home or something, so you don't blast us all with your super Alpha pheromones. Oh hey!" Alynna looked over at the two people exiting the elevator. One of them quickly dashed away from them, while the other stood there, his gaze trailing toward the retreating figure.

"Liam, sorry ... er, we had an emergency," Grant greeted the Alpha from San Francisco.

Liam Henney turned around, a frown on his face. "What? Oh yeah ... no worries, Grant."

"Lara!" Alynna rushed toward the other figure. "Hold up! Whatever you do, *do not* go into Cady's office unless you have some sort of forgetting potion handy! In which case, you're gonna have to share some with me!"

The young witch whipped around, her face as red as her hair. "Don't what? Oh, hey Alynna," she greeted her with a nervous laugh. "I was ...um ... just going to see Cady."

"Yeah ... um, about that," she linked her arm around Lara's, "why don't you step into my office first. Jeez, are you okay? You seem flushed. And what happened to your lipstick ..." Alynna happily chatted away, leading her away from Cady's door.

"I should go and help distract Lara, while Cady and Nick ... er ... yeah," Alex trailed off. He gave Liam a cordial nod and followed his wife.

"Liam Henney, right?" Frankie greeted the taller man. "Francesca Muccino, New Jersey Alpha."

"I remember you." The San Francisco Alpha's blue eyes twinkled in recognition, and he shook her outstretched hand. "The night of Alynna's ball."

Frankie laughed. "Yes, that night."

"The look on the brainless brigade's faces were priceless when you showed up," Liam quipped.

"Brainless brigade, huh? That's accurate. Yeah, well, I couldn't stand there and let them insult Alynna and her mom." Frankie chuckled. "And it was a lot of fun, too!"

Grant cleared his throat. "Well, Liam, sorry to delay our meeting. Why don't you come into my office and we can start? I'm sure Alynna will join us in a few minutes."

"I'm gonna go ... powder my nose," Frankie said. "Join me for lunch at the restaurant downstairs?"

"We all will," Grant said. To her surprise, he pulled her close and planted a kiss on her lips. "See you then."

Frankie watched them disappear into his office and shook

her head as she walked to the elevators. If Liam Henney was surprised by the public display of affection, he didn't say anything. Besides, he didn't have any room to criticize her, seeing as he was sporting a bit of red on his collar that looked suspiciously like lipstick.

———

Frankie spent the weekend in Manhattan with Grant, barely leaving The Enclave. She was in contact with her brothers and Nonna Gianna, who assured her all was fine and they were sorting out the paperwork, as well as looking at what it would cost to get the restaurant cleaned up. She tried not to think about the hard decisions that would be coming in the next few weeks, but Grant proved to be a good distraction, at least for the weekend.

The following Monday, Frankie went to Fenrir with Grant again, seeing as she didn't want to be cooped up in his apartment the whole day. Also, Grant told her they would start looking into who attacked her, and he wanted her to meet with his team so they could put their heads together.

"Morning, Jared," she greeted as she stepped out of the elevator. "Grant will be up in a bit; he had to pass by the 33rd floor."

The normally confident-looking young Lycan looked deflated today. Fear and apprehension rolled off him.

"Are you okay, Jared?"

"Huh? Oh, yes, Lupa, I'm fine." His eyes looked sad.

She crossed her arms over her chest. "Sorry, Jared, that's not going to work with me. My Italian mother senses are tingling."

"Well," Jared looked at his shoes, "Alynna ... I mean, Mrs. Westbrooke, she told me she had to tell the Alpha about me and John yesterday."

"So? Are you ashamed of him?"

"No!" Jared protested. "Not at all, but it's … the Alpha doesn't know about us. I'm afraid he might not approve."

Same sex relations weren't forbidden in Lycan society, but many frowned upon them. It was already difficult to produce Lycan children, even with modern technology and IVF. Some saw the lack of ability to procreate between homosexual Lycan couples as a loss to their kind.

Frankie's eyes blazed. "What? You're crazy, Jared! Grant doesn't care about that!" She walked over behind his desk and put her hands on his shoulders. "And if he does say something bad, you can bet I'm gonna give him a piece of my mind!"

"Who are you going to give a piece of your mind?" Grant asked as he approached them.

"Grant," she let go of Jared and walked over to him. "Do you care about who Jared dates?"

Grant frowned. "Of course I do."

"What?" Frankie put her hands on her hips.

"I mean, I know Patrick's a good guy, but does he make you happy, Jared?"

Jared nodded. "Yes, Primul."

"Then I care about that." Grant shrugged. "Now, will you make sure I get those status reports from Amata on my desk before end of day?"

Jared's face perked up. "Yes, Primul, I will."

"Good." Grant took Frankie by the elbow. "I'll be in my office."

As soon as the door closed, Frankie put her hand on Grant's chest. "Grant Horace Anderson."

He rolled his eyes. "Oh my God, you've been spending too much time with my sister. You two get on like a house on fire."

"Aw, you're such a softie!" She hugged him. "You know,

Jared was a wreck when I came in. He really thought you wouldn't approve."

"Why?" Grant frowned. "He should be with whoever makes him happy, right?"

She gave him a quick kiss on the cheek. He wrapped his arms around her waist and pulled her close.

"Uh-uh," she pushed him away playfully, "no stuffin' the muffin at the office." Frankie bit her lip to stop herself from laughing. She reminded herself to text Alynna that one.

Grant groaned. "Fine, then stop distracting me and let me work."

———

It was just before lunchtime by the time they finished their meeting in Grant's office.

"Thanks for all the information, Frankie," Alynna said as they stood up. "We'll get to work right away."

Frankie had told them all she could remember from the day of the attack. Her voice was calm and even, though some parts of the story sent a chill through her veins. Grant sat beside her, holding her hand and giving it encouraging squeezes whenever her breath hitched or she paused too long.

"Are you sure you have time for this?" Frankie frowned. "You just had a baby."

"Yeah, well, Lycan healing is amazing." Alynna patted her tummy. "And we have to find out who's trying to hurt you. Besides, you know the perks of working for the family business. I can work from home whenever I want but still get to bring Mika to work with me when I have to come into the office."

"I'll go through my own sources as well," Nick said. "We might ask you to work with a sketch artist to see if we can identify your attackers. Do you think you could describe them?"

Frankie shuddered but put on a brave front. "Of course." There was no way she could forget their faces.

"Alright, well, I think it's time we go." Grant stood, signaling that their meeting was over.

"Go where—hey!" Frankie whooped in surprise as her vision turned upside down. Grant put her over his shoulder in a fireman's carry. She giggled as she stared at Alynna and Nick's upside-down faces, their expressions a mix of shock and amusement. "Where are we going?" She waved to Jared, who stared after them, his jaw practically on the floor.

"One of the safe rooms in the building," Grant said matter-of-factly. "Just trying to keep everyone from being affected by our super Alpha pheromones."

CHAPTER TWENTY-EIGHT

"**M**s. Muccino." Jared's voice crackled through the speakers on the intercom on Grant's desk.

Frankie's brows knitted. "Jared? Are you calling me?"

Grant lifted his head from the paperwork he was signing and looked at her but said nothing.

"There's a delivery for you at reception, Ms. Muccino. The receptionist said the package came all the way from Jersey."

"Cannolis!" Frankie shot up from the couch.

"Cannolis?" Grant asked.

"Yeah," she slung her purse over her shoulder, "I was whining to Dante yesterday about how much I miss the cannolis from Muccino's, and I think he took the hint! I bet he baked me three dozen! Of each kind!"

She went to Grant and gave him a kiss on the cheek. "I'll be back!"

"Leave the gun," he joked.

"Take the cannoli!" she answered. As she left his office with a spring in her step, she could practically taste the delicious, creamy treats!

Oh God, didn't I just have a big breakfast with Grant two hours ago?

She took the elevator down to the massive reception desk. Fenrir Corp's headquarters was huge and they needed an army of receptionists just to keep things in order.

"Excuse me," she called to one of them. "My name's Francesca Muccino," she said. "Um, I was told there's a delivery for me?"

The young man frowned. "Yeah, I called it in. The guy was waiting here, but he said he had to use the bathroom. Let me go find him, Ms. Muccino." He stood up, then walked off toward the direction of the public toilets.

"Hmmm ..." There was something off and she couldn't quite put her finger on it.

She waited for fifteen minutes, according to the big clock over the reception desk. Finally, the receptionist came back. "I'm sorry, Ms. Muccino, I can't seem to find the delivery guy."

"What?"

"Yeah, he just disappeared. Maybe he had other deliveries to make."

"Oh," Frankie said in a disappointed voice. "Maybe it wasn't cannolis."

"Excuse me?"

"Oh nothing. Thank you anyway." She walked back toward the elevators.

The elevator took her straight up to Grant's floor. She knitted her brows as she realized Jared wasn't at his station. She shrugged. Maybe he went to the bathroom.

She opened the heavy wooden door. "False alarm! No cannoli!" she announced. "You'll have to—"

Frankie stopped short as the sickening scent of jasmine assaulted her senses. Jasmine and arousal. She saw red and let out a feral growl, her she-wolf clamoring to get out. When her vision cleared a split-second later, she knew she wasn't imagining it. Vanessa Bennet was spread eagled on the couch, wearing nothing but a smile, while Grant was standing over her, a white coat in his hands.

"Fuck me Grant, like you did last week! I've missed you so much! I want you inside me now!"

"*Bastardo!*" she screamed. Storming in, she grabbed the vase by the door and hurled it at Grant's head. It didn't quite make it and landed in a crash by his feet.

"What the? Oh fuck! Frankie!" Grant disentangled himself from Vanessa and got up from the couch. "This is a mistake!" He stalked over to her, reaching out to touch her.

"You bet it's a mistake!" She moved to strike him, but his hand curled around her wrist. "Let go of me!" She yanked her hand away from him. "God, I was so stupid!" Fury blazed through her, and she was glad she was too angry to cry right now.

"Frankie, please, listen to me. I lo—"

"No! I'm done! This is over! Don't follow me, don't talk to me, don't even come near me! I rescind your invitation to my territory!" She twisted away from him, headed toward the door, and yanked it open. The last thing she heard before the door closed behind her was Vanessa's sultry laugh.

———

Grant stood by the door, watching it close as Frankie left. "Goddammit!" He raked his hand through his hair. Rage filled his blood, but not white hot, but cold and freezing. Slowly, he turned back to the woman who was ruining his life.

"Get out," he said in low voice.

"But Grant, I'm all ready for you," Vanessa purred, her fingers between her legs. She let out a throaty moan.

Bile rose up in his throat. "Get. The. Fuck. Out." He threw the coat on top of her, grabbed her by the arm, and dragged her toward the door.

"But, Grant," she whined, struggling and digging her heels in. "C'mon, I told you, I'd do anything you want. Or you can do anything you want to me. Do you want me to suck you dry and let you come all over me? Or I can bend over and let you take me up the—"

"Shut up, Vanessa, just shut the fuck up!"

"You're making a mistake choosing her, Grant Anderson." Vanessa tugged her arm away from him. She wrapped the coat around herself and stood up to her full height, like a wolf posturing against an enemy. "What do you want with that poor little glorified waitress? You're the Alpha of New York and she is beneath you! That little—"

"I swear to god, Vanessa, you better watch your mouth!" Grant roared, a growl coming from his chest.

"What does she have that I don't, Grant?" Vanessa's face turned into a vile mask of hate. "Can't you see how right we are for each other? We would make the perfect match! Our bloodlines are pure, from great families. Our pups would be strong and powerful, while hers has been tainted by consorting with humans!"

"Are you really not going to leave?" Grant gritted his teeth.

"Not until you see reason or you throw me out by force!" She stood there, daring him to lay a hand on her.

"Fine!" Grant stalked to the door and yanked it open. "Jared!" he called angrily. "Call Nick Vrost! Tell him I need him. Now."

"Already done, Primul," Jared said with relish and cocked his head toward the two approaching figures. Nick and Alynna were marching down the hallway, and his sister was rolling up her sleeves.

"Primul," Nick said as entered the office, his voice icy.

"Escort Ms. Bennet out, please." Grant suddenly felt the anger draining from him.

"Don't touch me!" Vanessa's eyes grew wild. "If you do it, I'll bring the Connecticut wolves on your head!"

"Nick may be too classy to smack a biatch, but I'm not!" Alynna declared. She grabbed Vanessa by the arm, gripping tight.

"Go ahead and hurt me; it'll only make you look bad."

Alynna's voice turned sickly sweet, her lips curled into an evil smile. "Ms. Bennet, will you please come with me? Or will I have to tell your Alpha that I felt you were too dangerous and unstable around my pup, who happens to be in my office two doors down, which is why we had to toss your skanky ass out the door?"

"You wouldn't!"

"It would be our word against yours," Alynna dared.

Vanessa looked at Grant pleadingly, but, when the Alpha's face remained stony, her face fell. "Fine. You'll regret this, Grant Anderson," she screamed, vitriol dripping from every word. "Mark my words. You'll regret not taking what I have to offer. You and your entire clan."

"Let's go." Alynna yanked on her arm and dragged her out the door.

Grant sighed, and, by the time he turned around, Nick was already handing him a glass filled with whiskey. He took it and downed it in one gulp, then sank into the couch. "Christ, what a mess."

"Care to talk about it?" Nick sat down next to him.

"Frankie went downstairs to pick up a delivery from reception. She was gone five minutes when Vanessa walks right in. I was wondering how she got past security, but, apparently, she used Grayson's office to make an appointment and then sent Jared away to get coffee for our 'meeting.'"

"And then?"

"Well, I was confused, of course, and I asked her what she was doing here. She said she was here for me, then she took off her coat—she was naked as a jaybird under there—and plopped herself on the couch."

Nick stood up and headed towards Grant's well-stocked bar.

"That's where Frankie walked in."

His Beta visibly flinched. "Talk about bad timing. Why did Vanessa do that? Did the two of you ..."

"No," Grant denied. "I mean, a few years ago I may have flirted and danced with her at a couple of parties, but I haven't shown her any interest since then. She can't still think I want to date her." He shook his head. "I've been polite and kind, but only because she's related to Grayson."

"She probably planned to either seduce you or have Frankie catch you in a compromising position. Or both." Nick poured another measure of whiskey.

"Well, whatever her plan was, it worked. Frankie was furious and left. Fuck!" He slammed his fist on the leather couch. "Where could she have gone? What if she gets attacked again?"

"No worries, Alex is tailing her. Jared called me and Alynna just in time."

Grant sighed with relief. "I can't ... this is a fucking mess. I can't even go to her, she rescinded my invitation to New Jersey."

Nick shook his head. "What can I do for you, Grant? Can you fix this?"

"I don't know, Nick, I really don't know."

Frankie stormed out of Fenrir, determined to put as many miles between herself and Grant Anderson as possible. She would go home to Jersey. Of course, she didn't quite know how she was going to do that, since she had no car, nor enough money for a cab. Looking at her wallet, she supposed she could take the train and then walk home from the Barnsville stop, but that would take hours.

"Frankie," a male voice behind her said.

"What?" she growled, not really wanting to talk to any man, Lycan or human, right now. It was Alex Westbrooke.

"What happened?" he asked, concern in his voice.

"Nothing! None of your business." She started walking down the street, not really sure where she was going, as long as it was far away from Fenrir Corp.

"Hey, wait up!" Alex called. "Where are you going?"

"Home!" she declared, picking up her pace. But his damn long legs were no match for her shorter ones and he easily caught up with her.

"The Enclave is the other way."

"No, *my* home. Back to Jersey."

"Does Grant know—"

"Screw Grant Anderson! That lying, cheating bastard!" Tears flowed down her cheek, and she couldn't stop them even if she tried. God, she was making a mess of herself, and out here in public, too. She should have listened to her brain long ago and pushed Grant as far away as possible. Wiping her tears with the back of her hands, she kept walking away.

"How are you going to get back?"

"What? Why are you still following me?"

Alex shrugged and put his hands in his pocket. "Seemed like you could use a friend."

"Are you going to try and make me go back?" She stopped and put her hands on her hips.

He flashed her a smile. "I don't think anyone can make you do anything you don't want to do. That's probably why you get along so well with my wife."

Frankie was taken aback. *What was his game?*

"Look," he took a step toward her, "you wanna go back to Jersey? Let me take you. I got a car, my own car, okay? Not one of Fenrir's cars. And we don't have to talk or anything, but Alynna will never let me hear the end of it if I let you take the train all the way back to Jersey."

Frankie gave a defeated sigh. "Fine. Let's go."

The drive back was surprisingly pleasant. Alex drove a black Jeep Wrangler, not the latest model but one a few years old. He obviously took care of it, though he explained it had been in storage for months since he wasn't sure how permanent his move to New York would be. He chatted amiably, while Frankie silently looked out the window. He talked about his family back in Chicago, and Frankie was surprised that he came from a middle-class background. She found that Alex was a nice guy: easygoing, laughed a lot, definitely a good match for Alynna. After an hour and a half of driving, they arrived at her house.

"Thank you," she said gratefully as she opened the door of the Jeep.

"You're welcome," he said. "And Frankie?"

"Yes?"

"I hope ... well, I hope that whatever it is that happened between you and Grant, you can work it out. You're good for him."

"Yeah well ..." She shrugged. "Thank you again."

She hopped out of the Jeep and headed up the porch. After waving to Alex as he drove away, she turned and walked through the door.

CHAPTER TWENTY-NINE

I t was one week later when Frankie finally found the strength to go to Muccino's. She had been moping around the house in her pajamas, eating fast food and ice cream, and basically crying her eyes out before she went to bed. Her brothers didn't ask what happened, though they probably had an idea or suspected that she and Grant had a falling out. She shut out the world, turning her phone and her computer off. After allowing herself this one week of self-pity, she finally decided that enough was enough. She was Alpha, a leader, and her family and clan needed her.

Seeing the charred remains of the restaurant wasn't as hard as she thought. Outside, the building was still standing, but dark streaks of ashes marred the walls. The red awnings hung limply over the windows, which were covered with blue tarps. The firefighters broke down the doors in order to get to the fire, so now they were boarded up. The sign outside was hanging on its side and half the words were charred. It hurt, but it didn't feel like her heart was being ripped out of her chest, as she had been feeling all week.

The only moment she did cry was when she walked into her

office. The fire didn't reach it, but smoke and water from the firemen's hoses had. Everything was covered in soot, and papers, furniture, and books were all warped and waterlogged. She picked up her mother and grandmother's portraits, which had somehow survived, and hugged them to her chest.

"Ma, Nonna, I'm so sorry," she said, tears streaming down her cheek. She suddenly felt dizzy, and she ran to the wastebasket, where she threw up her lunch. It was too much, and the walls suddenly felt like they were closing in on her.

Dante was waiting for her outside, and she clung to him like a child. "I can't Dante, I'm sorry."

His arms tightened around her. "It's okay. I know it's hard."

They drove back to the house, where Nonna Gianna was waiting for them in the kitchen. Dante said he had to go and do some errands, leaving the two women alone.

"How about some tea then, *mimma?*"

She hesitated. "Alright."

Nonna Gianna put the kettle on and got two cups from the cupboard. "How are you feeling?"

"Awful. I thought I could go in there and be okay, but ... it's too hard." Tears welled up in her eyes.

"Shhhh ... it's okay." Nonna Gianna put an arm around her shoulder and pulled her close. "We'll get through this, don't worry."

"What if we can't? We've lost everything, and there's not going to be enough insurance money to rebuild."

"Then we will find another way."

"What if there's no other way?"

"And what if the sky fell tomorrow?" Nonna Gianna put her hands on her hips. "Francesca, stop it. What's done is done, and now we must pick up the pieces. We will find a way. We always do."

Frankie gave her a weak smile.

"Now, what about Grant?"

She frowned. "What about him?"

"I thought ... you know, the two of you were getting along. And that ... well ... I was hoping you'd settle down soon."

"I don't want to talk about it."

Gianna sighed. "Fine. Well, come eat then." The older lady stood to get a bowl from the cupboard. "I made some carbonara for lunch. You've been eating extra these days, probably from all the worrying."

"I don't want to eat," she said. "Or I don't know ... I threw up my lunch. Maybe I'll be hungry in a bit. Scratch that, I'm always hungry," she said with a laugh. "God, this whole mess has made my body all weird."

Gianna spun around, her face inscrutable. In two strides, she was beside Frankie, putting a hand on her forehead.

"Nonna, what are you doing?" Frankie looked up at the old lady with a raised brow.

"*Mimma*, how much have you been eating in the last few weeks?"

"What do you mean? Normal, I guess?"

"You had two desserts last night. And three servings of pasta."

Frankie flushed. "So, I've been eating my feelings, so what?" she huffed.

"And you threw up this morning?"

She nodded. "I couldn't stand seeing the restaurant ... like that."

Her great-aunt's eyes widened. "And your period? When did you last have it? Are your breasts feeling tender?" Her hand snaked down to Frankie's chest and squeezed her breast.

"I—oww! That hurt, Nonna!" The younger woman stood up, pushing the hand away. "What are you doing?"

The old woman chuckled and looked at her with sparkling

eyes. "Francesca, *mimma* ... your grandmother was the same and your mother, too."

"Same with what?"

"When they were pregnant. Ate two or three times more than they usually did, especially if it was a Lycan baby."

"Pregnant?" Frankie felt lightheaded when she said the word, and her hand immediately went to her stomach. "No ... it can't ... I get my birth control shots religiously!" Damn her genetics! "I'm not ready to raise a child!"

"Francesca, no one is really ready." Gianna patted her hand. "I never had my own, but I know what it was like for your grandmother and Adriana. And who says you'll raise your child alone?"

She looked up at her grandmother. "Grant doesn't ... he won't ..." She swallowed the lump in her throat, ashamed of herself for falling again for a man who lied to her, a man who told her he loved her and then cheated on her. "Grant doesn't want me. That's why I came back."

"Even if things don't work out for you two, Grant doesn't strike me as a man who would deny or abandon his own child! He's a Lycan and an Alpha!"

"It's not that ... I ..." A child would tie her to Grant forever. She would have to see him regularly, possibly with other women, maybe his future Lupa. And how would that work anyway? They were both Alphas. Would her child be both Alpha of New York and New Jersey? "We're not even sure if I am pregnant."

The older woman raised a brow. "You should take a test then. In any case, if I'm wrong, then you have nothing to worry about."

"Right." It was a mistake. She was 99% sure she wasn't pregnant.

But, exactly 5 pregnancy tests later, her 99% certainty went down to exactly zero.

"What do you want to do?" Gianna asked.

"I ... don't tell my brothers, please, Nonna." She had to think. No way she was going to get rid of the baby. Even the thought of that made her sick and her she-wolf snarled and growled at her.

Okay, okay, she told the wolf. *I won't think about that anymore.*

"But you will have to tell them eventually. Are you worried about them reacting to the news? You know they love you."

"Yes, but ..." Her brothers would have mixed reactions for sure. "I just don't want them to be disappointed in me."

"Francesca! Don't say that! They would never be disappointed in you."

Frankie sighed. "What do I do, Nonna?"

"You know you have to tell Grant, too, right? He's the father, and he has the right to know."

The thought of seeing Grant and telling him made her nervous. But Nonna Gianna was right. "I should see him." *We can work it out,* she thought as she rubbed her stomach. There was a child's life involved now.

CHAPTER THIRTY

She doesn't love you.
She wouldn't have left if she loved you.
She doesn't deserve you.

Grant should have blocked the unknown number as soon as the first message came in. Hell, he should have tossed his phone out. Vanessa Bennet was trying to get into his head and mess him up.

He continually tried to get in touch with Frankie ever since she left, but she wouldn't answer his calls or text messages. Seeing as he was uninvited from her territory, he couldn't even go to her. Sending someone in his place would only make her madder, and he didn't really want to involve anyone else. What a fucking mess.

His phone rang, and he was tempted to smash it against the wall. An unknown number flashed on the caller ID.

"What do you want, Vanessa?" he answered coldly.

"Why won't you answer me, Grant?" Vanessa whined. "I'm only trying to protect you from that gold digger! Can't you see, she only wants you for your money and your position."

"And you don't?" he sneered.

"Grant, I ... I love you."

"Shut up, Vanessa," he growled. "You don't love me. You don't even know me."

"But all this time ... I know you've been busy, but I haven't forgotten. You danced with me at the Fenrir Charity ball two years ago! You said I looked beautiful!"

"That was two years ago! I was being nice."

"You meant it! I could feel it!'

"Goodbye, Vanessa. I'm blocking you now."

"Wait! Don't block me, not until you see what I have to send you."

His phone chirped. With an impatient sigh, Grant opened the message. It was a picture of Frankie, looking beautiful in the same white floral dress she was wearing that one night at Muccino's. There was a man with her in the picture, standing close to her, whispering in her ear with his hand on her waist. Frankie was smiling, her eyes cast down.

Grant gripped the phone so hard the screen cracked. Fuck. A stab of jealousy pierced through him.

Kill, kill, the wolf growled.

He didn't need his wolf to tell him that. He wanted to kill the man in the picture with her, for putting his hands on Frankie. God, he needed a drink.

———

"Well now, I never thought I'd see you back so soon."

Grant sipped his drink and gave Tattoo Guy a sardonic smile. "Things have been busy at work, I'm afraid."

Tattoo Guy sat on the stool next to him. "You wanna talk about it?"

"You sure that redhead won't mind?" Grant motioned to the woman sitting on the couch, dressed in a scandalously short dress that showed off her gazelle-like legs. As soon as he'd entered Luxe, Grant saw Tattoo Guy and the redhead on the couch, the girl straddling his lap.

"Nah, she'll wait," he said and motioned for the bartender. "You runnin' into some kind of trouble?"

"Ha." Grant swirled the amber liquid in his glass. "It's more like trouble is running into me."

"Well then," Tattoo Guy took a small card from his wallet and slid it over to Grant, "Here."

Grant's brows furrowed as he took the card. Creed Security. Sebastian Creed, CEO. "You're a security contractor?"

He nodded. "Military and Private. Trouble is my game."

"Thanks. Sebastian." Grant put the card in his pocket. "I'll keep you in mind."

"No worries. By the way, you should go talk to that brunette over there." He motioned to a girl in a tight pink dress sitting by herself at one of the corner tables.

Grant eyed the girl. She was tall, slim, and looked like she was after a good time. He thought about it, sleeping with some random girl until he forgot about Frankie. He shook his head. "I just came here because I didn't want to drink alone at home." He dropped a couple of bills on the table. "See you around, Sebastian."

Sebastian gave him a two-fingered wave as he stood up with his drink and headed over to the couch and the waiting redhead.

Grant finished his drink, sent a text to his driver to pick him up, and walked to the elevators.

He was exiting the lobby doors when a blur came from nowhere. He reeled back in surprise. Pain shot through his jaw as a fist connected with his face. The punch caught him off guard and he stepped back, but his quick reflexes allowed him to recover and stop himself from falling over.

Shit, the mages!

He swung his fists, hitting his attacker in the face and then on his side, sending the other man tumbling to the ground.

"Who sent you?" he asked, towering over the man on the ground. His driver, Tate Miller, stopped the car on the curb and was already out, dashing toward him.

"No one sent me, you fucking asshole!" Matt Morretti looked up at him, his eyes filled with hate. Blood dripped from a cut on his lip.

"Jesus, Matt! What the hell did you do that for?!" He nodded to Miller. "It's okay, stand down." The bodyguard relaxed but kept his hand over the holster that was hidden under his jacket.

Grant extended his hand to help the younger man up, but he brushed it away, standing up on his own.

"I don't want your help!" Matt swayed at first but steadied himself. "You're gonna pay for what you did to Frankie!"

"Frankie?" Grant's heart sped up. "Is she okay? What happened? Is she hurt?"

"You know what you did!" Matt shouted at him. "You got her pregnant and sent her back to Jersey!"

Grant felt the bottom of his stomach drop. His ears started ringing, a buzzing in his head that blocked all other sound. Matt was saying something, but he tuned it out. *Frankie ... she's pregnant ... with his child.*

"... And then she was crying! Crying over you, you asshole! She thought I wasn't at home, but I overheard her talking to Nonna Gianna!"

"Matt," Grant shook his head, "I didn't know! I swear! She just ran off."

Matt looked confused. "Wait ... you didn't send her away because she was pregnant?"

"I would never!" Grant's shoulders sank. "I didn't send her away! Why would I do that? I'm in love her."

"She said you didn't want her!" Matt railed. "That's why she came back."

"No, no!" Grant ran his fingers through his hair in frustration. "There was a misunderstanding and she left! I swear to you, Matt, I would never hurt her or abandon my own child!"

A baby. He thought of Frankie, her belly swollen. Holding a perfect little child with dark hair. A boy. Or girl that looked like her. It didn't matter. Either would be wonderful.

Our pup, his wolf whined. *Must ... protect ...*

"I need to talk to Frankie," Grant said. "But she won't answer my calls, won't even let me go to Jersey."

"Do you really want to be with her? And the baby?"

"Yes," Grant answered without hesitation. "I'm going to do everything I can to make her listen and take me back."

Matt seemed appeased. "Well, we should think of a plan. Make her hear you out." He clapped Grant on the back. "So ... sorry punching you in the face, man."

He chuckled. "You did get me good. And sorry about hitting you back."

"No worries," Matt said in a good-natured tone. "If you're gonna be part of our family, you gotta get used to the fighting ... daddy."

Grant's face lit up at the word. Daddy. Jeez, he never thought he'd be so happy. A baby. A family. With Frankie. "C'mon, let me buy you a drink and we can talk. Miller," he called to his driver, "go and park the car. We'll be at the bar around the corner."

A little while later, they sat in a dive bar, not far from Luxe.

"So, why did Frankie leave New York?" Matt asked.

"Well ... this is a little embarrassing, but you should hear my side." Grant recounted the story to Matt, including how Vanessa was calling and texting him several times a day.

"What a psycho!" Matt said, looking at the text messages after Grant handed him his phone. "Oh and that picture?"

Grant frowned when he mentioned the photo of Frankie and that man. "Yes?"

"I posted that on our Facebook page last week, but that was taken months ago." Matt took out his own phone and showed Grant the picture. This one was slightly different, and it was bigger. Vanessa had obviously cropped out the rest of the photo. It showed that the picture was taken inside Muccino's, long before the fire had destroyed the dining room. Also, the man's other arm was around another woman, who was looking at Frankie with a smile. "That's our Uncle Jesse and his wife Amy. They came to the restaurant to have dinner for their 30th wedding anniversary, and we actually surprised them with a big party." He scrolled through the rest of the album, showing him all the other pictures from the event.

The Alpha sighed in relief. "I wouldn't have blamed her if she wanted to move on. But I'm glad it was just Vanessa being manipulative again."

"You need to make her listen, Grant." Matt frowned. "It won't be easy. She's been hurt before."

"You mean her dad? And your dad?"

Matt nodded. "And Jacob, too."

"Jacob?" Grant asked. "Who's Jacob?"

Matt sipped his beer. "Well, it's not my place to say, but ... I think she was about eighteen when this guy started sniffing around. You know the type: handsome, rich, arrogant. We all knew he was bad news, but Frankie really liked him and was sneaking around with him. One night ... well morning, really, she came home and my Ma was furious. They were shouting at each other and Frankie was screaming about how she and Jacob were in love and stuff. Anyway, to make a long story short, after he got what he wanted, he stopped coming by."

"And then?" Grant gritted his teeth. Hearing about Frankie and some guy, even if it was ten years ago, made his chest hurt. Jealously gnawed at his insides.

"Well, one day she came home and she was crying. I'll never forget it. My brothers and I ... well, we found out from some other people that Jacob was going around with some other girl, you know?" He paused. "It's a small town so everyone gossips, right? Apparently, there was some sort of confrontation and he humiliated her in front of his new girlfriend, his friends, and half the town. Called her a townie bitch."

Grant's jaw hardened. "Fucking asshole," he muttered.

"We were so mad." Matt gave an evil smile. "I was only thirteen. Dante was sixteen, I think, and Rafe was ten, but we all made him pay."

"What did you do?"

"We trashed his sports car. Dante actually went full Lycan and ripped up his leather seats. Then me, Enzo, and Rafe spray painted giant penises onto the hood and the sides." He took a chug of beer. "He was a dick, and now the whole town knew."

Grant laughed and clapped the younger man on the back. "Good for you." He probably would have maimed the man. For a moment, he wondered if he could get Alynna to track down this Jacob.

"Oh, and that's not all. Dante stalked him in his wolf form," Matt said with a grin. "Followed him and his new girlfriend around until he became paranoid. One night, Dante actually jumped them. Not to hurt them, right? Just to scare them a little. Jacob peed his pants and then abandoned his girlfriend to save himself. She spread the story around town and his reputation was wrecked."

"Well, remind me never to piss you guys off," Grant said wryly. "I think I'll stick with the punching." He stared down into his mug, his thoughts drifting to Frankie. His beautiful, strong Frankie. How she must have felt being rejected by all the men in her life, yet she managed to keep her life, her family, and clan together.

"You okay man?" Matt asked as he finished off his beer.

"Yeah, I'm okay. Want another one?"

"Naw, I'm good."

"I'm going to make this right," Grant vowed, rubbing his now-healing jaw before looking down glumly into his beer. "Assuming she'll still have me."

"Frankie is tough," Matt mused. "But I think you'll win her over."

"I hope so." Grant wanted nothing more than to race to Jersey, kiss Frankie senseless, and then put the biggest ring he could find on her finger. He wanted Frankie to be his, forever.

"Let's go." Matt stood. "Come back with me, and you can talk to her."

"I can't just do that, Matt." Grant shook his head. "I would be breaking Lycan law."

"So what?" the younger man said. "What's the worse she can do?"

"Well, I'll get a reprimand from the High Council, and then she could declare war on me. She could rally her clan members and attack us." Grant really didn't need that now.

"Shit, Grant," Matt laughed. "A slap on the wrist from the High Council? That's it? And war with Jersey? Have you seen the 'clan?' Except for Dante, Frankie, and maybe two other people, no one's under thirty. They're mostly out of shape rednecks and guidos. Believe me, no one will be waging war against you."

Grant downed his beer and stood. "Alright, I'll do it. Let's go."

"That's the spirit!" Matt gave him a bear hug. "Let's go to Jersey!"

The two men laughed and chatted as they left the bar. "Let me call my driver," Grant said, taking out his phone. "I should pass by—Matt!" He dropped his phone as a shadow behind Matt tackled him to the ground. The younger man struggled, but he was overpowered.

"What the fuck!" Grant looked around. Five men were closing in on them.

"Mr. Anderson," one of them said as he came closer. He was the tallest and largest of them. "You'll be coming with us now."

"Who the hell are you?" Grant growled. The air prickled with energy, and the various scents assaulting his nostrils told him they were all Lycans. His wolf was raring to get out, and he could feel the shift coming.

"That doesn't matter," the man said. "But if you don't come with us, we'll hurt your friend here."

"Grant, don't listen to them!" Matt gasped. The goon who tackled him had him in a sleeper hold. "Get out of here!" He howled in pain as the man held him tighter.

"Don't hurt him!" Grant calmed his inner wolf. "Look, what do you want? Money? I have it." He tossed his wallet to the ground. "And I have more."

Their leader laughed. "Oh no, Mr. Anderson. We just want you." He whistled and nodded to his men. "Cuff him. The other one, too." He turned back to Grant. "We're gonna go for a little ride."

CHAPTER THIRTY-ONE

F rankie paced the living room, looking at the phone in her hand. The contacts list was open with Grant's name highlighted. All she had to do was tap the green button to call him.

Shit.

Why was it so hard? Call him and tell him they had to talk. That's it. She wouldn't tell him about the pregnancy over the phone, of course. They would meet, and she would tell him in person.

The phone suddenly started ringing, and she gave a small shriek, dropping the device on the floor. "*Cazzo!*" she cursed and picked it up. It was Matt.

"Matt?" she answered. "What's up?"

"Ms. Muccino," a strange voice answered.

"Hello? Who is this?" Her brows knitted. "Where's my brother?"

"Ms. Muccino, we have your brother. And Mr. Anderson."

"Have him?" Frankie raised her voice. "What do you mean have him?"

"We've taken them both."

Her blood ran cold. "You have his phone." A chirp came from the phone and she quickly opened the message. The picture showed Matt and Grant, sitting on the floor of a dirty van, their hands tied behind them.

"Frankie don't try to—" Matt's voice came through the receiver.

"Shut up!" The sound of bone hitting bone crackled through, and Frankie screamed.

"No! Don't hurt him! Don't hurt them!"

"If you want to see them alive, Ms. Muccino, you'll come to the address we're sending to you now," the voice said. "And if you alert the authorities or the New York clan, we will kill both of them." The line went dead.

Frankie stared at the phone in her hand, unable to move. Her heart beat wildly, and a knot grew in her stomach. They had Matt and Grant. It was probably the same people who had attacked her. The phone chirped again, and a message from another unknown number arrived. Checking the message, she saw it was an address in Connecticut. Without another thought, she grabbed her keys and dashed out to her car.

———

Frankie programmed the address into her phone's GPS app and followed the directions. It was a two-hour drive according to her app, and she drove above the speed limit, crossing her fingers and hoping she wouldn't get pulled over. The sooner she got there, the better.

Go, go. Save our mate, her inner she-wolf, who was bubbling near the surface, urged her. The wolf also pumped adrenaline into her system. She had to save Matt and Grant. Get to them as fast as possible. *Oh please, don't let it be too late.*

The GPS led her to an old, abandoned building somewhere

between the border of New Jersey and Bristol. She pulled into the parking lot outside the building and carefully made her way to the large doors. The building was rundown, probably an old factory or warehouse. There were a couple of broken windows, and she could see light coming from inside. The chains that had kept the main doors locked were on the ground, and the metal creaked as she opened it.

The building was large and cavernous, opening into one main room in the center. There were three figures standing in the middle, and she couldn't quite make out their faces as the pendulum lights were hung high above them, obscuring their features.

"Come in, Ms. Muccino," the man in the middle said. Something glinted in his hand, and, as she drew closer, she realized it was the barrel of a gun, pointed straight at her. Her heart beat wildly in her chest, and the she-wolf was growling and screaming to get out.

Must ... protect ...

Calm down, she urged. She knew she wouldn't be able to shift fast enough to evade a gunshot, not at this range.

"Grayson?" she said, her voice incredulous as the man's face came into view. Beside him was Vanessa Bennet. However, she didn't recognize the third figure: a tall, large man with long, blond hair. "What's the meaning of this? And where are my brother and Grant?"

"Kill her now!" Vanessa spat. "Shoot her, Grayson!"

"Shut up, Vanessa!" Grayson said. "I told you, the plan has changed!"

"But it was a good plan!" she shrieked. "We get rid of her, Grant gives me a pup, and we take over New York!"

"It *would* have been a good plan if you could have sealed the deal!" Grayson's face went red. "But you couldn't even get him to fuck you!"

"You should have given me more time! I almost had him! I told you, he loves me!" Vanessa turned to Frankie, her eyes narrowing. "You whore! You spread your legs, and he comes panting after you! But don't worry. Once you're out of the way, Grant will realize he loves me. And he'll give me a pup!"

"Vanessa, I swear, if you don't shut up, I'm going to make you shut up!" Grayson roared.

"What do you want, Grayson?" Frankie asked.

"Why you, my dear."

"Me?"

"Yes. I will deliver you to the mages." He motioned to the tall, blond man beside him. "And, in exchange, they will give me what I want."

"The hell you will!" she shouted. "And why should I come with you?"

"Because if you don't, we will kill your brother," he said. "Bring them in!"

A door opened somewhere. More figures emerged from the dark; two of them were hunched over while three others prodded and pushed them forward.

"Grant! Matt!" she cried.

"Frankie!" Matt called. "You shouldn't have come!"

"Get out of here," Grant said. "Please Frankie ... go!"

"Shut up!" Grayson hissed as their captors pushed them onto their knees.

"Grayson, you asshole!" Grant snarled. "I should have known you were behind this! And you!" He looked at the tall, Viking-like man. "Daric. Of course, Stefan is behind this! He probably planned my kidnapping, too. What did he promise you, Grayson?"

"New York," Grayson admitted. "If only you had fallen into our initial trap. You were supposed to get away that night and then realize that the mages were getting stronger and bolder. I was ready, waiting in the wings to offer you an alliance, and marriage to Vanessa would have sealed the deal. Of course, once she had your heir, we wouldn't need you anymore." Grayson spat. "You could have lived a couple more months and seen your pup, but, as it stands, I'll have to kill you now."

"You think the mages are good allies? They'll kill you, too." He looked at Daric meaningfully. "They hate our kind. Stefan and the mages are only using you."

"Shut up, Grant." Grayson turned the gun on him. "You will die tonight, and then once you are gone, we will kill your sister, her family, and then your Beta and his wife. With no other heir or second, the High Council will have no choice but to appoint a warden for your territory."

"And that would be you, Grayson?" Grant finished.

"Of course." Grayson raised his gun. "I always hated you, you know. We should have been the most powerful clan in the world, not New York."

"No!" Frankie cried. She leaped toward Grayson, but one of his men grabbed her, dragging her away.

"Don't hurt her!" Grant growled. "Don't you fucking dare!"

"Oh, I won't hurt her," Grayson said. "I'll be handing her over to the mages. Don't know why they'd want a pathetic little thing like her, though."

Grant's eyes widened, and he looked at Daric. "I will hunt every last one of you down."

"Goodbye, Grant." Grayson cocked his gun.

"No!" Vanessa's piercing scream rang throughout the building, and she raised her arm, revealing the pistol in her hand. She shot once, but the kickback was so strong, she accidentally fired a second time. The bullet ricocheted off the lights, sending them swinging back and forth.

"Vanessa, what did you do?" Grayson screamed, his eyes scanning around him.

"I can't let you kill him!" Vanessa sobbed. The gun dropped to the ground.

Grayson looked at where she had pointed the pistol. "No! You bitch! You killed her! Stefan wants her alive!"

Frankie collapsed to the ground, the front of her shirt blooming with red.

"Frankie!" Grant shouted. "No!"

"No! Daric," Grayson grabbed the warlock by his shirtsleeves, "please don't tell Lord Stefan!"

"I'm sorry, Grayson. There is no more deal." With that, Daric disappeared into thin air.

———

In Grant's eyes, everything happened so fast, then it slowed down. One moment, he and Matt were on their knees, their hands bound in plastic cuffs, watching as Grayson threatened Frankie and revealed his plan. Then there was screaming, a gunshot, the lights swaying violently back and forth. Chaos surrounded them, and then time seemed to decelerate. He watched as red began to pour from Frankie's chest, and her body collapsed to the ground with a thud.

Grayson screamed in anger, then smacked Vanessa in the face. "You ruined everything, you bitch! We're dead! Dead because of you!"

"I can't let you kill him! So I got rid of his whore instead!" Vanessa shrieked.

"I'm going to kill you!" Grant roared. He broke away from his guard and began to heave and growl. The muscles underneath his skin began to move as his limbs grew longer and bigger. The plastic cuffs broke away. Dark hair sprouted all over his body, and, soon, he stood in full Lycan form.

"Shift, you idiots!" Grayson instructed his men. "And bring him down! Kill him!"

But they were too late. Grant was fully transformed, and he leaped onto the man on his right, ripping his throat out, then onto the one who was holding Matt like a shield. The younger man managed to get out of the way in time, and Grant sank his large teeth into the man's thigh, piercing the femoral artery. Blood gushed into his mouth, and he let it drip and drain, smearing his fur like war paint.

Once their two captors were down, he whipped around. Red, red everywhere. Frankie. Their child. She lay unmoving on the ground. His wolf eyes zeroed in on Vanessa and growled.

"No!" Vanessa cried as Grant's gigantic wolf cornered her. "Please, Grant, don't!" She closed her eyes, as if trying to bring on a shift. He bowed his legs, getting ready to pounce on her. As he jumped, however, he was hit on the side by a large blur. It sent him sprawling to the ground.

Grant's wolf rolled a couple of times, but he immediately got back on all fours. When he looked up, he saw five Lycans surrounding him, teeth and fangs bared, tails held horizontally. Grant bowed low, ready for the attack. Nothing mattered anyway. Frankie and his pup were gone. He would fight and defend himself to the death, take down as many of them as he could.

A howl came from outside, and, for a moment, the wolves surrounding him were distracted. Grant recognized the sound, and, in that split-second, he pounced on the closest wolf, dragging him to the ground. One by one, the wolves piled on him, their teeth sinking into his body, drawing blood. Pain shot through him as teeth and claws ripped into this body. He fought and tore away with all his might, but there were just too many of them.

All of a sudden, two large, brown wolves joined in, wresting his attackers away. As the two brown wolves (who he recognized as Alex and Nick) were battling two of the Connecticut wolves, the remaining ones flew off him, as if blown away by a strong wind. Lara stood a few feet away from them, waving her hand as she moved the air currents to send the Lycans crashing against the wall, knocking them out.

"Grant!" Alynna called as she stormed into the abandoned building. She was wearing tactical gear, a gun in her hand. "They're here!" she shouted into a headset. "Secure the premises! The Alpha is here! Have Medical on standby."

"Goddammit!" Grayson Charles, who had been watching in the corner of the room, screamed. He raised his hand, pointing the gun towards Alynna, who didn't see the Connecticut Alpha hiding in the shadows.

Grant howled and sprung into the air, knocking Alynna down. He howled in pain as the bullet dug into his massive body and lodged itself in his chest.

"Grant!" Alynna screamed from under the gigantic wolf. "No!"

The two blond wolves leaped at Grayson, knocking him to the ground. Nick's massive jaw locked onto his arm and ripped at the flesh, while Alex's paws held him in place. The Connecticut Alpha wailed in pain, then passed out as blood flowed from the torn meat of his arm.

"Grant," Alynna sobbed as she pushed the wolf off her. Already, the body was shrinking, returning back into its human form.

"Frankie ..." Grant choked, his eyes rolling back. "I love you ... I'll see you soon, see you both ..." Then his eyes closed.

CHAPTER THIRTY-TWO

"Oh God, no! Grant! Medical! Get in here now! The Alpha is down!" Alynna pressed her hand over the wound, trying to stop it from bleeding. "Grant!"

Alynna clearly looked surprised to see her. "F—Frankie?"

Frankie wrapped her arms around the body on the ground. "No! Grant please, no!" Tears streamed down her cheeks. "I'm sorry! I'm sorry. I never got to tell you ... I love you!"

There was chaos all around them. The Enclave's Medical team rushed into the scene with oxygen masks and a stretcher. Dr. Faulkner dashed to Grant's side.

"His pulse is very weak ... we're going to lose him!" he shouted to his team. "Please, Alynna, make way. We're going to do the best we can. Dr. Cross! I need you to assist!" he called to the young woman who was sprinting toward them, medical bag in hand.

"C'mon," Alynna said gently. "He's not ... he's still here, we can save him."

Frankie let the younger woman pull her to the side. Her

system was still seeped in shock even as she watched the two doctors work on Grant, their hands quick and efficient.

"We have the best medical team here, Frankie," Alynna assured her. "Did you check on Matt yet?"

"Oh my God, Matt!"

Her brother was standing next to Alex and Nick, who had cut his plastic cuffs. She rushed to him and put her arms around him. "Matt ... what were you doing here? How did they get you?"

"I was with Grant when we were jumped," he explained. "We were leaving the bar and these Lycans surrounded us and made us get into their van."

"But what were you doing In New York? With Grant?"

"Well ..." He looked at her sheepishly. "I was gonna make him pay, Frankie. I tracked him down and, as soon as I saw him, I punched him in the face!"

"What? Why would you do that?"

"He knocked you up, Frankie. I couldn't let him get away with it!"

Frankie opened her mouth and then closed it. Beside her, Alynna's eyes widened, while Alex's jaw dropped. Nick, on the other hand, had a smirk on his face. "I ... I ... how did you know?"

"I overheard you in the kitchen with Nonna Gianna," he explained.

Frankie shook her head. "Well that explains that ... but ..." She turned to Alynna. "How did you know where to find us?"

"Well, Matt isn't the only one of your brothers who has a habit of eavesdropping," Alynna said. "Rafe called me. He overheard you talking on the phone with the kidnappers. It was easy enough to hack into your phone and find the address they sent you."

"The last time the mages attacked, they caught us by

surprise," Nick began. "But this time, we were prepared. We've spent the last few months training and putting a plan into action in case something like this happened. We brought the whole security force, and the medivac chopper should be airlifting Grant back to The Enclave as we speak."

"Oh God ..." Frankie hugged Alynna. "Thank you ... so much. All of you."

"Well, I had to come and rescue my brother after all." Alynna's eyes sparkled. "And his True Mate."

"True Mate?"

"Of course!" Alynna pointed to her chest. The blood spread all over the front, and the bullet hole in the fabric showed where she had been shot. But there was no wound underneath.

"*Madre de dio*, I didn't notice! I just ... there was pain. I fell down and then ... I just woke up again! What happened to me?" She looked down, her hands shaking as she touched the hole in her shirt and the clean, unbroken skin underneath.

"Frankie," Alynna began, "you're carrying Grant's pup, right? If you are True Mates, that means nothing can harm you. The baby is protecting itself, protecting you. I survived a poisoning, Cady recovered from a stab wound, and, apparently, not even a bullet can harm someone carrying a True Mate offspring."

Her hand went to her belly. "I can't ... this is ..."

"This one is still breathing!" Dr. Cross called to the medical team, her voice ringing throughout the building. She was bent over Grayson Charles, who had passed out from loss of blood.

"Too bad," Alynna said distastefully. "Ugh, I hate that guy!"

Frankie looked at Grayson. "I know what you mean, but the High Council will take care of him." She glanced around. "Where's Vanessa?"

"She's here?" Alynna asked, frowning. "Shit. She must have

gotten away. I'll have a team try and pick her up. She can't have gone too far."

Frankie suddenly felt bone tired, the adrenaline finally leaving her body. "Grant ... do you think he'll be okay?"

Alynna's face looked hopeful, but her mouth was drawn in a grim line. "Let's head back to New York."

CHAPTER THIRTY-THREE

"How is he, Dr. Faulkner?" Nick Vrost asked as the older Lycan stepped into the waiting room. Beside him, Cady held his hand, giving it a squeeze.

"Alive," Dr. Faulkner said, but his face was grim. "The bullet was lodged in his chest. He lost a lot of blood. If he wasn't Lycan, he would have died in an instant."

"So he'll be okay?" Alynna asked. Beside her, Frankie sat silently, her eyes in a daze.

"I ... normally I would say yes, and we've done all we can." He shook his head. "I can't explain it, but it's like there's something holding him back."

"What do you mean?" Cady asked.

"Well, modern medicine can do wonders for the body," Dr. Faulkner began. "We can administer drugs that would have seemed like magic a hundred years ago and use advanced technology and techniques to heal broken bones and tissue. But there's still a big part of healing that rests on the body and, some might say, the mind. Grant's body is responding, accordingly, but his mind ... it's like it doesn't want to fight anymore. He flatlined once during surgery."

Alynna let out a cry. "Please Dr. Faulkner, what can we do?"

"Wait," the doctor said. "That's all we can do. Wait and hope and pray that he finds the strength to keep fighting."

The room was silent, the air heavy with grief.

"We have to do something," Alynna said.

Alex put an arm around her. "We've done all we can, babydoll."

"We should go get some rest," Cady suggested. "Grant will be fine by morning. I know it."

"Yes," Nick agreed, standing and helping his wife up from the chair.

"You can stay with us," Alynna said to Frankie, tugging on her hand.

The Jersey Alpha was looking straight ahead, unmoving, her mismatched eyes steely. "No."

"Frankie, you can't—"

"No!" she repeated. "I'm staying here. I want to see him," she pleaded at Dr. Faulkner. "Let me see him, please?"

Dr. Faulkner looked like he wanted to protest but then sighed in defeat. "Just you, Lupa."

"Thank you."

She followed him toward the hallway of private rooms in the medical wing, stopping in front of the third door on the left. He opened the door and motioned for her to go inside.

Frankie nodded, took a deep breath, and then entered the room. She suppressed a cry when she saw Grant looking pale and lying motionless on the bed.

"Grant," she called softly, slipping her hand into his. "Grant, please wake up. Please fight." Tears streaked down her cheeks, dropping onto the white, sterile sheets on the bed. She placed his hand on her belly. "I need you. We need you." She gasped as she felt a tiny spark in her belly when Grant's hand touched it. "Don't leave us. I love you."

———

He was falling. Slipping down a long slope. No, he was plummeting through the air, like he had jumped out of a plane without a parachute.

"Grant, please wake up. Please fight."

The voice ... it sounded familiar. *Frankie?* Memories rushed back. Yes, he was going to see her again. His sweet Frankie.

"I need you. We need you."

A spark of electricity jolted through him. *What was that?*

"Don't leave us. I love you."

She loves me? Leave you? No, I would never leave you, Frankie. But you left me. You died and you left me.

Falling, falling, dropping and tumbling down.

Wait, this was all wrong. Frankie. Frankie. Our baby.

"Frankie!" he called out, his hand grasping air. His eyes flew open.

"Grant?"

"Frankie?" His voice was weak and raspy, his vision was blurry, but he knew that voice anywhere. "You're ... Frankie ..."

Softly callused hands wrapped around his. "Yes, I'm here, Grant."

"I don't understand ..." He tried to sit up but felt dizzy.

"No, don't get up! Please, just stay down and rest. Do you want something? Water?"

He shook his head. "I need to make sure ... I'm awake and not dreaming. You're ... really okay?"

A warm body slipped in next to him, and slim arms wrapped around his chest. "Yes, I'm here. I'm okay. We both are."

He sighed with relief. "I saw you. The blood. You fell."

Soft lips pressed against his side. "I know. But our baby saved me, Grant. The bullet went through and then the wound closed up."

"What?" He felt dizzy again. "Feel ... so tired ..."

"Shhh ... I'll explain later. I promise I'm really here and I'm okay."

"Don't leave me, please, Frankie?" Consciousness started slipping away and he felt lightheaded.

"Of course not. I love you, Grant."

———

"Looks like you're going to make a full recovery," Dr. Faulkner said as he looked at Grant, who was sitting up in his bed.

After examining his wounds, he saw that Grant's condition had definitely improved. "I can't believe you were in such bad shape when you came in yesterday."

"Thank God." Frankie sat beside him, holding his hand, with a big, relieved smile on her face. After he had initially woken up, she stayed by his side the entire night. "I thought ..." Her face fell.

"Shhh ... sweetheart, I'm here." Grant squeezed her hand.

"God ... to think ... we could have—"

"I'm going to go call everyone, tell them the good news," Dr. Faulkner said and then left them alone.

"I'm sorry," Frankie began as soon as the door closed. "That last day in New York, I should have trusted you. Listened to you. Maybe this never would have happened if I did."

"Sweetheart, come here." Grant tugged on her arm, and she climbed into the bed with him. He wrapped an arm around her. "It's okay. I understand. I know it's hard for you to trust men.

But you have to believe me. I love you, and I would never leave you. I promise."

She nodded. "I know that now."

"Good." He slipped his hand over her belly. "You know, while I was asleep ... I thought I felt something, a spark."

"Was it ... our pup?"

His face broke into a smile. "I didn't imagine it, right? You're having my baby?"

She nodded.

"And we really are True Mates?"

"Apparently." She giggled when he tickled her stomach. "I just ... it's strange, right?"

"Yes." He kissed her knuckles. "I watched my sister find her True Mate, then Cady and Nick. I never thought I'd be as lucky."

She sighed and snuggled into his arms. "Me neither. I love you, Grant."

He sighed in relief. "I was hoping I wasn't dreaming that part either."

Frankie shook her head. "I'm sorry it took me a long time to say it."

"You mean you waited until you thought I was dead," he teased.

She swatted him playfully on the arm. "Beast," she joked and snuggled against him. "I think I felt it ... for a while now. I was just too afraid to tell you."

"And now?"

"And now I can say it. I love you, Grant Anderson."

"And I love you."

CHAPTER THIRTY-FOUR

"C'mon Grant, just tell me where we're going!"

"What part of 'surprise' don't you understand, Frankie?" Grant asked in an exasperated voice.

"But Grant ..." she whined and scratched at the blindfold.

"We're here."

Frankie let out a breath. The car stopped, and then she heard the click of the door opening. Grant guided her, taking her hand and helping her step out of the car.

A week had passed since the incident in Connecticut. Grayson Charles had recovered and was now in the custody of the Lycan High Council. His clan was in shambles, the power vacuum creating chaos. In their eyes, Grayson betrayed the Lycans by forming an alliance with the mages, not to mention offering them their own to serve as guinea pigs for their potion experiments. The Connecticut clan was calling for new leadership. His Beta, Logan Cooper, had taken over temporarily while they were trying to regroup. Grant knew him to be a good man, so he wasn't worried. He even threw his support behind Logan. Grayson's wife and child were put in protective custody since both were innocent, and, as far as anyone knew, Vanessa was gone. No one had seen or heard from her since that night.

"And where is here?" Frankie asked, crossing her arms. She'd been staying at The Enclave, as Grant refused to be away from her for even a single day. Since she hadn't been home, her brothers and Nonna Gianna had come to visit them as Grant recuperated. Dante, Enzo, and Rafe had given him a good ribbing, telling him that they were going to kick his ass for getting their sister pregnant out of wedlock, at least they would as soon as he was fully recovered.

"Just one second ..." Grant led her forward a couple of steps, then turned her body a few inches to the right.

Wherever they were, it was noisy. She could hear sawing, hammering, people talking, and heavy work boots stomping everywhere.

"Ready?" Grant asked.

"I've been ready since you blindfolded me."

"So impatient, my mate," he teased. Slowly, he removed the blindfold.

Frankie squinted, then shut her eyes quickly as the sunlight blinded her. After rubbing her eyes, she blinked a few times, and her vision cleared. She gasped at first, then held her breath as she tried to digest what she was seeing.

"Surprise!" Dante, Rafe, Enzo, and Matt shouted at her, their faces lit up with smiles.

Her brothers were standing in the parking lot of Muccino's, but, instead of the charred remains of the old restaurant, the building behind them looked newly painted. There were also about a dozen people walking around, carrying wooden boards, tools, ladders, and other construction materials. The Muccino's sign hung over the doorway and looked good as new, or better than new because it looked like it had never even been destroyed.

"Did you do this?" She looked at Grant. He didn't say anything but was smiling at her.

Frankie jumped into his arms, wrapped her legs around his waist, and gave him a big smack on the lips. "I love you," she said in between kisses.

"Get a room, you two!" Enzo called out, but he was smiling at the couple.

She slid down his body and squeezed his ass. "You bet we will!"

"Minx," he smirked.

"So, how did you do this?" She looked around her with amazement.

"Well, I thought it would be a good investment," Grant explained. "Muccino's has the best Italian food I've ever tasted, after all. And with a few improvements and some advertising, everyone will know it."

"Grant called us a couple days ago," Dante added as he approached. "He said he wanted to be our partner and start rebuilding as soon as possible. I said yes, but only if we make sure we restore everything back to the way it was. The way Ma and Nonna would have wanted it."

"Partner?" She looked slyly at Grant.

"Silent partner," he assured. "You guys will get to run the whole show. And there was one more condition."

"What was that?"

Dante held up a tablet and opened it, showing Frankie the screen. It was a picture of a corner shop in downtown Manhattan with a "for sale" sign outside. He scrolled through the gallery and it showed an artist's rendition of an Italian restaurant with a large "Muccino's" sign outside. "He wants to open a location in New York. And he wants me to run the kitchen."

Frankie's eyes grew wide, her mouth dropped open.

"Are you mad?" Grant asked. "I know it's a bit sneaky of me, going behind your back like this. But I did this all for you."

"Mad?" Frankie said in an incredulous voice. "You did this for me? Why would I be mad? Grant, this is the best thing anyone's ever done for me!"

"I'm glad you feel that way." He looked down at her, his eyes filled with warmth and love.

"C'mon, we have food!" Matt cocked his head, indicating that they should follow him.

They walked over to the back of the restaurant, and, to Frankie's surprise, there were several picnic tables set up, many piled high with food. Nick, Cady, Alex, and Alynna were chatting and laughing, while Nonna Gianna was holding Mika and cooing at her.

"Finally, you're here! I'm hungry!" Alynna shouted as they approached. She looked at the food, her eyes going wide as saucers. Dishes overflowed with pastas and meats, their savory aromas wafting through the air. There were five kinds of freshly baked pizzas and platters of various meats and cheese imported from Italy. Off to the side, the dessert table was piled high with all kinds of delectable confections and sweets, from cannolis filled with flavored creams to zeppoles fresh from the fryer and covered with a generous dusting of powdered sugar.

"Oh my God, when do you open in New York?" Alynna looked meaningfully at Dante.

Dante laughed. "Soon. I'll be moving to The Enclave, too, so I won't be too far away."

"I can't believe I'll be able to eat this everyday if I want! I won't have to defect to your clan after all." Alynna squealed with delight and gave Dante a kiss on the cheek. "You're gonna make some woman happy one day."

Matt and Rafe were handing out plates, encouraging everyone to pile on as much food as they could. They also called the workers who were fixing up the restaurant to join them, as there was definitely more than enough, even with two pregnant Lycans and Alynna.

Everyone sat down to eat as soon as they piled food on their plates. Frankie sat next to Grant, who had taken two helpings of Osso Bucco. Across from her, Alynna and Alex were joking, and, beside them, Nick was giving Cady a bite of his zeppole. Surrounded by family and friends and the man she loved, plus a baby on the way, she never thought she'd be happier.

Frankie had eaten about three helpings before she was finally ready for dessert. She put her fork into her tiramisu and felt something hard at the bottom of the plate. "Nonna," she called to her great-aunt, "did you drop an earring into the tiramisu again?"

The older woman pursed her lips together, as if she was stopping herself from smiling. "Oh really? Maybe I did. Can you dig it out for me, *mimma*?"

Frankie shrugged and dug in, trying to find the earring. As she pushed the crumbs and cream away, something sparkled underneath. "What the ..." She picked it up, brushed the remaining dessert away and held it up. "What?" It was a diamond ring. The princess-cut solitaire was probably three carats, and it was flanked by small side stones lining the platinum band. She gasped as it sparkled in the sun.

Beside her, Grant stood up from his chair and then got down on one knee. "Francesca Muccino, I love you. Will you do me the honor of being my wife?"

"I ... yes, of course!" Frankie answered, her eyes filling with happy tears.

A cheer erupted from the small crowd around them. Grant slipped the ring onto her finger (after quickly dunking it in a glass of water) and then picked her up in his arms.

"Let's elope to Italy!" she said dreamily as Grant put her

down. "I'll wear my grandmother's wedding dress, and we can have a small ceremony at the villa in Positano."

Alynna laughed through a mouthful of cannoli. "Yeah, right," she snorted. "Just try and get that idea past Callista."

Cady chuckled. "If I were a betting woman, I'd be betting against you, Frankie."

Frankie looked confused. "I don't get it."

"Oh you will," Alynna chortled. "Just wait."

CHAPTER THIRTY-FIVE

Frankie and Grant invited Callista Mayfair to dinner, and, as they were having coffee and dessert in the living room, they told her the good news. She was overjoyed when she found out about the baby but horrified when they told her that they were going to elope to Italy.

"No!"

"Please, Mother."

"Absolutely not!" Callista Mayfair put her literal foot down, her Manolo Blahniks making a clicking sound on the floor when she shot up from the couch. "I will not be denied a wedding this time!" She crossed her arms resolutely, and Grant sighed, then gave Frankie an apologetic look.

"This time?" Frankie asked, her face puzzled.

"First, Alynna had her City Hall wedding, and then Nick and Cady insisted on a two-week engagement," Callista railed. "Two weeks! That was hardly enough time to plan!"

"But you did a great job. I won't be waiting a year, Mother," Grant warned. "I want to be married before our pup is born."

"And before I start showing," Frankie added. She already had a wedding gown—her grandmother's. With a few adjustments, it would fit her perfectly, but not if she had already popped.

"And you will, dear." Callista patted her future daughter-in-law's hand. "But we will do it the right way! We will do it my way! Besides, *two* Alphas getting married? It will be the event of the century!"

"Fine," Frankie said, defeated. "Let's have a big wedding then."

Callista's face lit up, her eyes shining with tears. "Thank you, my dear! It will be a wonderful wedding, I will make sure of it! Everything will be perfect."

After a few more minutes of chatting, Callista declared she had to go and get preparations started. As Frankie and Grant walked her to the door, she hugged her son and future daughter-in-law, her eyes sparkling with happiness.

"You won't regret this," she declared as she left the couple alone. Callista was already dialing the number of the archbishop of New York by the time she was out the door.

"Thank you for indulging my mother." Grant kissed her on the lips. "I'd never hear the end of it if we eloped."

"I'm going to regret this big time, aren't I?" Frankie said wryly.

———

Frankie only *slightly* regretted letting Callista plan the wedding. The vivacious older Lycan didn't plan as much as take over the entire thing. If Callista Mayfair were going to wedding world war, she definitely would have vanquished her opponents and been declared victor. In less than a month, she sent out 300 invitations, booked St. Patrick's Cathedral on a Saturday morning, and put together an entire reception at the Waldorf Astoria with only minor casualties.

Honestly, Frankie was relieved not to have to worry about wedding planning. She had the groom, the dress, and the ring. That was all she cared about and needed. And she was way too busy supervising renovations for Muccino's in Jersey and starting construction on the New York branch to review place settings and flower arrangements. Besides, it was obvious her future mother-in-law was having a wonderful time with the wedding planning, and Frankie couldn't take that away from her.

The day of the wedding finally arrived. Frankie wore her grandmother's wedding dress, a beautiful tulle and lace concoction with a mermaid skirt, a cinched waist with a silk bow, and pearl buttons running down the back. The cathedral-length veil was a gift from Callista. She held a beautiful bouquet of orchids and lilies. Each of her brothers took turns walking her down the aisle, first Enzo and Matt, then Rafe, and finally Dante, who handed her off to Grant. Nick stood beside him as Best Man, while Nonna Gianna was her Matron of Honor.

"Should anyone here know of any reason that this couple should not be joined in holy matrimony," Archbishop Callaghan said as he neared the end of the wedding ceremony. "Speak now or forever hold your peace."

There wasn't even a slight pause when a voice rang out from behind.

"Grant! No! I love you!"

Vanessa Bennet came running down the aisle, her eyes glazed over. She was also wearing a full-length wedding gown. "You can't marry her! You love me."

"*Cazzo!*" Frankie rolled her eyes. "Hold this." She shoved her bouquet at Grant and picked up her skirts, intending to give Vanessa a piece of her mind. *Who the hell wears white to another woman's wedding?*

Before Frankie could even began walking toward the aisle,

Vanessa let out a pained shriek as a fist connected with her jaw, sending her sprawling to the ground.

"You. Will. Not. Ruin. This. Day!" Callista declared, her voice edged with danger as she rubbed her fist.

Alynna guffawed loudly from her seat on the groom's side. "Wow. I guess Callista's not too classy to smack a biatch."

"Take this trash out," Callista barked to the security detail posted by the altar. The two men hurriedly picked up the woman and dragged her away.

"Apologies everyone," Callista said sweetly to the crowd, who had grown silent. "Your Excellency, if you please," she nodded to Archbishop Callaghan.

The white-haired priest cleared his throat. "Um, yes ... alright, well, let's continue ..."

Frankie stared after her future mother-in-law as she composed herself and sat down next to her husband in the front pew. She was both terrified and in awe of Callista Mayfair.

EPILOGUE

"Any news yet?" Alynna asked as she stood up and walked over to the desk in the waiting room.

"I'm afraid not, Ma'am." The young Lycan nurse shook her head.

"Alynna, we've only been here an hour and you asked her the same question ten minutes ago," Alex said. He handed Mika to her. "Here, I think she wants mommy."

His wife sighed and took the baby. "Aww, Mika, are you ready? Ready to meet your cousin? I know I'm excited! Are you excited, honey?" She babbled to the baby, tickling her plump, rosy cheeks.

Nick Vrost stood up from where he was sitting, holding his son to his chest. The Beta patted the baby's back, as he wore a towel draped over his shoulder to protect his immaculate Italian-cut suit. Zachary Luther Vrost had his father's hair and nose and his mother's indigo blue eyes. Nick and Cady were over the moon and enjoying parenthood despite the sleepless nights and exhaustion.

"Don't worry, these things take time," Cady assured them as she put away her nursing cover.

"You just want to win the pot." Nick smirked at Alynna, referring to the betting pool where they had to guess the sex of Frankie and Grant's baby.

It started innocently enough when Grant joked to Nick that they should think about arranging their children's marriage to each other for the good of the Lycan race, to which Nick replied that they could end up being the same sex. Alynna bet ten dollars it would be a boy, since she said she wanted Mika married to little Zachary. Nick bet it would be a girl, just to tease her. Soon, everyone from Dr. Cross to Frankie's brothers was putting their bets in.

"It's up to like nine hundred dollars now!" Alynna declared.

"Don't you have a trust fund with about five times more zeroes than that?" her husband teased.

"It's not about the money, honey." She gave him a kiss on the nose.

"Then what is it about?" Alex asked.

"It's about proving Nick Vrost wrong," she said sweetly, eyeing the tall Lycan. "Don't worry Mika," she cooed to her baby. "I promise your future father-in-law will be nice to you, not mean like he is to me."

Nick let out a laugh, then was interrupted by a loud belch as Zachary burped out his lunch.

"Ew, never mind Mika." Alynna wrinkled her nose. "Maybe we'll find you a husband with better table manners."

The door to the side of the waiting room burst open, and Grant rushed through. He pulled his surgical mask down to reveal his ear-to-ear smile.

"Well?!" Alynna exclaimed. "Is it a boy or a girl?"

Grant grinned. "Both."

"What?"

"Twins. A boy and a girl." Nick and Alex immediately strode to Grant, then hugged and congratulated him. Cady stood up as well and gave her oldest friend a big hug and a kiss on the cheek.

"Alynna, don't you want to see the babies?" Alex asked as Grant ushered everyone toward the private rooms.

"Yeah, yeah, I'm coming." She was furiously scrolling on her phone.

"What are you doing?" Grant asked, eyeing his sister.

"I'm checking to see the betting pool on our Facebook group." She looked at Alex and Nick. "Who bet on boy *and* girl?"

"Actually," Cady said. "It was me!"

"You're so smart, my love." Nick gave her a kiss on the cheek.

"Aww, crap!" Alynna cursed. "Twins! I should have known! Between her super fertility, your mega-Alpha pheromones, and being True Mates, I'm surprised you didn't have a litter!"

"Well, now you have a matching set," Alex said with a laugh and clapped Grant on the shoulder.

"I think you should name one after me," Alynna said. "After all, you wouldn't have met Frankie if it wasn't for me."

"Alynna Horace Anderson," Grant joked. "Sounds like a terrible name."

"Ugh, let's just go see your kids," Alynna grumbled, still sore from losing the bet. "I just hope they didn't get your ugly mug."

They all filed into the recovery room where Frankie was lying in bed, two bundles in her arms.

"Congrats, momma," Alynna said as she kissed her sister-in-law on the forehead. "You squeezed two out of your vajayjay in one day! I can't believe it."

"Uh, it was exhausting," Frankie said with a smile. "But so worth it." She handed one of the bundles to Grant, who took it from her gently, as if he were handling glass. He kissed his son on the cheek.

"Are your brothers coming soon?" Cady inquired as she peered down at the bundle in Grant's arms.

"Yes," Frankie answered. "Things are a little hectic since Muccino's opened downtown, but Dante and Enzo are on their way as we speak, and Rafe is driving Nonna Gianna here. Matt should be off work at five and says he'll come straight here."

According to Grant, Frankie had gone into labor so quickly, there wasn't any time to warn everyone. She woke up that morning feeling tired and sore, and, as soon as she stood up, her water broke. It was a good thing that The Enclave's Medical wing was in the next building because Grant just carried her all the way there.

The group chatted excitedly and, soon, they were joined by Frankie's family. The din in the room grew louder and louder. Everyone wanted a turn holding the twins, both of whom had their mother's eyes, one green and one blue, but mirrored. The couple had yet to decide on names, so everyone was throwing out their suggestions ranging from lovely ("Adriana and Antonio!") to ridiculous ("No, Alynna, we're not naming them Fifi Crimefighter and her sidekick, Moxieboy.")

Grant looked down at Frankie, beaming at her. He sat next to her on the bed, his arm cuddling her close.

"How are you feeling?" he asked, pressing his nose into her hair.

"Tired. But happy." She moved closer to him. "And you?"

"Ridiculously happy." He kissed her forehead. He also felt a pang of worry. The stakes were much higher now that he had a wife and children to protect. But, for now, as he was surrounded by the people he loved most, he set his troubles aside and enjoyed the laughter and joy around him.

———

Dear Reader,

Thanks for reading this book!

Want to read some too hot to publish bonus scenes from this book AND a free Christmas story featuring the twins?

Then subscribe to my newsletter - it's free!

And you can opt out any time, plus you get **ALL my bonus content** including a FREE Book - The Last Blackstone Dragon.

Head to this website to subscribe: http://aliciamontgomeryauthor.com/mailing-list/

The True Mates story continues in Witch's Mate.

Want to check out what happens? Turn the page for a preview.

Get it now at select online retailers!

All the best,

Alicia

PREVIEW: WITCH'S MATE
ABOUT SIX WEEKS AGO...

L ara Chatraine tapped her foot impatiently in front of the private elevators at the Fenrir Corporation headquarters in Midtown Manhattan. The numbers ticked down much too slowly for her taste. The maintenance department at Fenrir had sent out a memo that morning saying they were doing some upgrades and the elevators may experience some slowdowns and even disruptions.

The delay was annoying and really put a crimp in her day. Though really, it was more that she was spoiled, since she never had to wait for the public elevators like everyone else. Since she joined Fenrir a few months ago, she had her own security badge and her palm print was already programmed into the system. These sets of elevators were for VIPs on the executive penthouse floor, their guests, and for those who worked on the 33rd floor (like her), which meant they were pretty much at her beck and call.

It was, of course, much different from the first time they had barged into Fenrir weeks ago, when she, her mother, and another witch from their coven had stormed through the doors, forcing their way inside. They were desperate to meet the CEO of Fenrir, Grant Anderson. Aside from being the head of a large multinational corporation, he was also the leader and Alpha of the New York Lycans, one of the largest and most powerful werewolf shifter clans in the world. Lycan and witch societies lived and thrived in secret, with humans blissfully unaware of their existence. The two factions were at odds with each other, though they had a tenuous truce. However, a group of former witches and warlocks, called mages, was trying to stir up trouble between the two. The mages kidnapped her cousin Cady and blamed a series of attacks against the New York Lycans on her.

Lara's mother, Vivianne, found out about the kidnapping and decided that they needed the Lycans' help to rescue Cady and prevent the mages from destroying them all. When Grant's gatekeepers and security team had rebuffed their requests for a meeting, they took matters into their own hands, sneaking in and knocking out anyone who stood in their way. Lara herself had used her powers to control wind currents to literally blow his doors open. They eventually convinced the Lycans to let them help find Cady.

Though they rescued Cady, the mages and their leader, Stefan, escaped. The New York Lycans and witches decided to work together, to try and stop the mages. Lara was now assisting the Lycans in trying to understand mage magic and find a way to stop them. Mages, after all, were former witches who turned to blood magic to expand their limited powers.

She sighed and crossed her arms. Her hours at Fenrir were flexible, and today she had taken the morning off since she and her boss/best friend, Dr. Jade Cross, worked late the night before. Now she was going for a lunch date with her cousin, Cady Vrost, all the way at the top floor in the executive offices.

The fine hairs on the back of her neck prickled with that sensation that told her someone was watching her. Whipping her head behind her, she saw a familiar figure.

"Ms. Chatraine." Liam Henney, Lycan Alpha to the San Francisco clan, nodded at her.

"Alpha," she acknowledged, then turned back to looking at the elevator doors.

Liam stepped up beside her. "Are the elevators running slow today?"

"Yeah," she confirmed. "Maintenance or something."

"Oh."

She stared up at the numbers again, which now seemed to be stuck just a couple of floors above them. From the corner of her eye, she regarded the Lycan beside her. She had only met Liam Henney once before, when they made their dramatic entrance into Grant's office. Liam was helping the New York Lycans figure out who kidnapped Cady and eventually helped them attack the mage stronghold. She remembered him clearly, with his electric blue eyes, his handsome, pensive face, broad shoulders, and tall, lean body she'd love to climb like a...

Whoa.

Where did that come from? Lara's cheeked pinked. But who could blame her? Liam was sexy and ridiculously hot. He had a handsome face, with a smile that made her stomach do flip-flops, and almond-shaped eyes turned down slightly at the corners, giving him an exotic look. His wide shoulders were encased in a well-fitting, and probably expensive suit, making him look powerful and sophisticated, but it wasn't just his attire or his looks that made him stand out. Liam Henney exuded a quiet, confident power that was understated, but it was definitely *there.* Just standing next to him she felt it and he could probably make her panties melt away with the right look.

Thank God, though, right now, he just looked annoyed. His brows were knitted as he stared up at the numbers, and Lara had to clench her fists to stop herself from reaching over and smoothing it with her fingers.

Oh God, what's wrong with me? And what is that? She wrinkled her nose. A fresh, citrusy scent tickled her senses.

Mercifully, the elevator doors opened.

"After you." Liam gestured to the elevator car.

She stepped inside. "Going to the top floor? I can get us there," she asked as she put her palm print on the sensor. "I'm meeting Cady for lunch."

Liam was about to take his security badge to place it on the scanner, but he stopped. "Yes...thank you."

As the doors closed, Liam settled right beside her and they waited in awkward silence.

1...2...3...the red letters indicating the floors counted up.

A heartbeat passed, and both spoke at the same time.

"So, what are you-"

"How was your-"

20...21...22...

"Go ahead," she said.

"No, you go," he said.

More silence.

30...31...32...

"I was just going to ask if you had a good trip from San Francisco."

"Ah...yeah. I mean, I actually came from Switzerland though. Lycan business."

"Oh. Uh, nice."

49...50...51...

Lara sighed inwardly. *Was this ride ever going to end?* It was also getting warmer, for some reason. Maybe they were also fixing the air conditioning. Good thing she was wearing a sundress and a light cardigan. Not exactly corporate wear, but part of the perks of her job was the casual dress code.

66...67...68...

There was more awkward silence, and Lara could feel his

eyes boring into the side of her head. Annoyed, she looked up at him. "What are you staring at?" she asked impatiently.

Liam opened his mouth, but a sound chimed, indicating they had arrived at the top floor. *Finally!* She moved forward to leave when Liam suddenly stepped in front of her, blocking the doors.

"Alpha, what's wrong?" she asked. "Hey, what do you think you're doing?!"

Liam's hand slammed on the close button, and then on the emergency stop. The lights dimmed and flickered inside the elevator, and he stepped towards her, forcing her to walk backward. His electric blue eyes glowed in the dim elevator, and her heart slammed into her sternum when she saw the hunger in his eyes.

Time seemed to slow down as the Alpha backed her up against the wall. She gasped as his large hands gripped her shoulders and Liam's dark head swooped down. His lips stopped a millimeter away from hers, but the moment they connected, time sped up again and all heck broke loose.

She should have pushed him away, asked him what his problem was. Really, all it would have taken was a wave of her hand. But the electricity and burst of power that shot through her the moment their lips touched shocked her. Plus, Liam was a damned good kisser. His mouth was warm and delicious, seeking hers out insistently. His hands latched around her hips, lifting her up against the wall. He grabbed at her thighs, parting them and pushing the skirt of her sundress up. Moving between them, he wrapped her legs around his waist. She gasped into his mouth in surprise as her hips slammed against him. Liam was sporting an honest-to-goodness boner down there, and from the size of it, it *was* true what they said about Lycan shifters. Damn, her panties were soaked in an instant.

A soft growl emanated from his chest and a hand buried

into her strawberry blonde hair. He pulled her head back, exposing her neck. Liam dragged his lips down the slender column, his teeth lightly grazing the soft flesh there. Lara whimpered, pushing her hips and grinding up against his erection.

His other hand crept up the back of her thighs, grabbing her ass and giving it a squeeze as he pushed himself closer to her. She shuddered as he found the perfect spot, the ridge of his pants-covered dick bumping up against her clit.

"Fuck!" she cried out before Liam's mouth captured hers again. The yummy citrusy fragrance was all him. His delicious scent wrapped around her, assaulting her senses. Her hands snaked around him, grabbing his shoulders as she pushed against him, her body winding tight as she could feel her orgasm approaching.

"Everything OK in there?" a voice crackled through the speaker. "Sir? I think we accidentally triggered the emergency button."

Lara whimpered in disappointment as Liam slid away from her. He blinked once, breathing heavily as he turned around and pressed the call button.

"Uhm, yeah...we're...fine in here," he managed to reply.

"Yeah, sorry about that, sir. We've been trying to run some upgrades in the background. I apologize for the delay, sir...you'll be on the top floor in a sec."

Silence filled the small elevator car. Lara managed to stand up on her own two legs without melting into a puddle. She smoothed down her dress and fixed her hair. Checking her reflection on the mirrored surface of the doors, she saw that her lipstick was definitely gone.

Liam turned back to her, his eyes wide and his face inscrutable. "I..." He rubbed the back of his head with his palm. "I'm sorry...I don't know what happened...fuck!" He sniffed the air. "You smell like...me," he growled and he began to stalk towards her.

Lara waved her hand and a gust of wind circled the both of them, whisking away his scent into the vent above them and making Liam stop in his tracks. "Not a problem," she said, hoping her voice didn't come out as a nervous squeak.

"Uh...thanks," he replied. "Listen, I-"

A loud ding interrupted him, and the lights flickered on. As soon as the doors opened, Lara sprinted out to the floor, dashing away.

What the heck happened? She shook her head.

"Oh, hey!" a familiar female voice called. Ignoring it, she kept walking towards Cady's office.

"Liam, sorry, er...we had an emergency," a male voice called.

"What? Oh, yeah...no worries, Grant."

"Lara!" Fast-paced footsteps caught up to her, and a hand grabbed her by the arm. "Hold up! Whatever you do, *do not* go into Cady's office unless you have some sort of forgetting potion handy! In which case, you're gonna have to share some with me!"

Lara whipped around to face Alynna, Grant Anderson's sister. "Don't what? Oh, hey Alynna," she greeted her with a nervous laugh. "I was...uhm...just going to see Cady." *Yeah. That's it. That's what I was doing. I totally wasn't making out with Liam Henney in the elevator.*

"Yeah...uhm, about that." The pretty brunette Lycan linked her arm around Lara's. "Why don't you step into my office first. Jeez, are you OK? You seem flushed. And what happened to your lipstick?"

"I was...er...I got super hungry on the way here and scarfed down a bear claw," Lara said quickly. "There was something wrong with the elevator. I think they shut down the air-conditioning...or something."

"Oh yeah, they've been doing those upgrades. Maintenance assured me they would fix it today."

"Is Cady OK?" Lara asked as they walked past Cady's office.

Alynna gave her a sheepish look. "Uh, yeah, about that...this is really awkward. But, well, Grant and his lady friend decided to have a bit of afternoon delight in the office," she explained. "Unfortunately, they must have released some super Alpha pheromones or something and the entire floor got...er...carried away."

Lara's eyes went wide. "So..."

"Yeah, *everyone* got carried away," Alynna emphasized. "Cady's door is still locked. And Nick's in there with her," she added, referring to Nick Vrost, Cady's Lycan husband and Grant's second-in-command.

"Oh," Lara said thoughtfully. She guessed that the moment the elevator doors opened, Liam had been affected by whatever Lycan sex voodoo was going around. A part of her was glad that he didn't just randomly kiss and feel up women in elevators as a habit.

Alynna opened the door to her office and led her in. "Yeah, sorry about that, but it was probably a good thing you guys didn't arrive a second earlier. Who knows what you guys might have seen."

Lara gave a nervous laugh. "Uh, yeah, true."

"So, why don't you take a seat?" Alynna motioned to the couch. "I'll send Cady a message and tell her to come here when they're...done."

"Thanks, Alynna," Lara said as she sat down. She looked around the plush office, trying not to notice that the other woman was picking up items that had fallen off the desk.

She sighed inwardly. *That certainly explained Liam's actions in the elevator.* Not that she thought he would suddenly be overcome with lust for her for no reason. However, there was no mistaking the burst of power she felt when their lips touched. She had felt a similar, though weaker version of it before. It was a few months ago when Cady and Nick's first touch marked them as True Mates.

Lara's stomach clenched. *No, it couldn't be.* There must be some mistake, a glitch in the universe. She and Liam Henney couldn't possibly be True Mates. Because if they were, then she would have to do everything she could to prevent him or anyone else from finding out.

Witch's Mate: Book 4 of the True Mates Series is out now. Get it at select online stores.

Lightning Source UK Ltd.
Milton Keynes UK
UKHW040732030921
389968UK00002B/377